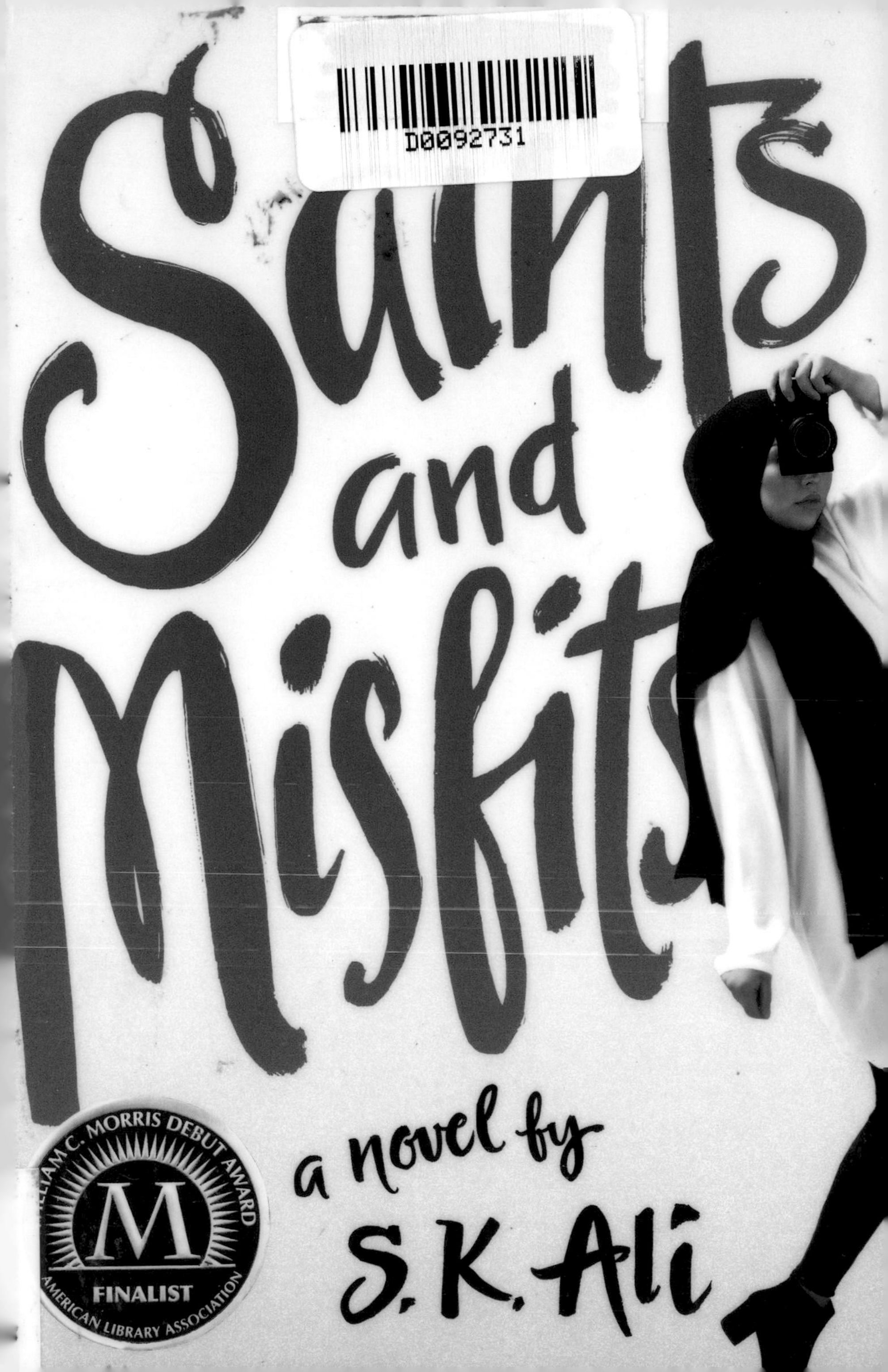
D0092731
Saints and Misfits
a novel by
S.K. Ali
WILLIAM C. MORRIS DEBUT AWARD
M
FINALIST
AMERICAN LIBRARY ASSOCIATION

Praise for *Saints and Misfits*

A 2018 William C. Morris Award Finalist

★ "This book is long overdue, a delight for readers who will recognize the culture and essential for those unfamiliar with Muslim experiences. This quiet read builds to a satisfying conclusion; readers will be glad to make space in their hearts—and bookshelves—for Janna Yusuf."
—*Kirkus Reviews*, starred review

★ "This timely and authentic portrayal is an indisputable purchase."—*School Library Journal*, starred review

★ "Ali's debut offers a much-needed, important perspective in Janna, whose Muslim faith is pivotal but far from the only part of her multifaceted identity. . . . A wide variety of readers will find solidarity with Janna, and not just ones who wear a hijab."
—*Booklist*, starred review

"A sympathetic and thoughtful study of a girl's attempt to find her place in a complicated world."—*Publishers Weekly*

"Ali brings to life a nuanced intersection of culture, identity, and independence. . . . Readers will cheer Janna's eventual empowerment."—*Horn Book*

"[R]eaders . . . will appreciate Janna's finding of a way to embrace her anger, receive support, and keep her faith."—*BCCB*

"*Saints and Misfits* is an engaging portrayal of a young woman and the abundance of differing, loving people who make up her extended family."—*Shelf Awareness*

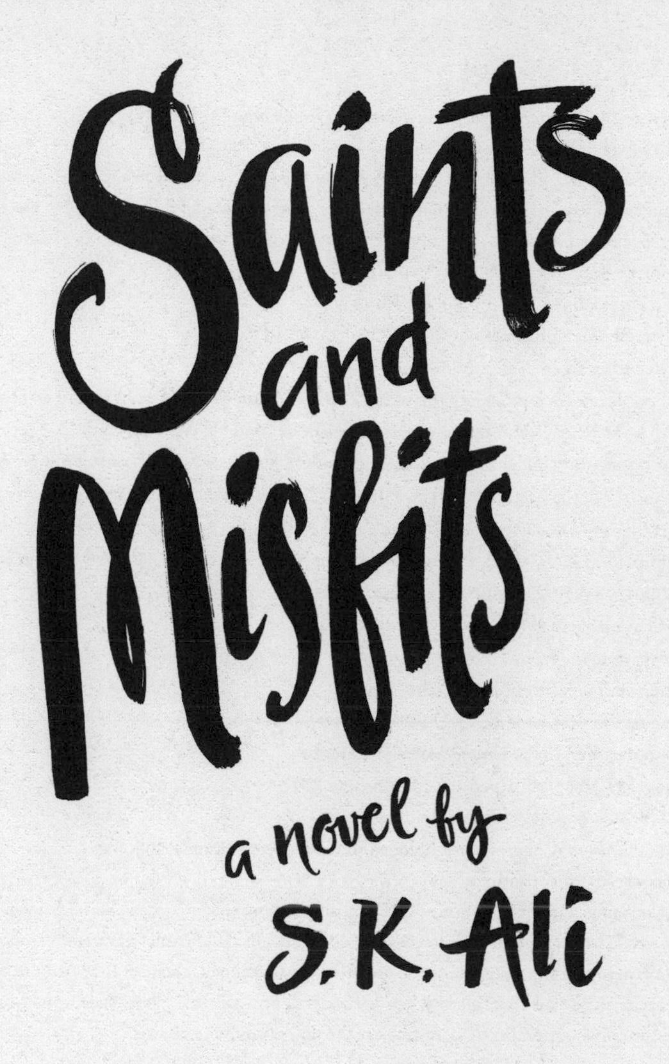

New York • London • Toronto • Sydney • New Delhi

An imprint of Simon & Schuster Children's Publishing Division
1230 Avenue of the Americas, New York, New York 10020

Hand-lettering by Nancy Howell

Also available in a SALAAM READS hardcover edition
Cover design by Chloë Foglia
Interior design by Hilary Zarycky
The text for this book was set in Adobe Garamond Pro.
Manufactured in the United States of America
First SALAAM READS paperback edition June 2018
10 9 8 7 6 5 4 3 2 1

The Library of Congress has cataloged the hardcover edition as follows:
Names: Ali, S. K., author.
Title: Saints and misfits / S. K. Ali. Description: First edition. | New York : Salaam Reads, [2017] | Summary: Fifteen-year-old Janna Yusuf, a Flannery O'Connor-obsessed book nerd and the daughter of the only divorced mother at their mosque, tries to make sense of the events that follow when her best friend's cousin—a holy star in the Muslim community—attempts to assault her at the end of sophomore year.
Identifiers: LCCN 2016041455 (print) | ISBN 9781481499248 (hardcover) | ISBN 9781481499255 (pbk) |ISBN 9781481499262 (eBook)
Subjects: | CYAC: Muslims—United States—Fiction. | Identity—Fiction. | Divorce—Fiction. | Sexual abuse—Fiction. | BISAC: JUVENILE FICTION / Social Issues / Adolescence. | JUVENILE FICTION / Social Issues / Sexual Abuse.
Classification: LCC PZ7.1.A436 Sai 2017 (print) | DDC [Fic]—dc23
LC record available at https://lccn.loc.gov/2016041455

To Rahmathun Lil A'lamiin

MISFIT

I'm in the water. Only my eyes are visible, and I blow bubbles to ensure the rest of me stays submerged until the opportune time. Besides the lifeguard watching from his perch, there's a gaggle of girls my age patrolling the beach with younger siblings in tow. They pace in their flip-flops and bikinis, and I wait.

The ideal time is when no one's around and no one's looking. But right now there's a little girl cross-legged on wooden bleachers peering at me from beneath a hand held aloft at her forehead, a smile on her face. I can't tell if the smile is a result of how long she's been watching me bob here in the water.

To check whether she's staring, I test her with a long gaze to the left of the bleachers, where Dad and his wife Linda are barbecuing. Their oldest son, Logan, round and berry-brown from a day in the sun, is digging a hole nearby, while the newest addition, Luke, lies on a quilt wearing a swim diaper.

Dad said I'd love it here because the beachfront cottage

they'd rented was one of the only two Cherie and Ed had let out this weekend. Secluded. Serene. Safe.

Ha. Cherie and Ed forgot to mention that the beach portion doesn't actually belong to them and is public property at all hours of the day. Party central.

I look back, and, hallelujah, the girl on the bleachers is gone. There's also a lull on the shore now. The lifeguard's turned to talk to someone behind him, and the beach girls are on the far right, peering at a sand castle.

I stand and cringe at the sucking sound as my swimsuit sticks to me, all four yards of the spandex-Lycra blend of it. Waterfalls gush out of the many hems on the outfit, and, as I hobble out of the lake, more secret pockets release their water. I'm a drippy, squelchy mess, stumbling toward Dad and Linda, picking up tons of sand as I move. I refuse to look around in case I see someone, everyone, watching me.

Maybe my face reveals something, because Dad starts right away.

"Janna, why do you have to wear that thing? You could have said, *No, I'm not wearing your burkini, Mom.*" He waves around long tongs as he speaks.

"Mom didn't get it for me. I ordered it online."

"I saw her hand it to you as we were packing the car."

"Because I'd left it on the hall table, Dad."

"It's her kind of thing. What's wrong with the way Linda's dressed?" He snaps the tongs at Linda. She's wearing a one-piece, just-had-a-baby, flouncy-at-the-hips number, and, really, I'd rather be in my burkini. It's black and sleek. Sure, when it gets wet, you kind of resemble a droopy sea lion, but at least it isn't pink and lime green like Linda's swimsuit is.

"Linda, you look great." I smile at her, and she smooths out her flounces.

"Too bad you're not her size—she could have lent you one of her suits, right, Linda?"

"Dad, I won't wear it. I'm a hijabi, remember?" I take a plate and add a piece of chicken from the platter.

"At the beach? Even at the beach?" Dad's gesticulating again and looking around—for what, I don't know. When he spies a woman unfolding a lounge chair nearby and starts talking louder, I realize it's for an audience. He wants an audience while he rants at me.

Maybe I should've listened to Mom and not come. My first vacation with Dad's family since my parents split when I was eleven and it's like I'm a visitor among the earthlings frolicking on a beach in Florida.

Before this, I'd only spent the odd weekend here and there with Dad at his house in Chicago. I was "Daddy's princess" back then.

The woman in the chair listens intently as Dad lectures. Linda's got a hand on his arm, and it's traveling up to his shoulder with a firmer grip, but he's still talking.

"How come you have to hide your God-given body?" He

turns a few burgers over. He's wearing a white T-shirt and red shorts over his God-given body. "It's not me who forces her to dress like that, that's for sure."

The woman looks at me, then at Dad and opens a book.

Linda places a hand on my glistening black back and hands me a can of pop. "I'll get you a burger when they're done," she whispers.

I move to sit on the bleachers before I realize the beach girls are sauntering this way again. I'm a swirl of sand art against a black canvas.

I duck under the wooden slats of the seats. Cradling my plate on crossed legs, I flip back the swim cap that's attached to my suit and undo my hair. Sand trickles down with the beads of water. Some of it falls onto my chicken.

Flannery O'Connor, my favorite author: That's who I need right now.

Flannery would take me away from here and deposit me into her fictitious world crawling with self-righteous saints and larger-than-life misfits. And I'd feel okay there because Flannery took care of things. Justice got served.

I forgot to pack her gigantic book of short stories because everything was last minute. I'd wanted to escape so badly that when Dad mentioned this trip with *his* family, I'd asked, "Can I come?" without thinking.

Mom had tried to put her foot down about taking a vacation right before exams, but, luckily for me, my brother

Muhammad is home for the summer from college. He talked her into letting me come. She listens to practically everything he says.

If it had been only me telling her I needed to get away, far away from Eastspring, she would've talked over me.

She didn't know I had to get away from a monster. And the truth is no one can know.

MONSTER

Fizz's house, last Sunday. Her twin sisters finished reading the whole Qur'an so there's a party. We listen to them recite; we eat; we laugh. Then Fizz and I sneak to the basement to watch TV. After ten minutes her mom calls for Fizz to come up and say good-bye to her grandparents.

I hang out with Rambo, Fizz's cat, on my lap, watching a movie review. A latch clicks, dulling the sounds from upstairs. Someone must have politely closed the door.

I'm laughing at the movie reviewer's imitation of an actor's wooden personality when Rambo's head turns, making me look at the stairs.

Fizz's cousin.

I stand, dropping Rambo from my lap, not even saying salaam.

I know him, know what he wants; he's brushed too close to me too many times at Fizz's family events.

He's standing in my only path of escape.

He comes straight toward me. No words, nothing.

I make a sound like a mix of please and no and help. I don't know who I'm talking to. There's nobody but him, and he is slamming himself into me like we're playing hockey. That's the stupid thing I see over and over in my head: the scenes from my brother Muhammad's extreme hockey moments video when the players slam into each other and lie tangled on the ice. Except we're on the ugly flower sofa and it's only one person slamming and I'm not wearing hockey gear, only a thin sweatshirt, and he's reaching under it.

The only screams I can muster are repeated whimpers of "Mom, Mom, Mom." I don't know if they float up to heaven, but as he tugs at my pants, the doorknob rattles and Fizz's mom's voice comes down. "Janna, open the door. The girls want to come down to watch a movie. Why is this locked?"

He gets up and backs away, adjusting his clothing. I run to the stairs, then stop. He's already gone to the spare bedroom next to the TV room and shut the door. It's only me to face everyone. Just me, Janna Yusuf, insignificant nobody, daughter of the only divorced mother at the mosque, someone whose sole redeeming feature is being friends with Fidda Noor, aka Fizz, of the famously pious Noor family. A family that boasts about Fizz's only male cousin: a Qur'an memorizer, a beacon of light for all youth.

I wipe my face and run upstairs to unlock the door and lock myself in the bathroom.

SAINT

I'm back from Florida and nothing's changed.

Muhammad is in front of the kitchen sink, chugging raw eggs from a carton for a new regimen he's on. Mom comes in and starts taking things out of the fridge, like she does every morning, to assess the day's offerings for meal options. Yellowing broccoli is on the menu today, so I pour myself a third bowl of cereal. I'm seated at the folding card table in the corner that Mom calls our "breakfast nook."

Muhammad wipes his mouth with the bottom of his T-shirt and turns to Mom. "So, are you calling *them* today?"

I shift, hiding my interest behind the Cap'n Crunch box, and hope they forget my presence in the room. I've been away for three days, so maybe they've gotten used to my absence.

"Called them already. Last night." Mom assesses a shriveled turnip, squeezing as she rotates it. "They said to come by after noon prayers to discuss the date of the next meet. Maybe

Wednesday if her dad can reschedule an appointment."

She stands up and almost gets pushed back into the open fridge. Muhammad lunges forward for a hug that makes a bear hug look dainty.

"Thanks! I'll go shower." He strips his shirt off right there.

"Ugh," I say. Bad move. They both turn to me.

"Aren't you going to be late?" Mom asks. "I told you the flight last night would get in the way of school."

Muhammad puts his shirt back on. "I'll give you a ride."

"No." I get up. "I'll walk."

"No, Muhammad will give you a ride," Mom says with that voice.

I shrug, picking up my backpack. Muhammad disappears into Mom's room and comes back out holding car keys. He's still in his pajama T-shirt, the one decorated with raw eggs.

We wait for the sole reliable elevator. The other one is always stuck on the fifth or fourteenth floor. The wait for either elevator is long on our floor.

"Who is *them*?" I blurt after five minutes.

"Who?" Muhammad looks around. Sometimes I can't believe he's studying economics at one of the best colleges in America.

"The *them* you're going to visit. The *them* you're going to shower for."

"Oh, you mean Sarah's parents?" He smiles a smile I've never seen before.

"Sarah? Sarah who?" Please not *Saint* Sarah.

Because I know why my religious brother would want to visit a girl's parents.

"Sarah Mahmoud. Your study circle leader at the mosque."

The elevator opens so I have no time to *gah*.

I get off at the lobby level with a huddle of people. The elevator closes on Muhammad's surprised face as he travels on to the parking level on his own.

Oh no they didn't. That's all I can think as I walk to school.

My brother fell for Saint Sarah without me knowing, and my mother is helping to arrange the possibility of them getting together. For life.

Sarah's "sainthood" means that to bestow her gaze on my brother she needs her parents' permission, which can only be sought once a would-be suitor has his parents call her parents to set up a series of chaperoned meetings. Even to get to know each other.

Mom's all for it because Saint Sarah loves Mom. Well, all mothers, apparently. When she first moved here, Saint Sarah surveyed the older women at the mosque to see what their areas of expertise were. Then she had them sign up to present things to the community. Mom did a talk on her thesis topic in college, "Patience and Forbearance as Markers of Resilience."

Saint Sarah: clear, glowing skin; perfectly proportioned, neat features with a big, ever-present smile flashing perfect teeth; a steely determined head; and a Mother Teresa heart. I forgot to add: The whole package is bow-tied in a billowy, diaphanous, organically grown hijab.

There's a very real possibility the most perfect Muslim girl on the planet may become my future sister-in-law.

REAL SAINT

It's Thursday. Mr. Ram day. He lives on the floor below us. He's old and tiny but sits up super straight like he's the general in a wheelchair army. My job, every Thursday after school, is to wheel him to the community center for Seniors Games Club, hang out there, and wheel him back.

Mr. Ram's son pays me abundantly for this and the other times I spend "elder-sitting."

As I take him to the elevator, I compliment Mr. Ram's clothes, to begin the walk right.

He's wearing a dark blue striped button-down shirt with a blue-and-white polka-dot bow tie.

On his head is a white fedora with a navy-and-gray feather sticking out of the band.

His shoes are a shiny black with white wing tips.

He removes his hat and salutes my compliment. "After

you," he says as we get into the elevator, although there's no possible way for him to go after me.

Once outside, we proceed without talking. I make sure to go around the bumpy parts of the sidewalk, giving a wide berth so that the wheelchair is easy to maneuver. Wheelchairs are heavier than they appear, and to make them look graceful, the person pushing has to do a lot of thinking ahead. I look down most of the time, but Mr. Ram looks up, waving at people as we pass.

When I was eleven and we first moved here, I'd go swimming at the community center at the same time as Seniors Games Club. Mr. Ram and I used to wait together for a ride back from Mom, and when he found out I was a reader, a real one, he became almost giddy. The week after, he brought along an illustrated copy of the Mahabharata, the Hindu epic.

"The Mahabharata is about the time after the Ramayana period." He watched me flip pages from the seat of his walker. "The Ramayana epic covers an age when it was easy for good to prevail, the lines of right and wrong being clear to see and understand. But the Mahabharata is when people knew the rules but didn't know the whys. They forgot them."

"Is that why there's a lot of fighting?" I held up a page with a chariot-filled battle scene.

"Miss Janna, every age has had that. It appears to be a by-product of civilization."

"It's like Lord of the Rings. My brother would like it." I stopped at a picture of a woman wrapping a blindfold on herself.

"That's Gandhari, who wanted to share her husband's blindness. Out of empathy," said Mr. Ram. "You see, she did something odd but for the right reason. She knew why she was doing it."

"She chose not to *see*?"

"For the rest of her life. Except once, when she removed the blindfold for her son."

"I can't believe it. I can't imagine doing that."

"It is like that wisdom about walking a mile in someone's shoes. Her purpose was to understand another's condition."

"So that makes it good?"

"Well, it makes her intention good," Mr. Ram said, getting up from his walker upon seeing Mom's car pull up. "Why we do an action is what determines its quality. A quality action or not."

"Well, I know why Muslims do things. Like why we pray five times a day." I closed the book and helped Mr. Ram turn his walker to face the right way to go through the doors. "It's to remember God more."

Mr. Ram nodded. "Yes, Miss Janna. Because when we just do things without a why, we become husks. Easily crumpled, no fruit inside."

There's a soothing rhythm to pushing the wheelchair, and now, in the lull it offers me, the monster's face reenters my mind.

Unannounced. When I block it, his fingers appear. When I fight that, his feet advance from the basement stairs. Each time I slay him, he reappears in parts.

I need an eraser that fills the entire screen of my brain.

Mr. Ram puts up his hand. That means stop.

Standing at the corner where our group of buildings meets the street is Sandra Kolbinsky's grandmother, Ms. Kolbinsky. Newly arrived from Poland six months ago.

She used to wear housecoats, but about a month ago she began wearing ankara- and kente-print dresses in dramatic color combinations. Today it's yellow and blue. I think she thinks Mr. Ram is African.

I stop and adjust my backpack, shifting the weight of an old clunker of a laptop.

"Ms. Kolbinsky, I'm still waiting for you to come along with us to games club," Mr. Ram says. "I can't think of a better honor than walking with you."

She laughs. "My daughter, she still didn't fill out the papers. She's taking a very long time."

"Do you want Miss Janna to get you another form? We can do that, right, Janna?" Mr. Ram twirls his hand in a questioning gesture.

"Yeah, sure, Ms. Kolbinsky," I say. It's going to be the fifth form I get for her.

"Oh, thank you," Ms. Kolbinsky says. "Mr. Ram, you

promise me you will teach me Parcheesi when I get there?"

"Oh yes." Mr. Ram leans forward. "I'll teach you until you can beat me with your eyes closed."

Ms. Kolbinsky giggles as I wheel ahead.

"Miss Janna, you have two more weeks until summer vacation," Mr. Ram says. "Are you prepared for your exams?"

"Will be in a couple of days," I say. "I rewrote all the important notes for every class and color coded them by relevance. Just have to study them now."

Mr. Ram is the only one I reveal my ultra-intense studying tendencies to. He approves.

He also knows about my Flannery O'Connor obsession. He'd been a book editor in India before he retired so he has a lot to say about her. It's just not the right things. He thinks she's depressing and joyless, killing characters suddenly just when you're getting to know them. I say she's a kick-ass monster killer, wreaking justice on her pages.

And who gets handed the worst of it in a Flannery world? Monsters hiding behind saint masks.

Um, yes.

Mr. Ram interrupts my mind's dip into that rabbit hole exclusively reserved for Flannery. "Did you decide about Caliban yet? Still believe that he is completely evil?"

"Mr. Ram, he attacked Miranda. That bothers me more than Shakespeare maybe meaning Caliban to be a dark man."

"So you don't want to dig deeper, then." Mr. Ram makes

a teepee with his hands. "I did a paper on foreign men in Shakespeare. That was a such a long time ago, so it must be old-fashioned."

We reach the edge of the sidewalk.

"Your friend is over there with a young man," Mr. Ram says when we're in the middle of the road.

Once we're across, I stop the wheelchair and look up.

Tats and Jeremy.

They're walking in the middle-school yard, their backs to us, Tats's ponytailed long hair bouncing with her steps.

MISFITS

I first noticed him in the spring when I took pictures of the track meet for the yearbook. My telephoto lens got the requisite shots of warm-ups and victory fists before it noticed someone packing away audio equipment at the announcer's table. Windbreaker jacket, a short, no-nonsense haircut, relaxed movements. I took some pictures, ignoring the little voice inside that said *Paparazzi! Stalker!* over and over as I zoomed in on a remarkable forehead.

(This is going to sound strange, but I found out, through careful study, that good-looking guys always have the right foreheads. High foreheads. Maybe it's because they balance the jawlines just so. Anyway, foreheads count a lot in my mind.)

Later I find out his name is Jeremy. He's the guy who runs the lights for our assemblies, the go-to guy for anything technical.

At the spring concert, he came over, asked if I needed

assistance setting up my camera. Kneeling to crank my tripod, I looked up, fell hard, and never recovered.

After a month, I developed this uncanny ability to sense his presence before I even saw him. That's how I became aware that he strolls through the sophomore hallways to get to some of his classes. That's also how I noticed he's a good friend of the monster.

This should have stopped me in my tracks. This, and the ways we don't fit. He's a senior; I'm a sophomore. He's white, of Irish background, and I'm brown, a mix of my Egyptian mother and Indian father.

He's Christian. I'm Muslim. The non-casual-dating kind.

But it didn't stop in me, the Jeremy fixation.

I told Tats, one of only two people who knows about him, that my brain, muscles, and eyes are starting to hurt from numbingly pretending I don't notice that he's less than four feet away from me like twice a day.

Tats told me he's in her drama club, tech crew. They meet Thursdays after school. (Onstage, not in the middle-school yard.)

MISFIT

At the community center, Mr. Ram and I check in at the front desk with the guy who runs program registration. He nods at me, comes around the counter to kneel by the wheelchair, and reaches his right hand out to do a special handshake that he's been trying to teach Mr. Ram.

I take another application form for Ms. Kolbinsky and turn to watch them. The guy is guiding Mr. Ram through the motions again, their hands vastly different in size, but close in color. "So, like this, shake, a hand tap, and then you clutch my hand, let go, and high-five, then finger tap with style, and point. You'll get it, sir, you'll get it!"

I don't know the front desk guy's name, but I call him Shazam! in my head. Shazam!'s been teaching Mr. Ram this handshake for almost two months now, ever since he started working here, but Mr. Ram still can't get it.

I dubbed him Shazam! because he saunters over periodically

to the foyer where Seniors Games Club takes place to shake hands again, deliver one-liners, and just like that—SHAZAM!—light up their faces before he walks back to his post.

Right now Mr. Ram's face is glowing with the happiness of the handshake. His mouth is open wide in a grin and he's shaking slightly, but no sound comes out: his Belly-Laugh smile, the gauge of his greatest point of happiness. I wheel him to his friends who are waiting, with chessboards spread, eager to see him.

I seat myself at a corner table and set up my laptop, away from the action.

"So, you related to Mr. Ram?" Shazam! is at the vending machine.

"No. He's my neighbor."

"I just thought, because, you know, you bring him here every week." He pushes buttons with one hand and pulls on his hair, a short Afro, with the other. "That's nice of you."

"No, I actually get paid to do it."

"So it's not nice of you?" He takes his Gatorade. Now he's facing me with a wide smile. A necklace of wooden beads hangs on his neck, the pendant disappearing into his white T-shirt.

"Yeah, it is. Because I still like doing it." I doodle clouds on my agenda. "Is that nice enough?"

"Sure." He takes a drink and salutes me with the bottle. "See ya—gotta get back to the desk. Might be some late gamers checking in."

I open my e-mail and read today's message from Dad: *Let go of that which clouds your success scenario. Dispense with the unnecessary.*

That's Dad for you. Every weekday he sends a message out to his mailing list. He thinks because he expanded his business, Lite Indian Desserts (LID), Inc., from a basement operation to national prominence he has the right to give everyone sound bites on success. He thinks he's the Deepak Chopra of capitalism.

There's an e-mail from Fizz: *Don't forget my birthday, tomorrow after school, my house! Xoxo, Fizz*

I peddle in e-mails because Mom thinks fifteen is too young for my own phone. She's the only mother who thinks so, according to Fizz.

I get to work editing Amu's postings on his website. Amu, "uncle" in Arabic, is Mom's brother and the imam, or prayer leader, of the mosque here in town. While he is smart and all that, his English has not kept up with the times, so he pays me to make it more accessible.

Every Thursday evening, Amu posts answers to questions he gets from the Muslim community on the website Memos from the Mosque. Some of them are downright unbelievable.

Today I'm looking at *Dear Imam, is it permissible to eat llamas?* And *Dear Imam, are we allowed to pray in a barn if there are pigs nearby?*

Apparently there are a lot of confused Muslim farmers out there.

Those I zap into the trash bin of oblivion. I filter two good ones and e-mail those to Amu. He'll work on them for a week and send them back to me by next Thursday.

I look over the answers he's written to last week's questions.

Dear Imam, are we allowed to keep hamsters if it's in a big LARGE cage?

Answer: Thank you for your question. I believe if we should examine your question together we shall find our answer. You herewith mention a cage, but you do not refer to it as merely just that, a cage. *No, you specify that it will be a* big *cage. And you do not even stop there. Quite emphatically, you add on the word* LARGE *in capital letters. I ask you why are you compelled to do this? Why do you feel it is necessary to be so exceedingly exact (if a bit banal) in your description of the roomy attributes of this said cage? Could it be that your conscience is* ethical *and you recognize what a* merciless *action it would be to cage a free creature of ALLAH? This is what He says on the subject in the Qur'an: "There is not a creature on the earth nor anything that flies on wings without its being organized into communities, just like you." Alas, the cage, no matter how spacious of an abode, would not constitute a community and would be utterly* merciless. *And Allah knows best.*

I trim the grandiloquent excesses on this and the other answer before e-mailing them to Amu.

He e-mails me back immediately. *Thank you, Janna. May Allah reward you abundantly. And do not forget to take pictures of the Mosque Open House on Sunday morning. Plenty of non-Muslims will be there so prepare for great inter-faith shots! We will use them for our website posting next week. God be with you.*

Amu the optimist. The same three non-Muslims show up to our open house every year. They get serenaded as though they're royalty because we get to post "Mosque Opens Door to Greater Community, and THEY CAME!"

But I don't want to think about Sunday. The monster will be there, pious and smiling, pretending nothing happened.

Freakily, I know I'll have to do the same: pretend.

If I don't, he'll flood my brain.

But I don't want him to access any part of me ever again. Not even a flicker of my thoughts.

MISFIT

Mom is home when I get back. She and Muhammad are sitting in the living room with a box of doughnuts on the side table. Odd, as we never get doughnuts, and Mom is never home before six. She has the afternoon shift at the library, sometimes even the evening one.

I say salaams and open the box. Two cherry-filled smothered in powdered sugar, my favorite. Very odd.

"You're home early." I take my first cloudy bite.

"I didn't go to work." She glances at Muhammad. "Muhammad and I were out shopping."

"Mom, let's get it over with." Muhammad leans forward. He's on the couch that he sleeps on. A huddle of blankets, towels, and Columbia U. sweatshirts cave in as he moves.

"Janna, sit," Mom says.

"I have studying to do." I'm suspicious now. Mom's not looking at me. She's shooting glances from the window to the doughnut box to the long-standing game of Risk between her and Muhammad on the coffee table.

"Mom, are you getting married?" I say, smiling. I've been privately practicing for the day she tells me. My part in it would be to look ecstatic. I like thinking up inevitable, awful truths and rehearsing my reactions so that I'm not caught off guard.

"No!" she says. "No, not that."

Muhammad laughs. "It's even better. Your bro is moving back home."

He holds up a hand for a high five.

"Why, did Columbia kick you out?"

"Muhammad will be working for a year." Mom leans forward, her eyes fixed on me. "To save money to continue college."

Okay. Why are they both staring so hard?

"He'll need your room."

"Ha. Funny." There are only two bedrooms in our apartment. Muhammad was busy away at school when Mom and I moved in, so neither of them belong to him. I shove the rest of the doughnut in my mouth to contain my emotions, jam squishing out the sides.

"He's changed majors, and it'll take more time to finish school now. We need you to be open to this."

I swallow.

"Please, Janna."

"No."

"There's no other option now. We can't pick up and move

suddenly. And he can't sleep on the couch forever."

"So you're going to make me sleep on the couch? How's that even make sense?"

"No, we'll rearrange my room so that you can have your own private space in it," Mom says. "I'm even downsizing my bed so that you can fit yours in. We picked one out today."

"No. I'm not four years old."

"We can get privacy screens so that it's an enclosed space."

Muhammad puts up a hand again. "I'm paying for those. Man, are they expensive."

"Mom!" I say, ignoring Muhammad. "You can't do this to me!"

I run to *my* room, passing my reflection in the hall mirror. I look like the Joker from *Batman*, with white powder and bits of cherry smearing the edges of my mouth.

My room is not a spectacular space done up like a Pottery Barn Teen room. That would be the room Dad's setting up for me at his house. Here, it's a secondhand bed by the window, a green dresser found on the curb, and a tiny desk that blocks the door when it opens. The special thing about my space is that it faces Tats's apartment in the building across.

Which I'm not even sure is special anymore.

I drop into bed and stretch an arm to pull the curtain across. I want dark.

I can't believe this. Muhammad is supposed to stay at

college until he finishes, then start his career and get married and never move back home.

I won't give in. I won't accept their arrangements for me. They didn't even ask my opinion. It's like when Mom didn't tell me she and Dad were divorcing.

For the longest time, I thought Mom and I packed up and moved on our own for an extended vacation while Muhammad stayed back to finish his last year of high school and Dad was on an important business trip in Chicago. They broke the news to me right before I turned twelve: Guess what? You had no say in it, but from now on your life will be like this. *Our family is divorced.*

I'd had no clue they didn't like each other anymore. I mean, I knew Dad wasn't home much, and when he was, they didn't talk a lot. But we still did things together.

There's life BD and AD—before divorce and after divorce—and in my head, the BD images, while faded at the edges, glow in the middle, like the filter Tats uses on all her Instagram pictures.

BD was after-school snacks with Mom, the kind with smiley faces on them, Dad timing my math facts at the kitchen table, the guest bedroom where Muhammad and I had our respective corners to plot major pillow-fight campaigns. It was me drawing at the coffee table in our sunny family room, sketchbooks spread out, TV on in the background.

I know memory can be selective and nostalgia deceptive,

but when the floor goes from underneath, I'd rather fall back than down.

It *had* to have been a better time than now.

BD is also when I started trying out hijab. Back then, at nine, I wanted to look like Mom. She wore jewel-toned scarves, and wrapping them around my head in front of the mirror was like trying on her heels.

One day I wore a purple one to school because it went with my sweatshirt. When I got home, Amu was visiting. He smiled on seeing me, but Dad frowned.

"She's young." I heard Dad from my bedroom; he'd said it with that much force. I padded to the top of the stairs to listen, my fingers playing with the tassels of the scarf around my neck.

"That's true." Amu's voice. "She doesn't understand it yet."

"She's just trying something. Let her be." Mom.

"You want to turn her into a mini you." Dad.

"No, Haroon, I want her to choose. And if it's to be like me, is that so bad?"

Silence.

Later I found out from Muhammad that Amu had been there to counsel Mom and Dad.

Mom had told him about it, but, apparently, I was too young to know that things were going downhill.

BD was going to the mosque together.

Except when it wasn't. Dad stopped attending due to

working on the weekends. That bothered Mom, but they didn't fight it out like couples do on TV.

Instead, Mom told me to draw what I'd learned at the mosque to share with Dad when he got home. So he gave me a pile of empty executive agenda planners from work, and every Sunday I went over my sketches with him.

My favorite sketchbook is on the shelf above my desk now: a leather-bound planner that holds the almost-finished biography of the Prophet Muhammad. The seerah, in graphic novel format.

I get off the bed and pull out the planner. I remember the day I started it at Sunday school. We were learning about how, although the Prophet was statuesque and walked nobly, he always, always stopped and stooped to smile at children. I *had* to draw a picture of that, without showing the Prophet's face, of course.

The colors I chose to draw with are all super bright and happy. So this proves it: BD *was* a better time.

I drop the sketchbook on my desk. Besides Tats, Mr. Ram is the only person outside my family who's seen it in full. He loved it and was always on me to add more. He made it seem like I'd be emulating the greatness of the Mahabharata scribe if I finished it.

Dad loved it too. Or acted like he loved it. I stopped working on it three years ago, when he married Linda, his administrative assistant.

That was the year I also started wearing hijab full-time.

And weirdly, when Dad first saw me with it, one evening on Skype, Mom had been in the background wearing a black scarf exactly like mine.

So, silence again.

Muhammad moving home means Mom will go back to telling him everything. I'll be "too young" to know stuff again, even about my own life.

Mom finds it too easy to exclude me.

No, I'm not giving up my room. I'm waiting this one out.

MISFITS

The next morning, I'm almost at the doors to school when someone beeps from the parking lot. I don't think it's for me until I hear a car pull up alongside. Muhammad.

I ponder ignoring him but know that he will make my life immensely worse, so I turn and walk toward the rolled-down window.

"Yes?"

"This is for you." He dangles a plastic bag out.

"What is it? English starts in five minutes."

"Look inside."

I shuffle closer and peer in. A phone. A shiny new one in a shiny new box.

Something I'm not allowed to have until I'm sixteen.

"Mom thought you'd want it earlier. To keep in touch with your friends."

"I know what a phone is for. And I know what bribery is for too. My room is worth way more." I leave him to ponder that one.

As I walk to class, Tats waves from the end of the hallway, where she's ripping off posters for one or another of the many clubs she belongs to. I start to wave back but drop my hand when Jeremy steps out from beside the trophy case. He's coiling up some wire from the school display monitor and sees my smile, frozen, when I see him so close to Tats. She glances at him, raising her eyebrows at me.

In English, as Ms. Keaton reviews rhetorical devices, I'm thinking:

Tats, how could you?

Am I not your friend?

I thought you were into Matt? Or did you realize, like the rest of the world, he's completely unattainable? And so you decide to help yourself to what you saw in my heart?

Whatever's happening between Tats and Jeremy must be developing at drama club.

The rest of the morning disappears in an intense exam-preparation lecture by Mr. Pape. There's exactly one school week left before exams, as next Friday is the official designated day off to study, so he tells us that he's going to cram the history of war into four days. He's a pacifist, so he spends a lot of time on ethics, standing by the window with one hand on his hip and the other hand ready to tousle his own hair when his speech gets too tragic. I sit in the back and write three different letters to Tats. They contain Amu's overused favorite words: "*un*ethical" and "merci*less*." I tear each one up.

At lunch, I avoid the cafeteria, where Tats would be waiting at our table, and log on to a computer in the library. Dad's e-mail says *Those who can't bear to look a bear in the eye are already dead. Stand and look before you fight or flee. It makes winning, and even failing, sweeter.*

I don't get that one, but I do know the bear is either Tats or Muhammad.

I decide to corner Tats in the locker room after gym, second-to-last period, the only class we share. I'm in an enriched stream, and she's trying out all the artistic avenues open to her. Which I'm kind of envious of. What would it feel like to want to become *only* a photographer, I wonder. But that wondering is very rhetorical because no way would I give up my straight-A+ report card to risk a dabble in hobbies.

Besides being artsy, Tats also has tawny hair. Have you ever seen long tawny hair? It's like the mane growing on your favorite fairy-tale horse, the kind your seven-year-old self dreamed about, frolicking through that meadow, underneath that rainbow.

It would be easy for Jeremy to fall for her is what I'm trying to say.

And me? I've got hair. It's just that since I started hijab, no guy other than Dad or Muhammad or Amu has seen it. So my hair has succumbed to the lack of maintenance that exists when the world doesn't judge you by it. I wear a celebratory halo of intercultural marriage, free to be, on my head: the tight curls of my Egyptian mother with the blue-black shine of my Indian father, amassed in a tight bun under my scarf.

Actually, I'd be lying if I said no guy has ever seen it. Tats has taken my pictures after makeover sessions in her bedroom. She said her brother once asked who her hot friend was after he'd accidently seen one of the pics. I pretended to get upset but secretly thought, *Really? Someone thinks I'm hot?*

We still do makeover shots occasionally. Then stop for long periods when the guilt gets to me. Or when Saint Sarah leads another session at the mosque on the powers of being free of societal beauty judgment—that my logical mind completely understands.

It's hard sometimes to move in obscurity when everyone else around you is so Instagram worthy. Even the person who's telling you not to care so much about looking great: Saint Sarah.

But gym class is girls only. I get to go hijabless for a glorious forty minutes. I'm partnered up with Simone, athlete extraordinaire, for our weights unit, so there's no opportunity to talk to Tats in class. Besides, I've been avoiding her bearish eyes until the opportune time in the locker room, pretending I'm really into perfecting my squats.

After class, people do their hair thing in front of the mirrors while I tuck it all in with one sweep of a scarf and a strategically placed safety pin. I'm always done first. And because Tats has that hair to maintain, she's usually done last.

I come out of the bathroom stall where I've been practicing my unaffected look and stand by the hand dryers to watch her toss the mane around. I'm readying myself to ask her a composed, nonrhetorical question—*Do you like Jeremy too?*—when the weirdest thing happens. She turns to me before I speak and takes a deep breath. Her eyes are wide and ingenue-like. If her favorite actress, Audrey Hepburn, had a younger, slightly less delicate-looking sister, Tats would be her, face-wise. Audrey is her favorite actress precisely for that reason.

"Jan, will you promise not to get mad at me?" she says. "It has to do with Jeremy."

I turn to the mirror and look at the ceiling lights through it.

"It's exciting news," she continues. "Just promise me you'll be all right with it."

The only response for that is to pick up my backpack and mumble, "Math class, late," before exiting the locker room. Before she sees my self-sabotaging, brimming eyes.

I've known Tatyana for a long time, standing by her to fend off stupid boys who've called her Tityana since sixth grade, because, somehow, she's scrawny (not slim but scrawny, as in kiddylike) yet amply endowed, like those things you spin and match up the different body parts of different people. In eighth grade I even put in detention time for a week, unrepentantly, for unscrewing the valve stems on one really uncouth boy's bike tires myself and then painstakingly deflating them, for her.

And now I'm fed up with her.

It's not like Jeremy's mine, so why am I so upset?

Don't answer that. It's totally rhetorical.

Enriched math class is all guys except for Soon-Lee and me. That would be okay if it were full of normal dudes. Instead it has people like Robby and Pradeep. Guys who make it a point to remind us we're the only two females in the class.

A whisper as I go up to answer a question on the whiteboard: "Look at that. I can't believe they let the only two girls in school without any booty into this class."

A note tossed to Soon-Lee after she works a formula aloud when no one else could solve it: *U sure you're not a guy? Wanna check again?*

And when Soon-Lee and I ignore their taunts: "I think some people are on the rag today."

MONSTER

After school I take the bus to Fizz's. She opens the door before I ring the bell and grabs the present from my hand as I'm about to yell happy birthday.

"Salaams. Sh. Get downstairs," she says. "Everything's set up."

I copy her stealthy walk, following her down the hallway, lowering each foot gingerly before lifting the next one. She lets me go ahead of her at the basement door, then shuts and locks it before scrambling down the stairs.

Fizz's younger sisters, Hana and Hadia, the twins, are sprawled on a love seat from the 1970s (pristine from being mummified in plastic wrap for most of its life), watching *Project Runway*. The oldest sister, Aliya, is cross-legged on the carpeted floor, folding a massive load of laundry. She's the most domesticated eighteen-year-old I have ever met.

"Finally!" says one of the twins. She clicks the remote, and the opening notes of *Pride and Prejudice*, the miniseries, begin to play.

"My mom's on the hunt for kitchen maids," Fizz tells me, ripping open a bag of chips. "She keeps talking about a birthday feast. Which means we'll be in the kitchen for hours, making something that will be eaten in ten minutes. Like homemade samosas or something."

I grab a handful of Cheetos and feed them into my mouth one by one as if I'm operating mastication machinery, contemplating how to tell Fizz about the latest development on the Jeremy front. She's the second person who knows about him, but only as a major forehead crush. I don't get into things too much with her because she's not exactly rah-rah about my liking a non-Muslim guy. Fruitless, she calls it.

Rambo joins us on the sofa with a far-from-nimble leap from the floor. He peers at the remainder of my chips cupped in my left hand, as if wondering what they are, so perplexed is his expression.

"Did you see him heave himself? He's on a never-ending diet and he's still a lardo," Fizz says. "Don't feed him."

Rambo tilts his head and looks into my eyes. His own eyes are blue and soulful. I sneak him one chip that he gratefully accepts before being pushed off the sofa by Fizz.

"It's his breed," Aliya says. "Let him be."

"He's prediabetic," Fizz says.

"Because of the stress you give him," Aliya says, folding Fizz's pajamas.

On-screen, Elizabeth Bennet and her older sister, Jane, give each other cuddly compliments.

There's a click, followed by footsteps on the stairs. Fizz's mom, Auntie Fatima, leans her head over the railing. Uncle Aziz, Fizz's dad, shows up behind her, munching on a samosa.

"Everybody, upstairs," Auntie Fatima says.

Only Aliya makes a move and stacks the folded piles into a laundry basket.

"FIDDA, HANA, HADIA—and, Janna, sweetie, if you want to—UPSTAIRS NOW!"

We shuffle to the dining room, where the gargantuan oval oak table is covered with evidence of a mass operation. Tupperware containing various candies are laid out at two, four, eight, and ten o'clock. Twelve o'clock has a box of clear plastic bags and twist ties.

"We are making loot bags," Auntie Fatima says. "For your party."

Fizz stands still. "What party?"

"Your birthday party." Auntie Fatima motions for Aliya to take the head of the table. Hana and Hadia snicker as they head to the gummy bear packs and bubble gum at two and four, respectively.

"No one told me about a party."

Auntie Fatima crosses her arms. "I didn't want to tell you because you would say no. As the chair of the mosque social committee, I have to be hospitable."

Fizz takes a seat in front of happy-face lollipops the size of my palms. "So, who's coming to my party? Six-year-olds?"

Aliya raises her eyebrows at Fizz in warning.

"What is wrong with being a good host? Giving out goody bags? Back home we always welcomed our guests with a treat, no matter how old they were, fifteen or fifty!"

Auntie Fatima marches around the table clockwise, making a sample bag to show us what we are aiming for: a muddle of cheap, kitschy candy. She tells us she'll be in the kitchen finishing the storm she's cooking.

"No, really, Mom, *who's* coming to *my* party?"

"Family and friends."

I freeze when I hear that. Family means Fizz's cousin Farooq.

Farooq the monster.

I dribble candy hearts into the bags passed to me from four o'clock.

Hana and Hadia get an idea to change the carefully organized composition of the loot bags, to add some pizzazz to the whole thing. Their passive-aggressive mutiny campaign gets limited to making bags with only red-colored candy or smiley lollipops by Aliya; she vetoed and confiscated the patent-pending eerie bags of gummy bears with their heads chopped off and lollipops with smeared smiles.

"What happened?" Fizz asks after Aliya puts on some

music and I scoot my chair over to nine o'clock. "Why do you look so down?"

I tell her about Tats's treachery. Tats and Jeremy out together when they should've been at drama club.

"I'm not surprised," Fizz says. "Some people have no morals."

I consider that. I don't know if that's even true. "Well, that's not who she really is. She's never done anything even close to this before."

"Anyway, it's a gift from Allah, isn't it?" Fizz watches my face for a reaction. "You can unlike him now. He's non-Muslim. I told you from the beginning to drop it."

I slump. "It's not easy like that."

"Come on, a Muslim guy, a *real* one, is what you need to focus on."

"Sorry, don't know any."

"First, check how much they've memorized the Qur'an. That will tell you what they're like."

I stop myself from picturing her cousin. I know that's who she's thinking of.

Instead, I see a husk of corn. An empty one. Because, like Mr. Ram said, that's what the monster is, just a husk with nothing inside.

I hate the husk.

"I know what I need to do," Fizz says, tapping my shoulder with a happy-face lollipop. "Imma jus gonna hafta find you some hot Muslim guy tomorrow night at the—"

"Fun-Fun-Fun Islamic Quiz Game," I say, groaning the words out.

The Fun-Fun-Fun Islamic Quiz Game is another brainchild of Saint Sarah. She wants the teens at our mosque to compete against other youth groups in our region and be the smartest Muslims or something. She is so nice that she let her five-year-old brother name the competition, as she told us on the flyer.

I'm laughing, but, really, what if I tell Fizz I don't want to find some hot Muslim guy?

We finish at five. Auntie Fatima declares that the leftover candy will go to the mosque to be distributed at the Fun-Fun-Fun Islamic Quiz Game.

The doorbell rings as we put away the Tupperware and box up the remaining candy. It doesn't stop ringing until almost every girl from the mosque is in the house. And some of their mothers. The monster, who has the whole Qur'an memorized, has been invited to say a few prayers and then disappear upstairs so the girls can "relax."

He's standing in the foyer talking to Uncle Aziz. I scuttle to the kitchen through the dining room and busy myself ladling things into bowls and serving plates.

"All meat. Not surprising." Someone tall and slim in a black gown is looking out the sliding doors to the patio, parting the vertical blinds to do so. She turns. It's Sausun, a sullen girl from study circle. "Like there are no Muslim vegetarians in the world."

"There's okra." I point a drippy wooden spoon at a pan.

"Of course there's okra. Probably covered in oil." She raises a perfectly sculpted thick eyebrow. Her eyes are hazel, and when paired with those eyebrows, they make a look-at-me combination. But she wears long gowns with Doc Martens boots and severe black scarves on her head, so she's not exactly a glamour queen. Kind of the opposite actually. "Okra is not edible in my book. Like something forgotten that's been foraged and forced on us. Like eggplant and mushrooms."

"Wow, you're really antivegetable for a vegetarian." I open the fridge. "There are potato samosas in here I think. I can reheat them if you want."

"No. I come prepared." She bends down and rifles through a laptop bag on the ground. "My own food. For such predicaments."

She holds up a bag of marshmallows with HALAL written on it in red writing. "Halal" means "permitted" in Arabic. Regular marshmallows may have gelatin from pork sources.

But all marshmallows need some type of gelatin. I make my way to Sausun.

"Want some?" she asks, dangling the bag. She rips it open.

"No, I just want to read the ingredients."

"It's halal."

"I know, but is it halal from beef gelatin? Or"—I scan the list—"fish gelatin. So that makes you a pescatarian. Because you eat fish, too."

"Thanks. For ruining my marshmallows." She continues shoving them into her mouth while watching me take out the samosas. Auntie Fatima returns from the living room, holding three bouquets of flowers.

"Oh, thank you, Janna. I'll heat those." She trades the samosa plate in my hands for the bouquets.

I hope she doesn't tell me to leave the kitchen. To go and enjoy myself.

Stop and smell the flowers, isn't that what they tell you to do in stressful situations? Closing my eyes, I bury my face in the blooms and inhale.

A snort of laughter from the corner of the kitchen greets my attempt at de-stressing. I open my eyes to Sausun's smirk.

What a . . . pescatarian.

Saint Sarah drifts in and kisses Auntie Fatima three times, saying salaam. There's a silk purple peony pinned at the side of her head, holding up her mauve scarf. It turns to me before she does.

"Janna! So good to see you." She comes over for a hug, but I hold up the mess of flowers in front of my face, with a smile, to indicate my unfortunate busyness.

She grabs them, bends to take a bottle of water from the case under the kitchen table, and strides to the dining room.

She's back before I can leave. A vase full of flowers decorates the center of the oak table behind her.

"I wanted to talk to you." Saint Sarah picks up both my hands and lifts them as if I'm a puppy she is examining. "Will you join our team for the quiz competition? We desperately need your brains."

"I have exams," I say. "Sorry."

"I heard you're working on a graphic novel of the Prophet's life," she continues, ignoring me. "So I thought you would be perfect for the seerah questions. There's a whole category of them."

Muhammad is already telling her intimate details about my life? Great.

I drop my hands. "I'm sorry, but I've got three important exams."

"Think about it," Saint Sarah says, smiling.

"Yeah, think about it," Sausun calls as I leave. She's eating samosas, an empty bag of marshmallows stuck under her arm.

I make the mistake of escaping into the family room. The monster is there on his own, fitting wires into the sound system. His back is to the door, so he doesn't see me. I find Aliya in the hall, arranging guest shoes in neat rows, and ask her to tell Fizz that I'm sorry, but I had to leave because of not feeling well. I actually *am* sick to my stomach. Aliya goes to get me a plate of food, but I'm already opening the door.

• • •

On the bus, I lean my head against the glass window. The scene outside turns from suburbs to city. The scene inside me is one I don't want to replay, but the remote control is not in my hand. Seeing him at Fizz's again is like involuntarily pressing play on a personal nightmare.

MISFITS

Saturday morning is prime exam-prep time, so I'm in bed studying when Muhammad knocks. He enters looking like a wombat. Not a cute one—one of those perpetually worried ones.

I don't know what happened with Saint Sarah's parents on Wednesday, but I do know that when I went to get a glass of water last night, he was up at three a.m., that special time of night Allah says if anyone has a really urgent prayer they need answered, ask it then. Well, Muhammad was up asking it, praying with this look I've never seen on his face. I think he'd call it sincerity, but I'd call it desperation. Uncharacteristically I did feel sorry for him and found myself saying ameen out loud after a particularly long prayer he muttered. He stood, yanked up his prayer rug, and took it into the dining room.

I mean, I realize Saint Sarah's parents are tough to crack. Imagine a Muslim version of the *American Gothic* couple, with a beard on the husband and a black hijab on the wife. I don't know how they begat Saint Sarah and her bubbliciousness. It doesn't make sense. Like in my family, our respective resemblance to each parent is obvious. I'm like Dad in a lot of ways. He dresses in black too, knows how to stay on course, never surrender, remain calm, and carry on. Like me.

Muhammad and Mom are easily lured, misled, and taken for a ride.

My brother holds out the same plastic-bag offering from his car yesterday and places it on the bed.

"Your phone." He takes a seat at the desk, his frame casting a moving shadow over its laminate surface as he swivels the chair to face me. "It's yours. And not a trade for the room. I bought it, but Mom's paying the monthly plan. It's too much of a hassle to return it now."

I look at the bag but resist the urge to check it out.

"So what happened with your visit to Sai—Sarah's parents? Why the middle-of-the-night prayers?" I ask.

"Her parents are not too happy that I switched majors. They heard from their friends I was going to study law. That's what they wanted."

"What are you going to study now?"

"You mean what have I been doing for the past year? Philosophy. I want to do my doctorate. Which is why Dad pulled the college funds."

"What?"

Muhammad's face is tight, like he doesn't want to get into it.

"He only agreed to pay if I did something that would benefit LID, Inc., somehow. Philosophy, no matter how I stretch it, doesn't fit the bill." He laughs. "Nor pay the bills, according to Sarah's parents."

He gets up and turns the chair back in position to face the desk. His eyes fall on the graphic novel, and he picks it up to flick through.

A smile flits his face. "My favorite scene."

He holds up a picture of kids sitting in trees, singing to welcome the Prophet to Medina.

I remember yesterday. "Why'd you tell Sarah about my book?"

"They needed somebody good at seerah for the quiz team." He walks to the door.

The slump of his shoulders stops me from yelling at him.

Mom is out for a hair and facial appointment, so I'm able to check out her room. There are three folded screens leaning against the wall, really pretty ones. Muhammad bursts in as I'm fingering the wood veneer on them, his phone in the air. "They're okay with it! Her parents are okay with me and Sarah continuing!"

"Yay." That's all I can muster. I let him have a high five.

• • •

Firing at Fort Sumter was a key catalyst action of the Civil War.

I take my exam notes into the living room. After ten minutes, I give up reading the same lines over and over. I have to get my camera.

Muhammad looks ridiculous, and I want proof.

Besides gliding along as though he's being transported on clouds, he also moves erratically, unsure of what to do next. He goes from kitchen to bathroom to dining room to living room and all sorts of combinations of those four rooms over and over. I consider sticking my feet out to trip him on one of the episodes of happy restlessness, but I'm afraid the noise of him falling would disturb Mr. Ram downstairs.

After careful positioning, I get one blurred picture of the whole thing.

Muhammad grabs my camera and keeps it away from me, via his typical flatulence threats, while he scrolls through my pictures.

Of course he finds and lingers on the stash of Jeremy's forehead pictures. "Very interesting. What do I see here?"

I run to my room, wondering how, merely a moment ago, I was *this* close to considering the possibility of maybe, perhaps, loaning him my room for a brief period of time. Now? No way.

There's no lock on my door, so I sit on the floor, leaning

against it, burning up, inside out, sinking my fingernails into my arms as I imagine Muhammad's face. We don't even fight like that anymore. Oh, what I would give to cat-whip his face into shape right about now.

That's when he knocks. And laughs.

Meow-hiss.

"You turd," I say.

"Oh, I'm the turd?" he retorts.

I stand and open the door in his face. The most excellent idea pops into my head.

"I can't believe what you're doing," I say. "I am so going to tell Sai—Sarah about this."

And, like I expect, my Ivy League brother stands still, a tiny sliver of fear encroaching on his face. Oh, I'm good at this.

"I've got pictures of my friends without hijab on my camera, and you, you sick pig, you're going through them?" I say. "Give me my camera!"

And right at the moment when the realization reaches his brain and numbs his body that he's probably seen Fizz et al without hijabs, I reach over and grab my camera. A masterpiece of how to cut your older brother down to size. Totally demolish him.

And make him forget about your forehead fixation.

But the guy bars my way out of the room.

"Wait a sec, freakoid," he says. "What about your crazy

pictures of . . . of . . . a guy's forehead? I'm sure Mom would want to hear about that late-breaking news."

I feel that squeeze of fear on my heart that invades on occasion, whenever "Mom" and "guy" are in the same sentence. But then I remember Fizz posing in her spaghetti-strap dress at Aisha's party last month. She would kill me if my brother saw her like that. She's the most modest person I know.

"Foreheads are nothing compared to seeing my friends uncovered," I say. "It's like peeking into their bedrooms."

He fidgets.

"Yeah, but I didn't do it on purpose," he says.

"Oh really? Your fingers were working through my pics due to some tic? Hand spasms?" I say, gaining strength again.

"Okay, then let's tell Mom about it when she gets home," he says. "ALL about it."

I blink into his stupid eyes. God, how could someone who finished a year studying philosophy be so, so, so petty?

Petty and, I have to admit, triumphant. There is no way I want Mom to see or know about those pictures of Jeremy.

"What do you want?" I say, defeated.

"Now we're talking," he says, leading the way to the living room. "I want you to chaperone some of my and Sarah's meets." And he actually smiles like, get this, a sheep.

I want to shear him (does it hurt the sheep to be sheared?

And if it doesn't, I don't want to shear him), but I stay quiet, listening to his dastardly plan.

"Right now, Sarah's dad or mom does all the chaperoning, at their house mostly," he says. "They suck the fun out of the whole thing, you know?"

"It's not supposed to be *fun*," I say. "It's supposed to be serious. Islam is serious. Marriage is serious. Who said anything about fun?"

"Well, Sarah is fun. I'm fun," he has the gall to say. "We want to know if we're fun together."

I make a puking motion.

"I don't want any part of this. I don't believe in early marriage anyway."

"But you believe in early foreheads?"

I make my best shut-the-hell-up face.

And then break down and give in. "Okay, so I like guys with high foreheads. So what?"

"A certain guy with a big forehead," he says. "Who is he? Maybe I can scope him out for you at the mosque."

I quickly change the subject at hand.

"What's in it for me—chaperoning your 'fun' interviews."

"Besides blackmail?" he says. "Well, there's also that matter of getting some reward from Allah for being nice to your brother."

"I can't believe you just did that. Use Allah and blackmail in the same sentence. You suck."

I go to the kitchen to check on what else he saw from my pics folder. I systematically erase each of Jeremy's pictures. He belongs to Tats now anyway.

"Remember we have a date tomorrow," Muhammad calls. "Dinner at her favorite restaurant."

As I head back to my room, I accidentally sweep his men off the Risk game board.

I'm so angry, I study the Civil War for four hours straight. I decide to *never* give up my room to Mom and Muhammad's confederacy.

MISFITS AND MONSTER

Mom opens the door to my room. She's wearing a new glittery scarf, and it's pulled back near her ears, highlighting long pendant earrings.

She never wears her scarf like that.

Sandra Kolbinsky's mom had started dating right after her divorce, and, in eighth grade, Sandra told me that a change in dressing signaled someone new in the picture.

"I'll be home late. Auntie Maysa and I are going out for dinner. She's here already, in the living room."

"By yourselves?"

"Auntie Ameera might join us. Why?"

"Just wondering. Are those new earrings?"

"No, they're old. Do you like them?" She stands in front of my dresser mirror and tilts her head to look at them. "Because I never wear them. They're too much, aren't they?"

"No, they're really pretty. It's just that, yeah, you never

wear stuff like that." I close my books. It's almost time to head to the mosque for the quiz game.

She slides the earrings off and puts them on the dresser. "You have them."

"No, Mom, I don't want them." I pick them up to give them back. They're heavy, and I can tell they're expensive from the way the stones feel.

"I haven't worn them at all. They sit there in my dresser because I'm not even sure I like them." She's leaving the room, but I follow her into the hall. "Janna, you think they're pretty so I'd rather you have them. Besides, Dad bought them for me."

Auntie Maysa pokes her head out of the kitchen, glass of water in hand. "What is this thing your mom doesn't want? That's too pretty?"

"Earrings." I hold them up for Auntie Maysa. "Pretty, right?"

"Oh yes. And Husna, you're wearing those. Especially tonight." Auntie Maysa puts the glass down on the counter and marches over. She takes the earrings from me and stills Mom's head to slip them back into her ears. "When are you going to realize that looking good isn't wrong now that you're divorced? Life doesn't end. It can start again. Especially tonight."

Auntie Maysa winks at me.

• • •

On the drive over to the mosque, Muhammad brings up Jeremy's forehead again.

"It has to be one of the Arab or Bosnian guys," he says. "Or Turkish. Turkish guys can have some foreheads."

I stay quiet, and dignified, like the North during the Civil War, and concentrate on the way the windshield wiper keeps missing this one part of the bird scat that Muhammad commissions it to take out. He sprays more and more cleaner and switches the wiper speed higher and higher, but the scat stays on. I totally admire its fortitude.

"Hameed!" he shouts. "I just *know* it's Hameed. Right?

My lips are sealed. *Bird scat. Bird scat. Bird scat.*

"What's the big deal? You know all about Sarah," he says. "You even got me interested in her."

"What?" I ask. "*I* got you interested in her?"

Forget bird scat, I had other scat to look into. The bull kind.

"Yeah," he says. "You kept talking about all the things she was doing at the mosque. And then I'd see her there, doing exactly what you said she was doing. With this big smile on her face the whole time. Nice, I sez to myself."

"Yeah, right," I say. "I kept complaining about all the things she was doing. Like this Fun-Fun-Fun Islamic Quiz Game thing."

"At least she's doing something," he says. "What're you doing?"

Bird scat. Bird scat. Bird scat.

"Oh yeah, I forgot—you're busy taking pics of guys' foreheads," he says, smiling.

I grit my teeth. I will resist.

As I pass the prayer hall, far behind Muhammad, who bounds ahead to join Saint Sarah, I see the visiting youth groups inside, in two huddles, prepping. Our group is downstairs in the cafeteria, where the game will take place.

Even though Fizz and her sisters are up at the front (upon orders of their mom), I stay at the back of the cafeteria, far from the makeshift stage, where team-member-selection deliberations are going on. Fewer chances of being called on as a contestant for the game.

I'm sitting on my own, scrolling through my new phone, adding numbers, when someone moves into my peripheral vision.

Farooq. Monster.

He's decided to hang out at the back too. I lower my phone. I feel it in my body, a seizing happening inside. I need to be aware.

I need to actively ignore him.

I deploy my intrigued-at-the-spot-behind-the-emcee's-head trick, but it's to no avail. He sits directly across the aisle, on the guys' side. This is one time I'm happy we have gender-separated seating at the mosque, but it still doesn't stop the feeling of ickiness that spreads over me when he's so close. He keeps up a steady flow of sidelong glances.

I'm trying hard to pretend he isn't here, but he's pretending I'm the *only* one here.

I get up and move to the first row, where there are a lot of empty seats. I'm taking long breaths in and out to calm myself when I notice Saint Sarah up on the stage, giving me a huge smile. And then I realize the emcee is repeating my name. Saint Sarah has picked me for her team.

Because of the monster, because I had to stand up to move, her gaze pounced on me.

I lumber up there, my legs feeling jointless, hatred for Farooq nearly crippling me with inertia.

When I get onstage, I notice the PICK ME FOR A CONTESTANT! signs on the backs of each of the front-row chairs. I have to fake a smile now, because what kind of loser would I be if I didn't mean to get chosen?

The team: my brother, Saint Sarah, Aliya, me, Sausun, and—get this—the Shazam! dude from the community center. From the shoulder bumps Muhammad is giving him, it's evident they know each other. I never noticed him before here at Amu's mosque.

We convene in the kitchen to talk "strategy" for the remaining ten minutes before we face the two teams from the other mosques. Saint Sarah takes over immediately, assessing the team, pondering our combined brain capabilities, assigning responsibilities—in general, doing what she does best: bossing around the rest of us.

I stay quiet even though I want to ask if there is a possibility of unjoining the team. And then I see him, peeking through the crack in the slightly open door.

It's him again. I know because I see his white thowb, a traditional long robe. He always wears it at Muslim events. Like he's some holy person.

He isn't moving, but standing at an angle where I can see him. His modus operandi at public events. He wants to break me.

Everyone else is talking, animated, excited, hopeful that this year, our first year, we'll win miraculously and then head to the regional Islamic Quiz Bowl competition, even though the other two teams are more experienced. Even Sausun has relaxed her ever-present frown.

"And what about you, Janna?" asks Saint Sarah. "Are you fine with seerah, or do you have another category in mind?"

Perverted, stalking guys, I think. I shrug.

"These are the topics: Qur'an, seerah, prayers, laws, worship, and general," says Saint Sarah. "We've divided most of them already but can reshuffle if you want."

I shrug again. He hasn't moved.

"She's really good with seerah," Muhammad contributes. "Remember I told you she's writing her own version at home, a graphic novel?"

He beams at me, like I'd say, *Aw shucks, bro. What a piece of sweet you are.*

"That was when I was like nine years old," I say.

Sausun snickers.

"But you're not finished. It's a work in progress," Muhammad says, not letting go. "Don't lie, Janna. I saw it on your desk even today."

He smiles at Saint Sarah as if he's expecting her to say, *Aw shucks, beau. What a piece of heaven you are.*

She clears her throat, clutches her clipboard, and says, "Actually, Nuah is interested in seerah too if you don't want it, Janna."

Shazam! waves his hands like he's conducting a plane landing in front of him. So that's his name, Nuah, the Arabic version of Noah.

"No, no," he says. "She can have the topic. If she wants it, that is."

He looks at me, one eyebrow raised into a medium-size forehead. He's still wearing a necklace of beads, but the pendant's out of his shirt now. It's a long wooden piece with a cluster of threads dangling from the end. He's wearing a tasbih, a necklace of prayer beads.

"It's a good topic; we need someone who's into it," Nuah says, smiling. "And I wanted the laws category too and, hey, guess what? It's still available. What do you say—you do seerah and I do laws?"

I nod, to shut down the focus on me. Aliya smiles and holds up a stiff thumb.

"Great," Saint Sarah says. "Team, let the games begin!"

We turn to go. Farooq moves away so there's no evidence he's been standing there the whole time. Except for the residue of his presence dripping over me.

How do you wash off what cannot be seen?

We win. I cry crocodile tears of joy to cover the real sadness of it all, and now there's a permission form for Mom to sign to let me go to the regional game, next weekend, in Chicago.

Muhammad goes out again as soon as we get home. Mom is still out, so I Google-Earth Jeremy's address, as I usually do when I'm alone. This time it's for nostalgia's sake, I tell myself.

A stash of candy is spread around me on the bed. Auntie Fatima was right: Goodies rock, especially because the winning team got to divvy up and take the leftovers home.

I'm eating a happy-face lollipop and admiring the turquoise-framed door on Jeremy's split-level bungalow when my new cell phone rings, jolting me with its novelty. It's my first cell phone call. Ever.

Tats. How in the world did she get this number?

I ignore it at first but then begin to wonder what she has to tell me that's so important on a Saturday night.

My threshold is five minutes, I tell myself. I'll let her talk for five minutes.

"Yes?" I ask. "How'd you get my number?"

"Your brother texted it to me this morning," Tats says. "Are you sitting down?"

"Yes," I say.

"So guess who I'm sitting across from? At Wishbone's?" she asks.

"Yes?" I ask, zooming in and out on the number 132 on Jeremy's door. There's a red Volvo in the driveway.

"Matt. He's with his mom and dad. And I'm with my mom and dad. He nodded. At *me*!" Tats says. "I took a bathroom break cause I just had to tell you. Can you believe it?"

"Yes," I say. How can she handle being in love with two guys at one time?

"Okay, I have to go back out there because, really weird, when I got up, I noticed his mom smiling at my mom. What if they start talking?" she says. "All right, I'm on my way back. Oh my God!"

"Yes?" I ask, mildly interested.

"They *are* talking. They're looking at the menu together. I'm going to die," Tats says. "Actually, I'm just going to calm myself down. I'll call you back. Are you up late?"

"Yes," I say, marveling at my ability to rely solely on this most simple word for our whole conversation.

I zoom out and switch to map view. From our condo, Jeremy's house is about five minutes away: walk down one straight, main road, turn left and then right, onto a quiet, leafy street. Across from this big, natural green-zone space with a lake. I wonder if he goes there often.

"Okay, if I can, I'll call you tonight. If I can. And, Janna, before I go, are you still mad at me? For talking to Jeremy?" she asks.

"Yes!" I say. Finally, a yes I really mean. "What do you mean, *talking to Jeremy*? About what?"

"Janna, I couldn't help it. Jeremy knows all about it."

"About?"

"You. He's highly aware of you now."

My mind freezes. "WHAT?"

"I'll have to fill you in," she says. "And it's not bad, Janna. It's actually really good—you're going to see. Oh God, Mom's waving me over. Bye!"

I close Google Earth. Now that he knows about me, it feels like I'm cyber-stalking.

MISFITS

"Tats called three times on the home line, while you were sleeping," Mom says when I enter the kitchen. Her freshly colored hair is tied up in a ponytail, and she's scrubbing the cupboard doors. "She said your cell phone is off."

She pauses, sponge mid-swipe. "I left the earrings on the dresser for you. Did you see them?"

I nod. "You sure you don't want them?"

"No, they're not me." She resumes cleaning.

I call Tats back while assembling my weekend breakfast: chopped bananas, peanut butter, yogurt, and granola. One of the variations of Dad's power breakfasts. *Fuel your ambition with assertive foods* was his message some time last month. It came with three recipes.

Muhammad is on his laptop, in the dining room, scrolling through job postings.

I stir my ambitious glop, standing and watching over his shoulder. Dog walker?

I call Tats again at her home number this time. It rings and rings.

Braille translator? Perfume sniffer?

"Muhammad?" I ask.

"Yeah?" he says, pausing on the posting for carbon manager to read the specs.

"Where are the philosophy jobs?" I ask. "Isn't that what you're studying?"

He turns to me and grins. "There is no job called *philosopher*, dear sis."

"As if I didn't know that," I say, redialing Tats's cell. I tilt my head to secure the phone between my ear and shoulder, and taste a big spoonful. I put too much peanut butter in, and my teeth find it difficult to wade through and locate the banana chunks.

"I'm just taking something for a year," he says. "How does furniture tester sound? For La-Z-Boy?"

"It sounds awesome if it means you'll stop hogging the whole table with your stuff," I say, plunking my bowl down in the one tiny space free of paper.

I dial Tats's home number again. In case I missed her being in the bathroom or something.

Come on, Tats, I think. *Pick up and give me the goods.* Last night I went over some scenarios and got almost giddy—a strange sort of giddy that was speckled with big drops of fear. But the feeling of possibility is intoxicating. *Jeremy and Janna* even sounds good together.

This could be the start of something exciting, scary, cozy, delicious—if I ever get through to Tats.

I call Tats's cell phone one last time, in case maybe she *was* in the bathroom or something, right at that precise time when I called earlier thinking she had been in the bathroom or something before *that* point in time. The power breakfast is getting soggy, but I can handle it, when *possibilities* exist.

Absolutely no answer—but still, doesn't rule anything out.

I put the phone down and realize, by the intense way Muhammad is scrutinizing me, that I have the remains of a dreamy smile on my face.

"Yes? May I help you?" I say, my mouth newly unstuck from peanut butter cement. "Don't you have a livelihood to pursue or something?"

"By the way, your friend Tatyana called a minute before you got up," Muhammad finally lets me know. "I told her you were sleeping, and she said not to call her back because she was going to her grandparent's cottage. She'll be back late tonight. Won't see you until Monday at school, she said."

"Thanks for telling me. *Now*," I say. "Thanks, Muhammad."

"No problem," he says, missing my sarcasm as usual or

ignoring it in that philosophical way of his. "It's the least I can do when you're doing so much for me tonight!"

He smiles at me—that smile again, a mixture of gratitude and hope and desperation.

"Sheep shearer, that's your next job," I say. "You can become a sheep shearer."

MONSTER

I'm on the bus with Fizz, en route to the mosque open house. She's telling me about Rambo's addiction to Wonder Bread, a sure feline prediabetic indication, but I'm not listening. Being the handy friend she is, she twists herself to smack me with her laptop bag.

"Janna," she says, holding tight to the strap overhead. "You're not here. And you're staring at that guy near the front."

I'm not staring at the guy near the front, but I know why Fizz thinks so: He's pretty good-looking; plus he falls into the admirable-forehead category. But I'm just having a zone-out moment, when there's nothing going on inside but it feels good against the blur of noise on the outside. A comfy vacuum.

I mouth an apology to Fizz and watch her rooting in her bag as the bus pauses. There it is, beside the tissue package she takes out, the little green book with embossed-gold writing that she carries around with her, *One Hundred and One Evils and Their Islamic Cures*. I decide against discussing the newest development with Jeremy revealed by Tats last night. Fizz is prone to remedying me and would invariably seek the answer to my "problem."

"So guess what? Your uncle asked Farooq if he would lead some of the Taraweeh prayers for Ramadan this year." Fizz beams at me. "His parents are like, *finally!* Farooq finished memorizing the Qur'an two years ago, you know. We don't get why your uncle took so long to ask him."

Now I know why I've been subconsciously cocooning myself in that vacuum of numbness. The prospect of the monster being at the open house is high. This knowledge must have been simmering under the surface of my thoughts.

The bus lurches away from a stop. I still the camera around my neck and shrug at Fizz. "Ramadan is in two weeks."

"Yeah, but it's barely enough time to prepare. I'm so excited for him. He deserves this after all the hard work."

I wish there were a way to still my heart. It feels like it's not mine and wants out of my body. I seal it shut with another shrug.

I can't tell her. I can't tell Fizz because she'd never believe such an unholy thing.

We get off at the next stop and run across the multilane road to the mosque. There's a large neon-on-black sign on the patch of grass by the road that says MOSQUE OPEN HOUSE: ALL ARE WELCOME!

The lawn is strewn with tables laden with wares because the open house is really one big superbazaar, a suburban souk, with haggling thrown in for authenticity. People are milling already, and I spot our regular non-Muslims, Cassie, Darren, and Julie, among them.

Fizz sets up her corner, selling scarf jewelry, and I snap some pictures of that. She made the decorated pins herself, melting and molding malleable plastic into interesting shapes, seated at a picnic table in her backyard a few weekends ago. I was there trying to convince her to go wildly corporate, while packaging the trinkets for her.

I look up after taking a picture of a basket of dangly American-flag scarf pins that Fizz thinks will sell like mad for the Fourth of July and see Julie seated at a henna booth across the aisle, with a big smile on her face. Time to take some strategic pictures.

I frame a shot of a woman in niqab, a face covering, decorating Julie's freckled arm with intricate designs of henna. I check the picture on the LCD display. Sausun is behind the niqabi woman, frowning into my camera. She ruined a perfect shot. I didn't even realize she was at the booth.

I fit the viewfinder to my eye again. She begins a scowl again.

I go over.

"My uncle, Shaykh Jamal, you know, the *imam* of the mosque here, needs pictures for the website. That's what I'm doing, Sausun. Is that okay with you?"

"Sure." She teases a part of her scarf that's hanging on her shoulders and lifts it across her face so only her eyes show. "There. Take the pic. I'm working toward this anyway. One day this will be me full-time so shoot away."

"You're really going to cover your face?"

"Niqabi all the way."

I get another shot. A great one, actually: two women with their faces covered, one with chunky Doc Martens boots on, beside an unveiled woman with a huge smile on her face, glancing at her arm being decorated with henna. Sausun drops her face veil when I wave thanks.

"Assalamu alaikum, Janna!" I turn to see Amu walking toward me. This weekend his white beard is cropped close to his face, and he is wearing a linen safari suit. He does that: go from a luxurious, long Moses beard and authentic thowb-wearing-imam look to a gentrified-summer-tourist-imam look, depending on the occasion. He gets criticism from the congregation for both getups. The conservative portion thinks he's being "liberal" if he wears non-Eastern clothes, and the liberal members of the mosque think he's not being of the people if he wears Eastern clothes. What they don't know is what I've noticed: When Amu wears Western clothes, he gives sermons on topics conservatives like to hear about, and when he wears Eastern clothes, his topics appeal to liberals. Like I said before, my uncle is very smart.

"Walaikum musalam, Amu." I return his greeting of peace

and give him a hug. He immediately turns to everyone around him and says, "This is my niece, you know! Janna, my sister's daughter."

He always does that to make sure he gets no flak for hugging me, a female. He told me once that being an imam meant a lifetime of getting scrutinized by Muslims for everything you do.

"Muhammad is over there helping out. He's been here for hours." Amu indicates the refreshment and snack area. There's a huddle of college kids setting up. "He told me he's moved back home."

"Yes, he changed majors."

"If he has to, I told him he can come live with me." Amu gives me a brief look before returning to scanning the crowd again. That look tells me Mom has told him my stance on Muhammad moving in. Amu's not impressed. "But I think he'd like to help your mom with things at home. That would be the best thing."

I check my camera settings. "What kind of pictures do you want, Amu?"

"Happy pictures. People enjoying themselves."

He waves Darren over. They walk across and pose for me in front of the clown jumping castle. With Darren's hair gelled and spiked high, the picture screams mosque website welcome page.

As Amu strolls away with Darren, I back out to widen the frame and crash into someone.

"Whoa," he says, grinning. "I wish I had a camera of my own, to get your expression."

The monster actually grazes my arm as he says this.

I fumble around the henna table and make it three tables over to a clothes rack, with as much nonchalance as one can muster when one's breathing is wheezy for no physical reason.

"Hallo! You look like a size four," a big man wearing forehead jewelry says, peering around the rack. "I have pink. You like pink?"

He holds up a sheer skirt with gold coins hanging off the waist, with even spaces between them. He gives it a shake and the coins jingle. Then he gives it additional shakes, at rhythmic intervals, and begins an Arabic song, swaying his hips.

I'm being serenaded by a belly-dance-clothing salesman.

I look around and see Muhammad in front of the refreshments table. Someone is tapping him on the shoulder and pointing at me. A couple of guys beside him are laughing.

He strides over to stand on the other side of the clothing rack, hidden from the big vendor.

"What are you doing?" he says.

"I'm on assignment, for Amu," I say.

"He told you to come over to this dude's table?" he says, leaning in to whisper. "The guy is not even Muslim."

"So?" I say. "I'm taking pictures of the *open* house. When we open the doors to the community? Ever heard of the concept?"

"The guy pretends to be Muslim," Muhammad says. "He comes here every year to sell us stereotypical stuff. Notice the camel bridles?"

I glance at the end of the booth and see hookah sets, golden swords, and blown-up black-and-white harem pictures from some previous era propped against, yes, camel bridles. The salesman leans in to see who I'm talking to, getting so close he bumps into my camera.

"Ah, this is your husband?" he asks, looking at my brother.

Muhammad grabs my arm like some backward, uncouth man and tugs me.

"I'm a photographer," I say. "This is my brother."

"Come on, we need help with refreshments," Muhammad says, indicating the yellow sign across from us that says DRINKS!

There's a whole crowd of Muhammad's friends hanging out there, guys with fledgling beards and girls with poufy hijabs, supposedly gender separated but, really, getting chatty with one another. The halal way.

I make a face at Muhammad and see Farooq hovering across from us, pretending to look at Islamic books.

A burly man wearing jingles on his forehead is a welcome sight at such times.

"I'm going to take some close-ups of this guy's table," I whisper to Muhammad.

He looks back at the refreshment stand. Saint Sarah has

arrived to bless the place it seems, from the way she's waving her clipboard around.

"It's for this thing I'm doing for my photography portfolio," I say. "This series called Real Fake. Stuff that is crazy ironic."

Either Muhammad is easily swayed by art mumbo jumbo or he wants to get back to schmoozing, because he begins backing up.

"Wait," I say. "Can you tell Fizz's cousin over there that she needs help at her table? Thanks."

He nods and whispers, "Be on guard," before turning away.

I accept the pink skirt from the belly-dance guy and hold it up. Through it, I see Muhammad sending Farooq on his way to Fizz's jewelry stand. The monster looks over once more before he turns down the aisle, but I shield myself with the gauzy fabric.

"No, that is not for your face," the belly-dance vendor says. "You wear *this* on your face."

He hands me a mock veil. I jingle it and he laughs. I vow to stay at the real fake booth and help out. You know, to educate the man on real Islam, while protecting myself from a scary Muslim dude roaming these parts.

It's a good thing that only I know about Farooq, because that only leaves one person, me, to ponder the irony of the situation.

• • •

The belly-dance vendor, Mr. Khoury, is a Christian from the Middle East. "Okay, yes, I'm not Muslim. But I like this open house. And you like the stuff I sell?"

I nod and click pictures of his table. The truth is people do stop to buy his wares. Embroidered fabric wall hangings mostly. They're actually nice—dark colors entwined in geometric patterns.

Those and the battery-powered plastic swords. Little kids are going crazy for them.

"Do you have any kufis, sir?"

I look up at the familiar voice. It's Nuah, formerly the Shazam! dude, holding books and wearing a T-shirt that says HI, MY NAME IS RANDOMLY SELECTED under an airport symbol.

"Kufis? I don't know—do I?" says Mr. Khoury, spreading his arms open over his tables. "I've got lots of things, so maybe I'll have kufis, too?"

"Kufis, caps for your head?" Nuah circles his curly hair with one hand and, with the other, waves at me in acknowledgment. "The traditional kind?"

"Now that's funny." The vendor puts his hands on his hips. "How do we get a cap on that hair? It will be like squeezing small socks on a bear."

He pantomimes the action with both hands, grunting to animate it further. Muhammad glances from across the aisle, where he's handing out lemonades to three girls wearing identical outfits. He queries me with a series of head tilts. *Everything okay?* he mouths. The girls turn to look at me.

Nuah laughs. "The kufi is for my little brother. He has a buzz cut, not hair like mine." He tufts his Afro.

"Ah, I see. Then I think I may have some in my van. It's like a warehouse in there." Mr. Khoury looks at me. "Will you watch my table for me, my assistant?"

"Now, *that's* nice of you," Nuah says after Mr. Khoury leaves. "Assisting this merchant gentleman here."

"Actually, I'm taking pictures for the mosque website."

"Some would say that's even nicer."

". . . aaaand I get paid to do it. It's part of maintaining my uncle's website." I pause my picture taking to see his reaction.

"So if my calculations are right, you're pretty loaded. This gig and Mr. Ram, you must be raking in the big bucks."

"Those are not even part-time jobs. You're the one with the real job."

"Correct." Nuah puts his books on the table to pick up one of the popular plastic swords. "Also correct is that I head to college in one more year. You know the tortoise and the hare? I'm the tortoise, and the racetrack's my bank account. I've been saving for years."

"Where do you want to go?" I lower my camera. This topic always excites me. I've been dreaming of college since middle school.

"Ah, you mean my finish line? Caltech, engineering." He swings the sword in the air like a lightsaber, both hands on the hilt. It responds by lighting up and making a clanging sound. When he slashes the opposite way, the sound changes slightly. "Pretty nifty toy."

"Yeah, those are bestsellers." I glance at his books. *The Content of Character* by Shaykh Al-Amin Mazrui and *The Study Quran*.

"Hope you didn't take pictures of that, kids walking around with swords in front of the mosque. That's all we need, more images of 'violent Muslims.'"

Mr. Khoury returns, holding a bin. He opens it to reveal flattened caps arranged in neat rows. He takes one out and pulls it open. It's a red fez, high and tapered at the top with a hanging tassel.

He motions for Nuah to come closer and places the fez on top of his head. I lift the camera and snap a picture.

Muhammad is by the table. "What're you guys up to?"

"Brother of my assistant, what do you think?" Mr. Khoury asks, motioning at Nuah.

Nuah poses for Muhammad, his hands resting on the hilt, sword pointing down, the fez sitting precariously on his hair. I take another picture.

Nuah takes the cap off and places it on the table along with the sword. "Here comes the *man*."

He advances toward someone and brings him forward. It's the monster.

"This guy here is helping fix up my recitation of the

Qur'an." Nuah's arm is around him as he turns him toward Muhammad. "On his own time."

"Dude, I know this guy from when we were kids. You're the one that's just getting caught up with the scene. This guy here is gold." Muhammad shakes the monster's hand.

"Thanks for getting your uncle to set me up to lead Taraweeh, man." The monster crosses his arms. I move behind Mr. Khoury and turn to look at the wall hangings draped on the dividers backing his stand. My eyes travel along the black lines of a gridlike design.

Muhammad told Amu to ask the monster to lead prayers at the mosque?

"No problem. Who else but you? You ready?" Muhammad.

"Yup, pretty much. Gotta brush up in the next couple of weeks."

"Me too, brushing up before Ramadan." Nuah's voice. "Got the *Study Quran* to prep."

"Don't think he'll need that, bro. He's got it memorized." Muhammad, laughing. "The *whole* Qur'an, now that's something. Not a lot of us can say that."

"The whole book? Wow." Mr. Khoury moves in his excitement. I shift along with him, now looking at a navy-and-burgundy wall hanging. "Qul'li ma dha ya'qulu al-Qur'anu ani'l Yasue?"

No one says anything. Then Muhammad: "He's asking you to tell him what the Qur'an says about Jesus."

The monster doesn't answer.

"You know Arabic, right?" Mr. Khoury moves again.

"I'm not Arab; I'd have to read up on it." The monster, his voice lowered.

"I can tell you what the Qur'an says about Jesus. . . ." Nuah, but Mr. Khoury interrupts him.

"So you memorized a book, but you don't know what it says?" Mr. Khoury sounds incredulous. "A book you say God sent?"

"It's a lot of work, to memorize it all. People go to classes for years." Muhammad.

"But that's like my boss gives me instructions, and I just memorize them. I don't even know what the instructions are. And then my boss asks me if I did my job, and I recite his instructions back to him!" Mr. Khoury is waving his arms. I feel the moving air they generate. "My boss would fire me!"

"Lots of people do understand the Arabic. Some who memorize the Qur'an may not, but maybe for them it's a first step in their study." Muhammad. "Anyway, many read the English translation. We do know what the Qur'an says."

"So this gold guy here who memorized what he doesn't understand, what is the big deal? You agree or don't?"

Mr. Khoury presses on, and I slip through a gap in the rear dividers.

• • •

On the way home, Fizz points out a girl who gets on the bus with us and whips off her hijab as soon as she sits down, stuffing it into her bag.

"So why does she wear it?" Fizz wonders. "I feel like asking her that. If she doesn't like it, be like Miriam. Miriam goes around everywhere without hijab, even the mosque."

"Maybe that girl does like it," I say. "Just not wearing it everywhere. Maybe she's gaining strength by wearing it to the mosque."

"That doesn't make sense," Fizz says. "Choose it or don't choose it. Don't sit on a fence. Admit it—that's weak."

"Maybe," I say, clicking through my camera, looking at some awful pictures of hookahs and plastic swords, thinking, *What's wrong with being weak?*

I mean, I know Fizz isn't weak, except when facing her mother, but I know I can go wobbly-kneed in all kinds of scenarios.

I show her the picture of Nuah posing with the fez.

Fizz smiles. "Nuah. He goes to my school, a junior, new here. By the way, thanks for sending Farooq over. I was swamped at the table. Maybe girls started coming because of him."

No comment.

Fizz gets off, and I go on to my creaky building in the midst of a congregation of old condominiums, neither retro cool nor demolition ready—yet. Ms. Kolbinsky is leaning on the fence by the entrance, eating grapes from a bag. I wave at her, and she offers me some grapes. I trade two for a samosa from the box I'm bringing back for Mom.

"My daughter, she still didn't do the papers." Ms. Kolbinsky takes a bite out of the samosa. I watch her reaction.

"Not too spicy for you?"

"No, I make spicy food. This is good spicy."

"Mr. Ram likes spicy food."

"Maybe I can cook him something."

"Ms. Kolbinsky, I'll give you the new form I got you. Maybe tomorrow."

She waves good-bye with her bag of grapes.

Muhammad stayed back to clean up at the mosque and Mom's not home, so I let myself into an empty apartment. I have some quiet time to e-mail Amu the picture of himself with Darren and the one with Julie getting henna, the only good pictures I took today.

As I clear the bed to study, I think about Amu's pointed remark about Muhammad staying with him. That bothers me, but not because my brother won't be living here with us. I'm too used to him not being around. It bothers me because Amu looked disappointed in me.

The monster is going to lead Ramadan prayers.

I see his hands raised in takbeer to begin prayers, with everyone standing behind him in neat rows.

The same hands.

I block it by slamming my backpack on the desk.

I take out my math textbook and toss it on the bed.

I hate him. People think he's great: Fizz, Amu, Nuah.

My brother thinks he's great.

Sinking to the floor, I rest my head on the bed.

Why do I have to bear his evil in me?

It's his evil. So why is it me that's hurting?

SAINT

Mom knocks as I'm putting on my hijab to go to the restaurant with Muhammad and Saint Sarah. I didn't want to go before, but I'm really dreading it now that I found out Muhammad is in love with Farooq. *He set up the Ramadan gig for him.*

"Thanks for going with them. I appreciate it," Mom says. She sets a laundry basket on my bed. It's my hand washables, ironed and folded.

"Can I borrow some of your scarf pins, Mom? I can't use my magnet ones on this scarf. Too thick."

"Sure. You know where they are, same place." She starts opening my drawers to put away my clothes.

"Mom, I'll do that. See, this is another reason why I refuse to share a room." I turn to her at the door. "You're always babying me."

She lets go of an open drawer and raises her hands as if

she's facing a cop with his gun drawn. "Just trying to help you because you're busy, but if you want me to leave, I will."

I head to the dresser in her room. As I open the junk drawer, a flyer, one end snagged in a crevice in the wood above, unfurls.

MEET YOUR MATCH!
A New Kind of Muslim Marriage Service
Operating in YOUR City on Select Dates
Enjoy dinner and then proceed to a roundtable-
style series of introductions to interested,
HIGHLY eligible singles in your area.
We welcome everyone!
Eastspring: June 12

June 12 was yesterday. Mom's long-pendant-earrings day.

I close the drawer and decide to change my scarf.

"I think I have it. I've been thinking about it since you told me about your forehead thing." Muhammad, giddy about his date, is driving silent me. "Now I'm pretty sure the guy in your pics is white. I can tell."

I stare ahead.

"So, I'm thinking, the whole day, yesterday and today, I didn't see one guy that fit the description at the mosque. None of the white guys there have such prominent foreheads." He turns to check my face. "By the way, I'm trying to help you."

I make no sound.

"So, I think, this guy is not Muslim." He looks at me again. "And that's okay. It happens."

I can't help it when I hear that. "Yeah, I know: Melissa, Samantha, and Jennifer."

"Fourth grade, sixth grade, and seventh. Crushes from long ago."

"What do you want? Why are you Sherlocking me? I'm already doing this date thing for you."

"I'm helping you like I said." He turns the car north onto the main street of Eastspring. "Sometimes you just have to find alternatives. And then it hit me today, while at the open house, at that table where you were taking pictures."

I turn to him. What is he going on about?

"You know who I can see you with? And who has kind of a big forehead? Farooq, Fizz's cousin." Muhammad stops at a light and beams at me. "You love Fizz's family, so it's like a bonus."

I close my eyes and turn away.

"Okay, suit yourself. The guy is the real deal. If you knew him, you'd completely agree."

When we arrive at the restaurant, Harold & Fay, Saint Sarah is waiting by the doors, wearing a flowery summer dress with high platform sandals. Her scarf is held up by a pink peony tonight. She flings her arms out when she sees us and envelops me in a tight, perfumed hug as if she hadn't seen me this afternoon at the open house. Then she proceeds to link arms with my stiff self as Muhammad opens the door for us.

I get a feeling that it's going to go downhill from such a grand entrance, so I give myself some advice as we step into the uptight, uptown restaurant: *This is about them. Don't make it worse than it already is. Keep your mouth shut, except to open it wide to eat the most expensive appetizer and dessert on the menu on Muhammad's tab.*

But then she, Saint Sarah, squeals when she finds out that I'm an appetizer, no dinner, and yes dessert person too, like her.

"I knew you were amazing, Janna!" she says, as if being like her immediately catapults me into another class of human beings.

It keeps getting worse, the squeals, every time she finds out another thing we have in common (all of which she's teasing out of me with the precision of a brain surgeon). A weird, completely alien feeling suddenly pierces my heart for a brief, fleeting moment. I feel sorry for my brother, who is trying to daintily eat this tiny piece of deepwater char with mustard greens, preserved fennel, and watercress puree while interjecting what he thinks are witty observations to divert the attention back to himself.

She's forgotten about him.

When Muhammad flops back in his seat, apparently giving up on us and his food—his plate a work of art, swirled from more fork action then eating action and resembling the deep murky waters from whence the fish came—the feeling of sympathy flees, and I decide to sprint to the front lines. I'm going to decimate him for linking me and the monster so effortlessly. I'm going to annihilate him.

To do it properly I know I have to wait to spring efficiently, intensely, in such a way as to get to the jugular of the whole thing in one or two swipes.

I get my opportunity when the waiter brings the dessert menu.

"Yum, dessert!" I say, mustering excitement from the thinning air.

"Ooh, this is going to be good!" says Saint Sarah. "What will it be for you, Janna?"

"Well, let me see . . . will it be oozing chocolate lava cake at sixteen dollars or the caramelized runny butter tarts at fourteen dollars or the . . . ," I say, trailing off.

Then, expertly, I stop and look up, stricken.

"What is it?" Saint Sarah asks.

"Nothing," I say. "I think I won't be having dessert," I add meekly, closing the leather-bound menu with a faint sigh.

"Why? You can't only eat breadsticks," Saint Sarah says, glancing at me, then at Muhammad as she notices my "surreptitious" peeks at my brother.

"No reason," I say. "Except that I'm actually full. Buffalo mozzarella breadsticks with pumpkin seed sauce, you know."

She looks at me again, adjusting her cotton-candy-pink hijab in wonder.

"Muhammad," I say, turning to him and leaning forward to gaze thoughtfully into his eyes. "I forgot to ask: Did you get that job you applied for? Or are they saying the philosophy thing is not cutting it? Like the others did? Mom's been wondering too, because of the rent increase."

"Oh," says Saint Sarah. She closes her menu too.

Muhammad stares at me, confused. I love that look on his face.

"Sorry," I say, giving what I hope is a tinkly laugh. "I forgot: Don't discuss finances—or lack of—at the dinner table. Sorry, Muhammad."

His eyes narrow. He's getting it and will soon gather the forces of his puny yet searing rejoinders, so I stand. "I need to go to the restroom. Sarah, are you going to come with me so that we keep this halal? I don't want to get in trouble with your dad for leaving you guys alone."

Saint Sarah gets up, looking at my brother with a mixture of pity and confusion. I love that look on her face too.

My back feels prickly all the way to the restroom, so I guess Muhammad is sending daggers my way.

In the restroom Saint Sarah shows me her new way to secure her hijab, as if I'd asked. I'm feeling victorious so I humor her, even letting her redo my hijab in the latest style.

When we get back to the table, there's a big sampler plate of *all* of the restaurant's desserts waiting for us. Muhammad stands up, pulls out my chair for me with a flourish and then Saint Sarah's before sitting down with a smile.

Saint Sarah smiles this soft smile back at him, and I realize right then and there, they're already an item.

And wham! Just like that, I understand why she focused on me during the whole dinner. She knows she only has me to win over so she'd gotten right to work.

I thought I was the stealthy one, but her? She's stealth with a smile.

MISFITS

Today is the hottest day thus far in the year, and that means most everyone will act annoyed as soon as I step into school. Because they'll be stripped to the teeniest clothes they're legally allowed to wear. And me? I'll look like I'm going on an Arctic expedition.

The first thing off everyone's lips will be *Don't you feel hot in* that*?* "That" meaning my covered-from-head-to-toe self. They'll act like their eyeballs will boil from the steam coming off me.

A kind, good-hearted person might be touched that people are being so empathetic to the personal weather condition of others, but the more *I* hear it, the more I fume. Thus, getting hotter. So I need to dress carefully today.

Tats says I wear too many layers, so I choose my thinnest shirt made out of T-shirt material. It's weathered near the neckline, like worn enough to see my bra strap, so I yank it off and put a tank on underneath before putting it back on. The shirt also kind of goes up at one side, because it's an asymmetrical cut, so I have to pull a short skirt over my jeans to cover the way it hugs my hips. With my scarf on, I realize that I'm layered again, and it's all in black. I pick up my backpack and do a silent scream at the mirror.

I'm not like Fizz. As soon as summer comes around, her family whips out these loose cotton tunics in colorful designs that her grandma sends from abroad. Sure, they keep cool, but I don't feel like looking like an exhibit at an international museum of exotica. I get called "exotic" enough at Fenway.

Fizz et al go to a Muslim high school. You're allowed to look different there because, apparently, it's a bastion of difference. They wear their hijabs in twenty-one different ways, according to Fizz. She wears the pull-on kind.

I have to wait until lunch to talk to Tats. We have a "temporary" cell phone ban currently at school due to some infringement of the rules by the regular ruffians, so now we all pay by being denied our civil right to text in the hallways. It's supposedly temporary, but it lasts until school lets out next week. Collective punishment, anyone?

Ms. Keaton stops me as I'm leaving English to let me know that my final timed essay has to be on *The Tempest*. I asked her earlier if I could do any of the literary works we'd studied this year. "You can do Flannery O'Conner next year for your independent project."

"Ms. Keaton, do you think Shakespeare demonized dark men by depicting Caliban in that way? A friend of mine thinks so."

"There are diverse ways of reading texts, depending on who you are. We all access books differently." She zips up her laptop case. "But it's true: Sycorax, his mother, was of North African background."

Mr. Ram must be concentrating on that part, while the only thing I see is that Caliban tried to assault Miranda.

In history, Mr. Pape does an interesting exam review period, where he puts the desks in a rectangular formation with one historical war image on each desk. We have to discuss among ourselves and put the images in an agreed timeline order. Then we're to stand behind an image of our choice and talk briefly about the topics the picture triggers in us. I stand behind the image of the woman in the war effort poster, raising her fist. *We Can Do It!* I'm sure I can talk about the way things changed for women during both world wars.

Lauren Bristol is beside me, behind the image of the mushroom cloud after the bombing of Hiroshima. She's been in my classes since I moved here but never says anything more than hi to me. She travels in the upper echelons of Fenway High, and getting a hi from up there is good enough.

"Discuss with the person next to you what you're going to say," Mr. Pape says. "Take three minutes."

Lauren looks to her left side and then at me and turns to

choose me. I glance at who she gave up as a partner. Sandra, Ms. Kolbinsky's granddaughter, who people call Mustache because of a port-wine stain birthmark under her nose. I was friends with her in middle school, but then she changed, and by the end of freshman year, she turned quiet, almost mute.

The guy at my right has already chosen his friend next to him, so I turn to Lauren. Sandra leans against the wall, partnerless. Mr. Pape heads our way.

"Janna, Lauren, make a group of three with Sandra." He motions for Sandra to join us.

After he leaves, Lauren turns her back on Sandra again and faces me. "So, what are you going to say?"

"That the Second World War, like the First, resulted in a lot of changes for women," I say, leaning out to address Sandra, too, who is slumped on the wall once more. "Because women were seen as being valuable to war efforts, and they kept things going with the industries back home."

"Okay, and my picture reminds me that no one thinks about the tragedy that results when places are bombed," Lauren says. "This image reminds me of the human costs of war and why no one has ever used nuclear weapons again. We're done."

I look at Sandra, who's standing by the picture of the naked girl running after being burned by napalm in the Vietnam War.

"Sandra? Your turn," I say.

Lauren stares at me and excuses herself. She stops to talk to Mr. Pape and heads out of the classroom.

"This picture reminds me of why war sucks," Sandra says, watching Lauren leave.

"I heard the girl in this picture lives in Canada," I say. "Well, she's a woman now."

"She's okay?" Sandra asks. "I thought she'd died."

"She's a spokesperson for peace or something."

"That's cool," Sandra says. "Okay, so this picture reminds me of why it's important to work for peace."

I smile at her just as Lauren rejoins us. "Sorry, had to take a bathroom break. My hair."

Her hair looks exactly the same as when she left: straight, dark and shiny, parted perfectly to showcase her profile.

Mr. Pape calls us to attention and starts the timeline presentations from my far right.

Lauren leans over to me. "She feels herself. In class."

"Who?"

"Mustache. I've seen it."

I'm quiet for a minute, pretending I'm listening to Mike talk about the development of cannons. "In this class? Because I haven't seen it."

Lauren straightens up. She doesn't say anything again.

Sandra follows me out to the cafeteria after history. It's sophomore lunch, and the halls are mostly empty.

"You know, your grandma wants to go to the games club at the community center really badly," I tell her.

"Yeah, but my mom's too tired to look into it. She works two jobs."

"Can you get your grandma to sign the forms? You can fill out the rest yourself."

"You have them?"

"I'll get them to you tomorrow." I make a mental note to add it to my agenda. "She's hilarious, your grandma. She likes Mr. Ram and doesn't hide it."

Sandra laughs as we enter the cafeteria. Tats waves me over.

I walk to our table in the corner, beside the entrance to the serving line. When I look back, Sandra is not behind me but sitting on the steps leading into the cafeteria pit, unwrapping a sandwich. Something tugs at me.

"Mind if Sandra sits with us?" I ask before I can stop my mouth that has a direct line to my heart.

"Why?" Tats says. "I thought we were going to talk."

Jeremy and Janna, my brain says.

The way Sandra slumped on the wall in history, like it was normal to be ignored, that's what gets me.

"I don't know. Maybe because today's the first time I heard her say something since ninth grade?"

"All righty then. We'll talk in gym I guess."

I catch Sandra's eye and point to the spot next to me. She shakes her head.

I shrug and pull my lunch out of my backpack. "Are we allowed to check our e-mail? Or is that part of the ban?"

"I checked mine." Tats chews on a carrot stick.

I read Dad's message: *Take your reward when you see it within reach. Don't question your luck. Success belongs to you.*

A bag is placed on the table next to my Tupperware of rice. Sandra slumps into the chair beside me.

I talk about the woes of living at Fairchild Towers for the rest of lunch period with Tats acting out the more colorful neighbors. Sandra sits and watches us, laughing once in a while.

Ms. Eisen informs us that we're going to continue our weights unit until Tuesday, after which point whoever shows up for the last classes will play softball in the field. "Tomorrow we'll be recording our abilities. I'll use the results as an evaluation for your final grade."

Tats raises her hand. "Can we have new partners?"

"No, everyone back to your assigned partners."

Tats and I say good-bye to each other, and I head to where Simone is waiting for me, soccer legs planted firm, mat spread out.

The only thing to do now is to meet Tats on the roof after school.

Only seventeen people, seventeen untouchable people, know about the roof. Even Lauren isn't in that high of an echelon.

Since Tats's brother was a member of the untouchable crew during his time at Fenway High, and since she heard him in his senior year bragging about it one day to his girlfriend, when Tats was hiding in his room, back when she was in the eighth grade, to see what her brother did there with his GF, and since she wrote the exact method of getting up on the roof in her diary to preserve it until we got to Fenway, we became the sixteenth and seventeenth people to make it to the top of the school. When he graduated, her brother handed over the key, dangling on an España key chain, to the old teacher's storage room, through which you could access the roof hatch.

It's apparent we're the only ones who hang out there just to talk, judging by the paraphernalia cluttered around the place. Some of the items, I have no idea what use they had. But if it's on the roof, it's probably illegal in some way.

By being there simply to talk, peacefully talk, we're almost blessing the place, you know?

"First," Tats says, settling against the itty-bitty vent, the safest place not to be seen from below, "did you know Matt sort of waved at me today? Like this."

She stands up, gets a guy swagger on, and then picks up a hand for a second, up to her hips, and drops it.

"And it was from across the hallway," she says proudly. "The two girls with him even looked me over. All because our families ate at Wishbone's at the same exact time. That is what is called *cosmic*."

I want to jump topics but I know she needs to unload, so I look impressed.

"And my mom's joined his mom's book club. That's the bad part," she adds, sitting down again.

"Why's that bad?" I say, thinking Muhammad would get so excited if Mom joined something with Saint Sarah's mom. It would get them to be friends and then pave the way for him and her to live happily ever after.

"Um, don't you know what those book clubs are for? They're therapy sessions. She'll be talking about her problems, me included, and next thing you know, Matt's going to hear all about it. It's at his house every two weeks." Tats sighs. "I tried to stop my mom. That's why she joined for real."

"Maybe he'll like you more, the more he hears about you secondhand. It's worked for others," I say, thinking again of Muhammad and his weird claim that my talking about Saint Sarah had prodded him into falling for her.

"Oh yeah, I'm sure he's going to like hearing about my 'learning' condition," Tats says. "Mom never lets up on that."

"Oh," I say. "Want some halal gummy bears? No piggy gelatin."

She takes a handful, picks a green one out, and bites off its head.

"Ugh, these aren't real gummy bears," she says, flinging them away. The headless one lands next to the remains of a joint. Evicted for being different.

"So," I say. "Jeremy?" I slowly arrange the remaining halal gummy bears in a circle on the roof in front of me, to contain myself, to bring myself down to earth. Actually, below earth, sublevel, into the depths of unfortunate occurrences.

I have this thing I do when I'm looking forward to something, when I notice myself getting overexcited, where I don't think of the great possibilities in detail—only the awful ones—so that when it turns out to be something amazing, I'm genuinely surprised. In an unpracticed kind of way. It may not be part of Dad's prescription for living successfully, but it's kind of the best thing if you have an active imagination.

These are the possibilities I've been wallowing in regarding Jeremy and me:

1) Tats told him I liked him. He said he'd walk by the sophomore hallway to give me my eyeful for the day, because he's into charity.

2) Tats mentioned my name as a potential photographer for end-of-year drama club pics, and he said he wanted to know how to spell such an interesting name. She told him to check with me as she had no clue.

And the last, most terrible one:

3) Tats mentioned my name as a potential photographer for end-of-year drama club pics, and he said he knows the right guy for me. His good friend Farooq.

I clear my head of that possibility.

"Oh, yeah," Tats says. "Okay, so, we're on a cleanup break at drama club and Jeremy's doing inventory of the lighting equipment with Ms. Jones and I kind of stand by, pretending to wait to talk to Ms. Jones, but I'm really observing him, right?"

I nod. I'm evening out the colors in the gummy bear circle, so it's balanced.

"And then he turns to me and smiles. This really nice smile."

I suppress the stab of jealousy that immediately makes itself known, right below my heart.

"I wave and say, 'Are you Jeremy?'" Tats continues, with this faraway smile on her face. "Because I've heard about what you did with the lights last year for *Macbeth*."

The knife of jealousy is reaching up. If it actually pierces my heart, I think I'll throw the gummies at Tats.

"He says yeah," Tats says. "And then, get this, we get dismissed early, and as we're leaving, he says, 'You're the girl who hangs around with Janna, right?'"

I freeze and stare at Tats. "What?"

And then I understand.

"Oh, wait, I know," I say. "It's because he's friends with this guy, Fizz's cousin. That's why."

Tats blinks at me.

"So you're going to finish my story for me?" she asks.

"Okay, finish," I say, settling back to continue the gummy bear collective.

"So I say, 'Yes, that's me, but how do you know Janna, 'cause she never mentioned it,'" Tats says. "Isn't that funny?

You mention him like four times a day. But I had to move carefully, right?"

I stay quiet because I'm about to explode. Either from the agony of waiting as Tats meanders through her story, the agony of finding out that it had something to do with Farooq, or the agony of carrying around so much potential happiness.

"He said, 'Actually, I don't know her; I've just seen her places.' Like a wedding he went to, his friend's brother's wedding. He said you were the only one from Fenway High there besides his friend," Tats says.

Farooq's brother's wedding in the fall. I'd been there with Fizz. *He'd* been there? He'd noticed *me*?

"And, Janna, he had this in-ter-ested look in his eyes, soooo . . ." Tats pauses. "I couldn't hold it in. I said, 'Oh yeah, I think Janna mentioned you being there, at the wedding. Yeah, actually, she's mentioned you a few times. Actually, lots of times.'"

"TATS!" I yell.

"Wait, wait, wait," Tats says patiently. "Because then Jeremy said oh."

I wait. I want to give her a few minutes before I push her off the roof.

"Then he looked down, looked up, looked around, looked down again, and said . . . drumroll, please," Tats says.

I stand up to get ready to push her off before walking back to the hatch, to get away from the scene of the crime.

"He said, 'Is she with someone? Like going out with anyone?'" Tats stands up and beams. "He likes you, Janna! You, you, you!"

She grabs my hands and we shriek. Then I stop.

"What did you say?" I ask.

"I said you were engaged to this guy from back home from when you were three, but otherwise no," Tats say.

"Funny. Tell me what you really said," I say, proud of the way I'm controlling my excitement.

"I said, 'No, she's not with someone. Have anyone in mind?' And then we both laughed. That's why you've seen him around, dude," Tats says, picking up her bag. "We have to go. This is around the time the smokers come up here."

"Wait," I say. I bend down and arrange the gummy bears into a heart. In the middle, I put a green bear (Jeremy) and a yellow bear (me) looking at each other.

After school I head to the kitchen and pour cold chocolate milk into the quaint old teacup with roses that Teta, my maternal grandma, presented to me last Eid. I stick in one of those long wiggly plastic straws that Mom kept from when I was four and sit on the window ledge in the living room, sipping slowly while smiling at the birds. I swear I can hear Snow White yodeling that lovely song she does somewhere off in the distance. (So, yes, I start humming along.)

I forget Muhammad is home, and, while he's not too sharp

in the intuition department, he wanders into the living room for some reason to stand and watch with nary a sound. When I stand up to add some graceful actions to the soundtrack, he snorts that laughter that he reserves solely for me. It's the kind of laughter that makes one want to act like a three-year-old and throw a tantrum—precisely because it is how an unkind grown-up would laugh at a three-year-old doing the Disney-princess thing with all due seriousness. It's a let-me-puncture-your-balloon-of-happiness laugh.

But, like I said before, Muhammad is not too intuitive, so he accepts my excuse that I'm practicing for some school play and not experiencing serious pangs of love. He goes off to pour himself some chocolate milk too.

Fizz calls, and I have a moment of uncertainty. I haven't practiced keeping the J excitement from my voice yet, and she's too good of a friend not to notice something so uncharacteristic of me: cheerful, enthusiastic hellos/salaams followed by comments observing the wonderful things around us humans. She'd definitely see through the fairy magic enveloping me, and I have absolutely no plans to update her, so I let the phone ring.

When it starts ringing again after a pause of three seconds, I pick up. It's Aliya, using Fizz's phone.

Aliya lets me know that Muhammad has dropped off my permission form for the regional Quiz Bowl and that two cars are going to Chicago on Saturday. Saint Sarah's tiny car has already filled up (let me guess: Muhammad is one of the passengers) and do I want to go with her, Nuah, and an extra guy to keep Nuah company (no idea who)? I say sure, sure.

Then she reminds me to brush up on more seerah, to be really ready, as there might be an audience for the competition. I say I've already reviewed stuff. Then she says we're meeting on Friday at Saint Sarah's place for a last practice. I say okay. Then she asks if I want to talk to Fizz. I say no and hang up quickly.

I'm afraid.

How did Fizz morph, in my mind, from a best friend with a no-nonsense attitude into this stern, judgmental person in the span of a few days? I can see the look she would have given me if she'd materialized on the roof when I was shrieking with Tats. She'd have reached into her bag for the green book with the gold title and flipped through the pages, her eyes never leaving me, and found the page on fornication, zina:

> *A Muslim is not to long for the things that lead to zina, such as kissing, being alone, and touching, for all these things are haram and lead to the greater evil which is zina. Do not come close to it.*

But I won't, I tell Fizz in my head. I won't do it, come close to it. I just don't know how to tell my heart to stop. Or to not choose Jeremy.

And I don't know how to tell it to stop smiling now that he chose me back.

For the rest of the evening, I study *The Tempest*. I fall asleep with a smile on my face even though I'm doing grim work. When Mom wakes me up for evening prayers, I'm clutching an old Franklin Covey agenda, one that contains a series of arguments to prove Caliban's depravity.

MISFITS

Ms. Eisen blows her whistle in the gymnasium. "The weights challenge comprises the first part of your exam. I want to see records of everything. Get your clipboards, girls."

Simone lets me go first. I pick up the weights and begin my squats.

After watching me for a while with her pen poised, Simone lowers her clipboard. The blank spaces on the chart tell me that she hasn't recorded anything.

"You know you can go up, right? It's better to do heavier weights and fewer reps," she says. She's one of those natural athletes who can do any sporty thing under the sun.

"But this is what I've been doing since we started weights. I don't want to change it now when we're getting marked for it."

"Are you feeling it? Tell the truth." Simone scrutinizes me as I extend my arms, having come up from a long squat.

"Not right this instant." It's true I haven't broken a sweat since we started.

"Do you feel it after class at any point?"

I think about it. "I'm not sure."

"Then you're settling for lighter weights, because the answer to that should be *It kills me*." Simone walks over to the rack of weights and points at two of them. "Here, this should do it."

She's pointing at ten pounds. Five times more than my regular weights.

"What? That's too much!"

"Don't waste time. Fewer reps, heavier weights." She walks back to the mat. "I'm just trying to help you."

I pick up the weights, and my arms fall immediately with the burden. Simone's tapping the clipboard.

Grunting, I get into position.

"Start!" Simone barks.

I squat and stand, sure I look like a weightlifter at the Olympics as my legs wobble. Sweat beads assemble on my forehead, ready to cascade.

"Good! I can tell you can feel it now." Her pen moves across the clipboard. "It's going to *kill*—I promise you. You're going to love it."

The front of my shirt is soaked as I switch to lunges. A swirl of hair releases itself from my ponytail. Others join it, frizzy and free.

"I'm impressed," Simone encourages me. "This is what it's all about."

I move on to mat exercises and after the last crunch lie there spread-eagle and panting, my hair a tangled ball around my red face.

Tats sticks her head in and obstructs my view of the ceiling.

"Get up," she says. "You have a visitor."

I get to my feet, pulling on her hand because my core is *done* for the day. I look over at the locker room, expecting some mutual friend of ours, but Tats shifts me to face the weight room, a separate facility that is connected to the gymnasium through an inconspicuous door.

Jeremy is there, raising his hand for a small wave.

If it had been the 1800s, I would've fainted right there.

As it's the twenty-first century, I go like this: 😮

Recovering, I wave back meekly and weakly, my mind scrambling to make sense of this latest development. My hair is showing to a guy. A guy unrelated to me.

To a guy I freakin' like.

This is so against my religion, I'm actually *flummoxed* for the first time since learning the word.

I turn to Tats, who's grinning like she's proud of her baby's first step.

"What the hell?" I ask her, smiling lightly in the general direction of Jeremy, who is beaming and kind of acting like he's waiting for me to walk my frizzy-hair self over to him.

"This is his spare period, and I was like, perfect, an opportunity for Jeremy to see the real Janna!" says Tats. "But what happened to your hair?" she whispers. "And why are you soaking wet? Ugh, is that sweat?"

"Tats, how long has Jeremy been here?" Has he seen my whole Olympian efforts?

"Since the beginning. Why?"

Simone hands me the clipboard and positions herself, taking a deep breath. There's an assemblage of enormous weights parallel to the mat, ready for her.

I pretend to watch her do sets of squats while grasping huge weights. The girl has Madonna arms.

"This is so not cool," I say to Tats, unclasping my bangs from a barrette halfheartedly holding them. I flip them over correctly, along the most flattering part in my hairline. "He's not supposed to see my hair, remember?"

Tats leans over and smooths the back of my hair. "Relax, it's just one guy. And it's just your hair. Dead matter according to Mr. McKay."

"Actually, it's my arms and legs, too," I say, looking at my T-shirt and shorts, feeling exposed, wishing Mom's coverall prayer outfit would suddenly appear. It's like a hazmat suit, with a skirt instead of pants.

"You're wearing huge culottes compared to Lauren's awesome teeny shorts," Tats reassures me. "And arms are like nothing, especially in your loose top."

"Why don't you just call them my state-issued phys ed pantaloons and balloon blouse while you're at it?" I say, getting irritated at the way she's periodically grooming me and then glancing Jeremy's way.

Jeremy's talking to Ms. Eisen, and whatever he's saying is making her laugh. I forgot, he's like some star on the baseball team.

Simone stops. "How many sets was that?" she asks.

"Um, six?" I say.

She repositions and begins again.

"Tats, get him out of here. I don't feel right about this," I say. Should I grab Simone's workout towel, a facecloth, and lay it on my head like a doily at the center of a coffee table? Or beeline to the locker room?

"Jan, just pretend you don't see him," Tats says. "He has every right to use the weight room. And tomorrow, put some leave-in conditioner in your hair before class."

If Jeremy wasn't looking over right at that point, I would hit her on the head with the clipboard.

Ms. Eisen walks over to us.

"Tats, disappear; Eisen is on her way," I say, moving my pen across the chart in a series of squiggles. "Get to your partner now."

"My partner's away, so Eisen already did my exam," says Tats. "Hi, Ms. Eisen."

Ms. Eisen nods at her and then motions for Simone to stop. "I need to talk to Janna here."

"Me?" I ask.

Ms. Eisen takes the clipboard from me and hands it to Tats. "Tatyana, take over for Janna. Janna, walk with me."

I succeeded all year in escaping Ms. Eisen's radar by being the average Jane or, in my case, the average Janna, and doing everything so-so. How is it that with less than two weeks left to go until year-end, she's walking with me now?

"Janna, I'm going to get a male student, a senior, to help me with our last couple of gym periods. I want to play softball to finish the year off, and Jeremy's on Fenway's baseball team. I'm telling you because of your hajeeb."

When she'd first used "hajeeb" I'd kindly pointed out it was hijab. She told me some words were too hard for her to pronounce, so "hajeeb" it is in gym class. Tats said I should have asked her why she has no problem pronouncing Genevieve's name.

A good question I dare not ask.

I glance at Jeremy as we pass him. He's pretending he isn't aware of us, but I know he didn't need that much concentration to roll up his left sleeve.

"Well, it's going to be outside, right?" I say.

"Yes, but we'll be doing drills inside first—especially tomorrow, with that heat wave forecast."

"Oh, because if it's outside, I'll be in hijab anyway," I say. "It's okay, Ms. Eisen."

"Well, I was telling you, not really asking your permission."

Ms. Eisen begins walking away and then turns back and says, "Don't you need your hajeeb right now? Five minutes till bell rings, so go get changed now."

She blows her whistle to gather the other girls.

I jog to the locker room, but before going in, I go Bollywood and pause to look at him again. He's standing and watching me, in my pantaloons and frizzy hair. With a nice smile on his face, like he likes what he sees.

Right at that moment, I feel like the most beautiful girl in the world.

Soon-Lee scribbles me a note. *This is crazy. Want to study today? After school?*

I nod. When we walked into math today, Mr. Mason handed out a ten-page package, copied back to back, entitled "A Course Review." As I flipped through, I noticed that there were at least four topics I didn't remember learning anything about. A hush fell over everyone as we went through our notes, the textbook, and "A Course Review," trying to find links to what we were taught this year.

Mr. Mason is looking at his phone, with his feet up on the desk.

Soon-Lee flips her hair to the left side, twists the ends, and begins working out a problem in her notebook. I peer over to see what she's deciphering.

Mr. Mason looks up. "A question, Janna?"

"Sir, I don't remember some of the topics in this package. Is everything in here going to be on the exam?"

"Everything." He goes back to his phone.

Robby pokes me with a pencil. I turn to him with a frown. His package is open to the second-to-last page, and he's pointing at the bottom. There are the remains of a website name that's only been half blocked off. I check the other pages in my package. They all show a rectangular outline near the edge of the page, like letters have been covered up before being photocopied. It's evident this is something Mr. Mason pulled from online somewhere.

No wonder it doesn't match what we've done in class.

Robby leans in to whisper. "We didn't learn half this shit."

Soon-Lee glances over. I point out the website remains to her. She goes through her own package, disbelief growing on her face.

"So which one of you is going to let Mason know this isn't fair?" His voice a thick whisper, Robby peers up at both of us from his slumped form on the desk.

Soon-Lee stares at him over her dark glasses. She peels a sticky note off a pad. Her pen moves across the yellow paper.

She passes it to me. *Why does it have to be one of US? MAN UP Robby.*

I crumple the note and drop it on Robby's desk, a smile on my face. He reads it and gives Soon-Lee the finger.

I pick out a highlighter from my pencil case and commence

highlighting each topic we haven't covered. There's a lot.

From behind Soon-Lee, Pradeep passes Robby a note that makes him crack up and nod.

"Robby, may I suggest you concentrate on your own learning." Mr. Mason raises his eyebrows. His phone is on his desk, and for the rest of the period he watches us.

"Maybe it's an experiment," Soon-Lee says. "A twisted experiment where he wants to check how well we can teach ourselves."

We're in the library at a pair of study carrels. Soon-Lee's got her iPad propped up, and it's been running a steady supply of YouTube videos demonstrating the new concepts we need to learn.

I show her Dad's message for today to make her feel better: *To spring back after failure, you only need two things: energy fueled by the memory of past successes and a vivid mental image of your success scenario. It's in your grasp if you spring immediately.*

"What does that even mean?" She pauses from recording formulas into her notebook. Her writing's gone from tiny, perfectly formed letters to chicken scratch.

"It means we need to concentrate on beating this thing with a positive attitude."

"We have less than a week before the exam, Janna. There isn't anything positive about that."

Familiar hyena-like laughter reaches us from the bank of

printers and photocopiers along the half wall separating the checkout area and the book stacks. I motion to Soon-Lee, whispering, "Robby and Pradeep."

We make our way to the bookshelves behind us. Through the gaps in books, Robby and Pradeep are visible, standing by a printer. Pradeep's backpack is open, and he's shoving in each freshly printed page.

"There's no way they should be this happy right after that math class," Soon-Lee whispers. "Unless . . ."

She steps out from the bookshelves, a pen still in her hand. "Hey, guys, what's up?"

Pradeep zips his bag and shoulders it. "Nothing, just wondering what that smell was. But then you showed."

Robby laughs and thumps Pradeep on the back. "Korean BBQ, meet Mr. Hacker."

"Shut up, man." Pradeep heads out through the turnstiles, clutching his backpack in his arms. Robby scrambles after him.

Soon-Lee beelines to the printer they were at, still humming as it prints out a blank page that says seven of seven. She pushes the menu button and selects *Jobs list*, from which she presses reprint.

The machine starts up again and spits out another seven pages. I turn the printout over. It's an exam, with the same website link from our course review lining the bottom of each page.

"What was that your dad said about springing immediately?" Soon-Lee says with a grin.

I let her make a copy for me. But that doesn't mean I'm going to use it.

After school I lie in bed, a buzz of thoughts swirling in my mind: hoping Fizz doesn't call again, debating whether to wear my hijab to gym tomorrow, wondering if Jeremy is going to talk to me in the morning. I'm also mustering the courage to take a careful look at the exam. As I sit up to rummage in my bag for the contraband matter, Muhammad barges in. "Dad's on Skype."

Muhammad sets up his laptop so that we're sitting on the couch with the window behind us, the rest of the apartment strategically hidden from view. We'd agreed that this is the best setup for video chatting with Dad as he sometimes starts asking about Mom's buying habits if he glimpses anything new in the apartment. I guess he's careful about his child support payments being put to good use.

"Greetings, people of Eastspring. What's the latest from the hinterlands?" Dad's wearing a suit and tie, but I can tell he's at home because he's holding Luke on his knee. We call the baby laddoo, like those Indian dessert balls, due to some serious chubbiness all around and due to the fact that Dad's company is one of the premier prepackaged Indian sweet makers in North America. We call our other half-brother, Logan, laddoo too. The laddoos are a year apart.

"Hi, laddoo," I say, waving. "Dad, we're going to Chicago

this weekend. For the Islamic Quiz Bowl tournament. Are we going to see you?"

"Coming here? Your mother never told me," says Dad. He starts frowning, swatting the laddoo's hands away to stop him from stuffing the tie into his mouth.

Muhammad nudges my knee with his. "We just found out this past weekend," he says. "We're driving up for the day with others, so maybe we can have dinner together."

"Nonsense, you have to stay with me for the night," Dad says. "You can take the bus back, or, Mo, why don't you drive up on your own?"

"Because he wants to go with Sarah," I say.

Muhammad nudges my knee again, harder.

"Sarah? And who is Sarah?" Dad's brows are knotting up.

"Sarah is this girl who I'm getting to know, for, you know, marriage purposes," Muhammad says.

"Your mother never told me anything about that," Dad says. "I thought we'd agreed on an open communication plan. I don't want to be finding out that you're getting married in this way."

"I'm not getting married, Dad," says Muhammad, stepping on my toes.

"Ouch!" I say. "Dad, he's getting mad at me because I'm telling you all this."

"Is your mother there?" Dad asks. "I would like her to be involved in a renewal of our essential agreements. That our family operates in the same way regardless of whether we are a merged entity or not."

"No, she's not home from work yet," I say.

"Okay then, enlighten me as to what this marriage business is all about," says Dad. "I hope you're a little more clear with this than with the idea to switch college majors."

Muhammad talks fast for five minutes, making it seem like Saint Sarah is this amazing catch: smart, giving, kind, friendly, et cetera, et cetera.

"But is she down-to-earth? Fun?" Dad asks. "Because you want someone *cool* to be with, for the lack of a better word. Not uptight. It makes for a better future."

I make a sound.

"Yeah, she's awesome," Muhammad says.

"Yeah, she's the one who planned the Fun-Fun-Fun Islamic Quiz Game!" I say. "See, Dad? She's really f-u-n. Ouch! Muhammad!"

The laddoo starts crying on seeing my plight digitally.

"No, no, Janna's okay," I say, smiling brightly. "See? Happy Janna!"

The laddoo's lips tremble once more before settling back into his satisfied chubby face.

"Oh yes, I'm getting an excellent idea," Dad says. "I'll ask Linda if it's okay for your whole team to stay here, with us. How many of you are there?"

"Six," Muhammad says, a spark of excitement entering his

eyes. Which is funny because Dad never elicits that kind of response from him.

"Plus one," I say to Muhammad. "Apparently, we have an extra person in our car. A guy."

"Then it's not a problem," Dad says. "You know we have more than enough space up here."

Dad has an eight-bedroom house with a basement that has four more bedrooms in addition to the nanny suite. Dad's version of "lite" Indian sweets for "better" Indian restaurants was the key to his success after years trying to peddle the crazy-sweet stuff.

"How do you guys like that?" Dad asks. "I can get to know this Sarah girl as well then."

"I'm game," says Muhammad, a sudden strange seriousness replacing the previous glee in his eyes. "If everyone else on the team is fine with it."

"Me too," I say. "I can't wait to squeeze that laddoo!"

The laddoo gurgles and flails his pudgy hands forward toward me, smacking the keyboard. The screen goes blank.

We wait, and then Muhammad closes the laptop.

"Brilliant, Janna," he says. "Just the thing we need—the whole team to see how Dad lives."

"What do you mean?" I say. "Oh, you mean Sarah? That she's going to see that Dad's not Islamic?"

"It's not only her," Muhammad says, picking up his laptop. "It's everyone."

"But then why'd you act excited first? When Dad brought it up?"

"Because it seemed fun. And, for a sec, I forgot about what he was like."

"You're awful," I say. "You're ashamed of Dad?"

He's walking away, toward Mom's room. I follow him, this thumping feeling growing in me.

"You think more about what others think than about how you feel about Dad?"

"Well yeah, if his essential agreements include dictating my life into being a copy of his. I don't want to marry a Linda and live like a coconut. Brown on the outside, white inside." He closes the door on me.

Dad is stiff, arm's-length-only family to Muhammad, mainly due to their different views on Islam. Muhammad and Mom are becoming a team. And then there's me. Dangling in the wind.

I pick up Fizz's call right after that. I'm moving in a haze of anger at Muhammad, so it doesn't register it's her calling.

"Guess who's been asked to cover for Sarah as study circle lead while you guys are gone to Chicago?" Fizz asks.

"Uh, no?" I say.

"Uh, yes," Fizz says. "I said no way. Me? Lead a study session?"

"You'd be good, you know," I say, warming up to the fact

that we had a focus to our conversation, other than the one I'm avoiding. "You'd be totally in charge. Not like Saint Sarah, flaky."

"We're reading Ghazali, remember? Which I didn't even choose," Fizz says. "How am I going to get people to reflect? You need to be Zen to do that."

"And you think Saint Sarah is Zen?"

"She's got that yoga look. Remember how she got us to reveal all our prayer flaws so easily?"

"She's just got the look. You've got the guts to get people talking honestly, with no BS."

"I'm not doing it," Fizz says. "I'd rather work on my flaws on my own than talk it all out with the study group. What's the point of figuring this stuff out anyway? Just get people to do their prayers on time, five times a day."

I stay quiet. We're reading *Inner Dimensions of Islamic Worship* by Al-Ghazali for study circle, and so far I haven't found one flaw that I *don't* have in my worship. I used up four pages of my 2011 Moleskine agenda writing them out. Rushing is my number one problem, and since figuring that out, I actually began slowing my prayers and working on my "conscious awareness," as Ghazali calls it.

"How's school?" Fizz asks. "Did you find out what Tatyana—"

"Oh my gosh, I forgot to tell you—Dad wants the whole Quiz Bowl team to stay with him in Chicago!" I say.

"What? Why?"

"Because we'll be there anyway. It's going to be kind of fun, don't you think? Too bad you're not coming."

"Yeah. Aliya's car is full. What about Sarah's?"

"Full," I say quickly. "I actually have to go now. Study for history and math."

"Okay," Fizz says. "What about Jeremy?"

"Oh yeah," I say. "Tats just told him I was best friends with you, and that you were Farooq's cousin."

"Oh. That's all?"

"Yeah. I really have to go now . . . salaams."

"Waalaikumusalam warahmathullahi wabarakathu," Fizz says. (Which is Arabic for extra heapings of kindness ladled on top of the simple "peace be upon you" we usually say to each other. Which makes me feel tons worse. Which makes me feel really really low. Which is why I take a long shower with Mom's expensive hair conditioner. And then spend two hours working on my hair. Which is why I go to sleep with cascading curls, ready for gym tomorrow.)

MISFITS AND SAINTS

Muhammad and I are at the breakfast nook checking e-mails and eating cereal when both our phones make a simultaneous beeping sound. It's a text from Dad.

Confirmed: hosting 7 kids this weekend. Going to call the caterers for a super breakfast.

"Hope the food's halal," Muhammad says.

I kick him under the table, and my cereal spills. Muhammad laughs as he takes his bowl to the sink.

"Why do you hate him so much?"

"Hate's a strong word." He's filling up the sink with soapy water and sliding in dinner dishes from last night.

"Here, you need to hear this, Dad's message for today: *Share your home, your time, yourself. Share and you enlarge your networks and widen the possibilities to achieve your success scenario that much faster.* See, this message is read by—whoa, the last I checked there were about four thousand people on his mailing list. Now this is read by nine thousand and sixty-two people. He's encouraging all these people to go out and do things."

"You read his messages every day?" Muhammad stops sponging to look at me. It's a weird look, almost like he's looking at someone in the hospital.

"They help my day, okay?" I secure my phone in its zippered compartment in my backpack and stand up.

"How does that message help your day? He's telling you to share so that you can get what you want. It's like he's saying that he invited all of us this weekend so that he can maximize things for his business. We all know what his success scenario is: make loads of money."

"You're just a hater." I yank the front door open. "And a mama's boy."

The last thing I hear as the door closes is his laugh.

I doodle in history while Mr. Pape reviews points of view. Sandra is sitting next to me, peeling an old student council vote sticker off her desk with precision, lifting this end, then that corner, making her way around the edges carefully. I look up from my picture of a hideous Muhammad in an apron and catch an intense stare from Lauren, who's at the desk nearest to the door. It's a glazed gaze. I turn the corners of my mouth up and do a little wave. She registers me, softening her face with a smile. Then she lifts the end of a lock of hair and drapes it under her nose and nods toward Sandra, a smirk on her face. I turn back to my doodle and pretend to be intent on my work.

When we pack up to leave, I notice I've doodled a huge mustache on my brother. It's scribbled in quite ferociously.

I let Sandra go ahead of me and wait for a bit before I head to the cafeteria. It's bothering me that Lauren's homing in on me like that. Maybe I'll cool the reacquainting with Sandra for a while.

But when I get to our lunch table, Sandra is already sitting beside Tats. And like yesterday and the day before, she doesn't say anything, just sits there and eats. Tats has run out of impersonations, and I'm quiet, aware that when I passed Lauren's table, her friends muffled their chatter.

We have a subdued lunch, and I wonder if Tats and I will end up muted like Sandra by the time school lets out next week.

We get to the locker room early. Tats places her backpack on a bench and pulls out an enormous transparent makeup bag. She picks out two tall canisters from among the makeup. "Leave-in conditioner and/or mousse. I didn't know if you wanted to go for the slick look or big curls."

I unwind my hijab and stick it in a cubby. Taking a claw clip out, I shake my hair side to side in slow motion as if auditioning for a Pantene commercial.

"WOW!" Tats puts the hair products down and rushes over to me. "You don't need my help! Your hair looks amazing!"

"Thank you, thank you very much," I say, grabbing the mousse canister to use as a microphone. "I'd like to thank my mother for suddenly becoming so obsessed with her hair and thus investing in the best conditioner in the world. Also, for buying us a top-of-the-line curling iron just two weeks ago. Thank you, Mom, for making this moment possible."

"But doesn't she wear a scarf everywhere?"

"She's been trying new stuff out. It's like she just remembered that she has hair and a face. After the divorce, I mean," I say, remembering that Linda has great hair. And always manicured hands. "You should see all the new makeup she, I mean *we*, have."

I open the zippered compartment at the front of my backpack to reveal a sample from Mom's makeup collection, most of it acquired recently. I refuse to link the purchases to the Meet Your Match flyer in her dresser. No, just no.

"Okay, let's do your face."

I succumb to a bit of lipstick and mascara. We put the makeup away as the rest of the girls come in. I change in the bathroom stall and wait until I hear Lauren's voice trail out of the locker room. When I come out, it's only Tats and me. "Thanks for waiting."

"You're wearing a tracksuit?"

"Yeah." I look in the mirror and zip the jacket up all the

way. I'll be hot, but it will feel better than wearing shorts and a tee. I can only do so much.

We walk out into the gymnasium and head to where the girls are sitting down, by Jeremy's feet. He's got a catcher's mitt on, and he's throwing a ball up and down. I sit at the edge of the group, wrapping my arms around my legs, willing him not to see me yet. I want to have a moment to take a breath. I know I look good, but, oddly, I don't want him to intentionally look at me. Maybe if it's by accident, it would feel better?

A long, blaring whistle invades my thoughts. Ms. Eisen is coming out of her office, her whistle stuck in her mouth. It emits another long screech.

I look around like everyone else to see what the problem is.

"Janna Yusuf, get up! Did you forget there's a male present? Go get your hajeeb!"

I'm so startled that her words don't sink in. So I continue to sit there dumbly. Then Tats, who's more with the program, steps up to the plate with her input.

"Ms. Eisen," she says, her tawny hair almost bristlelike beside mine, "Janna doesn't need to wear her hijab for gym. It's in her religion. In the Qur'an."

Some of the girls laugh. Miriam laughs the loudest because she's Muslim—one who doesn't wear the hijab but still knows the Qur'an, still knows that it has no verses on gym class.

Ms. Eisen blows the whistle again. I get up and walk to the locker room, trying to decide if I should act like I'm shocked there's a male present, or if I should rock my silky hair for all its worth in its last foray in front of Jeremy's eyes.

I end up hunching over and slinking away, shame curdling inside me then reaching its fingers to wrap tight around my body. So tight that it squeezes tears out of my eyes. She just embarrassed me in front of the whole class. In front of him.

I don't come out of the locker room again. Tats comes looking for me, but I'm pretending to take a shower, so she leaves after trying to talk over the waterfall. I'm actually wearing my tracksuit and standing in the water, thinking of those lyrics about love going to waste.

As soon as Tats leaves, I peel off my soaked clothes and dry my hair back to its fried frizziness. Then I stuff that frizz into my black hijab, cover my body in black layers, and take the roof key from Tats's pencil case.

Someone broke up the gummy bear heart collective I left up here. They squished the two gummy bears in love. Smeared remains, colors entwined, cling to the asphalt.

Is Allah upset at me?

I sit there and let the heat wave coil over my covered self.

When the bell rings, I walk home without stopping by Tats's locker as usual. I want my bed before anyone else gets home.

Through the double doors, I notice a familiar figure in the lobby and slow down, briefly debating whether I should go around to the back of the building, near the dumpsters.

Instead, I pause by the mailboxes and take out a textbook from my backpack.

Mr. Ram is parked by the fake-plants extravaganza. He's staring out the wide windows at nothing.

I open my textbook and direct all my attention to it, walking nimbly, so as not to catch his eyes. I don't want a tour of his memories today.

"How's the book coming along? The book about Prophet Muhammad?" Mr. Ram calls out as the elevator doors open and I'm about to sneak in. I stop in the doorframe and let the sensorless doors slam hard into my shoulders. Why is he asking about that now? He's Hindu, so why does he even care about my seerah book? It's not the Mahabharata.

I retrace my steps, walking backward. I don't want to talk to him, but I just can't let the elevator doors close on his stiff and proud back. I'll have to see him when I take him out tomorrow, and ignoring him now would mean a double dose of those pursed lips and teepee fingers later on. Maybe like a kid he'd even tell his son about my rudeness, and I'd lose my first job ever. I stop and sit on the ledge that keeps all the fake plants at bay, beside his wheelchair, refusing to look at his face. I'm not in the mood to act nice.

"Mr. Ram, I don't want to work on it. That's the truth," I say, staring at his plaid sleeve. "I'm not going to finish it."

"Why?"

"I'm not that person anymore. I'm old, not the little kid

I was when I started it," I say. Why is he wearing a lumberjack flannel shirt with pearly snap buttons tucked severely into high-waisted dress pants today? And a plaid scarf (that doesn't match the shirt) around his neck? His inner temperature monitor must be way off, because the lobby is stifling hot. People at school who groan on seeing my summer look would positively melt on seeing Mr. Ram.

"You're old?" Mr. Ram laughs. "Miss Janna, do you know how old I am?"

He leans forward and lifts a shaky hand to his heart.

"Seventy?" I lie. I really think he's ninety-six, but I don't want to hurt his ego. I don't know if it still hurts people's feelings at that age to be thought of as older, but it's better to err on the side of caution.

He laughs again, this time doing his Belly-Laugh smile. At least one of us is having a good day.

"Ninety? Ninety-one? Ninety-six? Ninety-nine?" I say, looking right into his eyes, which are tearing up because he's having so much fun. I can't stop myself from smiling on seeing his face. It's like a baby's, his mouth slack and loopy like he can't fully control his smile.

"No, no, slow down." He puts his hand out to my arm, patting it to stop me. "I am at the great age of ninety-three."

He stops smiling and places his hand back on his wheelchair armrest. "What do you think of that?"

"Um, I think that's old but not too old?" I say.

"Yes, exactly that." Mr. Ram beams at me. "You're a smart girl; that is what I always tell my son. That is why I told him you have to be the only one to walk me—you know that."

I nod. He always tells me that. Only I'm allowed to walk him, he tells his son, nobody else. He makes it seem like there's a lineup of people waiting to do my job.

"I'm not too old. That is exactly what I am. I grow in years, but some things, they stay the same," he says. "Who I am inside this body, what I know to be true, that all stays the same. My kernel is me all the time. I let no one change that, Miss Janna."

"Okay." I have no idea what he's talking about.

"You don't remember the day you showed me that book you made about your prophet? After I showed you the Mahabharata? You liked it so much; you were so proud of yourself."

Then he just looks out the window again. And doesn't speak anymore. Am I supposed to go now? He's acting really strange today, like he's on slow mode.

"Mr. Ram, why are you here alone?"

"My son left me here. He takes me with him to pick up Ravi from school every day. I told him to go by himself today. I'm tired, so he'll be tired pushing me."

"Mr. Ram? I have to study. I have exams." I hold up my textbook as testimony and get off the ledge.

"Yes." He nods at the window. "But you didn't get a poem from me yet."

"Oh." I sit back down, suppressing a huge sigh of impatience. Mr. Ram used to recite things to me when he was in a good mood as though he was giving me gifts. When I was eleven, it was okay because I excitedly called myself a poem collector and wrote down his words as though they were precious. I was really into tongue twisters and funny Shel Silverstein stuff back then, and I loved reciprocal reciting, surprising him with things he'd never heard. But now? Now I want to curl up in bed in mortification, imagining Jeremy's face as I slunk away from gym.

"This one is by Rabindranath Tagore. It is about the birth of my country."

I nod, glancing at the elevators. The good one is making its way down again. I hope the poem is only three floors long.

Mr. Ram straightens his already erect back, fixes his eyes on me, and begins, his words precise and loud, like he memorized them for school in India.

Where the mind is without fear and the head is
held high;
Where knowledge is free;
Where the world has not been broken up into
fragments by narrow domestic walls;
Where words come out from the depth of truth;
Where tireless striving stretches its arms towards
perfection;

Where the clear stream of reason has not lost its
way into the dreary desert sand of dead habit;
Where the mind is led forward by thee into
ever-widening thought and action—
Into that heaven of freedom, my Father, let my
country awake.

He closes his eyes on finishing.

I pat his arm and whisper thank you, infusing it with as much authenticity as I can. Then I speed-walk to greet the elevator that's lumbering open.

I open the dashboard on Amu's website. There must be someone else out there with the same problem as me. Someone must have asked a question about this.

Non-Muslim love, I type into the search field. It pops up immediately.

Dear Imam, I love to wear non-Muslim clothes. Especially the fashionable ones from the mall. (The one here in town.) But my brothers, all three of them, they dress Islamically, in long kurtas and thowbs, like the companions of the Prophet. When I'm with them, I stand out like a sore big toe. (We're all bald too, except they wrap their heads in turbans, like at the Prophet's time, so lucky them. They call it Islamic—I call it convenient!) Imam, how do I change and become more pious like them?

Answer: First, let me commend you on your interest in following

Islamic precepts in your life. However, I did not know, until I read your question, that clothes have a religion. In the Qur'an, clothing is referred to as a cover and as items of beauty: "Indeed, We have bestowed upon you from on high [the knowledge of making] garments to cover your nakedness, and as a thing of beauty, but the garment of God-consciousness is the best of all." There's no reference to a specific style of clothing. As long as it meets the requirements of Islamic modesty and cleanliness, it can be a "thing of beauty," a fashionable item if you will, of any culture. If your brethren disagree, please do ask them how exactly Abu Jahl and Abu Lahab, those men bent on killing our beloved Prophet, were dressed. Were they also not wearing the same garments that are now claimed to solely represent Islam? If they were to materialize in our midst today, those among us without true knowledge of our religion would rush to authenticate them as exemplary Muslims, based on their appearance. Meanwhile, the garments of these two evil men—time-stamped, yes, with the fashions of the Prophet's time—encased hardened hearts. Thus, we wear clothing on the outside to cover and beautify, but our insides are equally important. If our outsides look pious but our core is not mindful of Him, we are not true servants of God. We must constantly strive to align these. That is the beautiful struggle of being a believer. In closing, I want to add clothing is cultural, and Muslims belong to ALL cultures of the world. (So go ahead, cover that head with a baseball cap. Or a turban. I hear they are quite fashionable these days.) And Allah knows best.

I smile. Amu's awesome.

• • •

After dinner, Mom opens my bedroom door as I'm perusing the bootleg math exam. I have no time to erase the stricken look on my face, but, lucky for me, she associates it with the conditioner and curling iron that I left on the desk.

"Did you have a girls party to go to today? Why all the hairstyling?" she says as she picks up the iron and winds its cord around it.

"Just trying something new," I say, placing the exam sheets in the middle of my math textbook. My fingers shake, as feigning nonchalance is hard with Mom scrutinizing me.

She shoots a pointed look at my hair, which, I have to admit, is a tangled mass held back by a headband. I shrug and highlight random things in my math notebook.

"They're delivering my bed tomorrow." Mom takes a seat at the desk. "Janna, I know your number one concern is privacy. What if I make a promise that nothing will change in terms of that. I'll treat your space as a separate room. Completely."

"I really doubt that. I'll be right there. It'll be easy for you to treat me like I'm seven."

"You mean when you used to beg to sleep in my room?" She looks at the picture on the wall above my desk. It's a photo I took of the decorative pebbles in front of Dad's house.

"I just know you'll tidy things in my space, like it's your room, like you always do. Maybe even check on me."

"No, I wouldn't." She sighs and turns to me, her eyes blinking like they're wet. "Muhammad being home will be helpful for me."

Amu's face flashes in my head. How does that happen?

"Mom, I'm trying to study."

"I know, but I'd like things settled for Muhammad. For us."

"You mean for Muhammad, period." For some reason I feel angry instead of sad when I see this affecting her. *It was your choice to leave Dad,* I want to say.

"Janna, think about what you're saying."

"I'm saying you only care about him." My throat closes on that, and I want to cry after saying it. Muhammad and Mom are becoming united in my head. But I'm on my own.

My phone beeps with a text from Tats. I HATE Ms. E. But guess what? J likes your hair. He thinks it's hot. ☺

"If I only cared for him, why wouldn't I just *order* you to hand your room over?"

"I'm studying." As I'm about to click the phone off, another message pops up. He wants to talk. When?

"Well, I see you're making good use of the present we got you." Mom stands up.

"So it *was* a bribe." I'm trying to click off when three more messages appear, annoying beeps punctuating the air. When hot hair? ☺

When hotness?

When?

"Do you really think that's what it is?" She doesn't make a move to leave. "If so, maybe you need to give it back then."

Powering the phone off completely, I place it on the side of the bed closest to the wall and keep my hand on top to ensure its security. The idea of Mom taking it from me and finding Tats's texts is making me sick. "Okay, Mom, I don't think it's a bribe. I know you meant it as a present to show you care about me. Not just Muhammad."

Making sure my voice doesn't sound robotic while just saying what she wants to hear is hard. I look up at her to see if it works.

She turns and leaves, closing the door behind her. I don't catch her face, but the stiffness in her back tells me she's not impressed with me.

I power the phone back on and delete all of Tats's messages.

SAINTS

I decide to buck trends and be hot, temperature-wise. If a bunch of people can jump into icy waters for polar bear plunges in the cold of winter, I see no reason I can't wear my favorite clothes when it's ninety degrees outside. Four layers of diverse fabrics: denim, Lycra, cotton, sweatshirt, and a slick (and thick) pashmina to knit the whole ensemble together. All in black, my feel-good color.

Comfort clothes are a must today.

Mom's queen mattress, box spring, and headboard are resting against the wall beside the front door. Muhammad appears carrying the disassembled lengths of the bed frame, held together like it's an Enfield 1853 rifle-musket and he's marching to the Battle of Fredericksburg. (Sad fact: The North suffered more than twice the casualties in that skirmish.) He does a Three Stooges move when he sees me, turning suddenly and feigning surprise at missing my head with the bed frame.

I glare and stuff a breakfast bar and a lunch bar into my backpack. My plan is to head to school earlier and miss the drama of dismantling Mom's room.

At school, I sit on the steps by the side doors that lead to the hall where English is. Normally these doors are locked, but if you wait long enough, someone opens the door from the inside for whatever reason. Okay, usually a nefarious reason, like smoking or making out.

I take out a granola bar and cradle Flannery's complete stories in my lap. With the first taste of oats 'n' honey, I fall into "The Life You Save May Be Your Own." It's shady here due to an old oak tree standing sentry beside the steps, and I'm doing okay so far.

But the light shifts, maybe a cloud moves, and that or something else makes me look up, toward the front of the building. Jeremy's getting out of his car in the parking lot, his arm outstretched, opening the door. I lean back and lift Flannery up to my face, thinking Tats would call this *cosmic*, me reading the line *Are you married or are you single?* just as Jeremy appears on the horizon.

His arms appear in my mind. The arms I saw when I searched for him in last year's yearbook. He was standing with some of the guys from the baseball team, strong, tan arms crossed so hard across his chest that the veins etched an imprint in me. I never knew until that moment that you could look at someone's arms and want them around you so badly.

I wonder if Flannery ever felt that way. There was only one guy linked to her and only one recorded kiss. According to her notes, she didn't think much of that kiss. According to his notes, neither did he.

I lower the book, thinking Jeremy would be gone into school by now.

He's walking toward me. He's in the middle of the lawn between me and his car.

I look around for help and then gather the remains of my breakfast and stand up, flushed, realizing just how hot it is. Oh God, I can't talk to him now; I don't know what I'd say; I don't have Tats with me. All this time I'm holding Flannery open on the page that says, right at the very top, *Are you married or are you single?*, fluttering it around as I move in ambivalent ways to collect myself.

Was there ever a bigger geek than me? *Ya Allah, save me from my geeky self,* I'm praying when the side doors open. Soon-Lee spills out, holding her boyfriend's hand. "Hi, Janna."

"Soon-Lee! Can we talk? Something serious." I'm walking away from the steps, backward, increasing the space between Jeremy and me, with Soon-Lee the monkey in the middle.

"Sure," she says, letting go of her boyfriend. He shrugs and puts his hands in the pockets of his Bermudas.

Jeremy is almost at the steps when I back myself into the corner where the arts wing juts out.

"The exam, did you look at it?" I gaze over Soon-Lee's

petite shoulders. He's standing on the steps, like he's waiting for me.

"My conscience only let me look at the parts we didn't learn about. Here, look." She bends over her open messenger bag. I look. Still there, thumbing his phone.

"See, I even blocked the questions we should've known all about with a Sharpie." She holds up a stapled set of papers that look like a formerly classified, now somewhat declassified CIA document. "Ethical or what?"

"Good idea. Can I get a copy of that?" He's talking on his phone now.

"Course. Want my notes, too? On the topics Mason didn't teach us?"

"Awesome."

Soon-Lee turns to look at her boyfriend. He's wandered off to stand by the fence across from the steps, watching us with his elbows resting on the metal railing.

I glance again at Jeremy and catch his eyes. He smiles in the middle of his phone conversation.

"Who's *that*? And why are you hiding from him?" Soon-Lee adjusts her dark frames to peer at me.

"I'm not." I reach out for the papers she's holding.

"Oh come on. Who's he waiting for over there then?"

"I really don't know." I flip through the exam as Soon-Lee leans against the wall beside me.

"He's hung up. And now he keeps glancing over. Don't

worry—I'm looking at Thomas and just using my powerful peripheral vision to relay this information to you."

"Does he look happy? Confused? Annoyed?"

"He looks hot. As in temperature hot."

"I wish he'd just go in."

"Oh my God, is he stalking you?"

"No! He's not stalking me! No way." I'm sure I said that a bit too loud. I'm afraid to look his way to check.

"Aw, he likes you then?" She turns to me, her left shoulder pressing into the bricks. "And you so like him back. It's written all over your face."

"Soon, are you coming back to me soon?" Thomas calls.

Jeremy's no longer on the steps. He gave up on me. Yes!

What is wrong with me?

"Sorry, math troubles," Soon-Lee says as we join Thomas again. "Thomas, do you know the guy that was standing here just a minute ago?"

I hit Soon-Lee with Flannery.

"Yeah, Lauren's cousin?"

"Lauren? Lauren Bristol?" Soon-Lee's incredulous.

"As in the bitch herself." Thomas drapes his arm around her shoulders, pulling her close.

After agreeing to a study session on Monday, I make my exit with a wave, walking to the more accommodating, less happening, front doors.

Lauren's cousin?

• • •

History is awkward because I can't stop myself from glancing at Lauren periodically to find the Jeremy resemblance I've been missing all along. She's nothing like him, from hair to facial features to stature to style. She looks old money, with the tiny, perfect diamonds in her ears to prove it. I don't get why she's not in a private high school.

Mr. Pape seats himself on top of an empty student desk. "Last day for questions before exam week."

"Okay, do you have to be antiwar to pass the exam?" Oliver says, amid laughter. He occasionally takes Mr. Pape on when he's bored. Usually on points related to his love of the right to possess guns.

"No, but if you're pro-war, articulate your position clearly in the essay portion, using proper citations, and you get an A."

"See, I don't like that: Why'd you call it pro-war? It's called antiterrorism."

"Sure, sure, whatever you call it, just do a good job with your reasoning."

"Are you antiterrorism, sir?"

"Of course. I'm antiviolence."

"So, why do you cut up antiterrorism tactics?"

"I don't believe more violence solves the problem of violence. Anyway, my opinions don't constitute the exam."

"They do, if you designed the exam." The class goes silent for a second before a few guys begin hooting.

"Oliver, if you see that the exam is, in any way, unfair to your beliefs, you can take it up with the office. But not before you have evidence of it." Mr. Pape's knuckles on the desk are white, the only telltale sign he's getting stressed.

"I have evidence plenty in all the stuff you've given us." The guy behind Oliver makes a sizzling sound.

Mr. Pape stares at Oliver.

I slump down on my desk. I hate, just hate, this.

Sandra's hand rises in the air. We look at her.

"Mr. Pape, how detailed do we have to get for the short-answer questions?"

"Thanks for asking, Sandra." He jumps off the desk and strides to the board and begins to talk about the perfect short-response algorithm.

I give Sandra five. Her first oral contribution the entire year, and it cut the tension like a birthday cake knife.

"He waved at me again. From five o'clock," Tats says as we make our way to our table at lunch. "Did you see it?"

I look at Matt and his friends. They appear to be laughing, huddled over a phone. "No, I missed it."

"So, what if one day I went with my mom to her book club? At his house?" Tats takes a seat. "Would that be weird?"

"Kind of," I say, unwrapping my second granola bar of the day. "What if he's not even there? I can't imagine him hanging around when his mom's book club is happening."

Sandra plunks down beside me.

I look at Tats, wondering if she's going to change the topic of conversation.

"No, not to see *him*. Just to see his house, you know?" Tats takes out a saran-wrapped tray of sushi from her backpack. It has a big LAST BATCH OF THE DAY SALE sticker on it.

"I think that's stalkerish," I say.

"What do you think, Sandra? Is it stalkerish to go to a guy's house when he's not home? A guy you like?" Tats picks a roll up with her chopsticks and looks at Sandra.

"I don't know," says Sandra.

"Do you like someone?" Tats asks, before opening her mouth wide to shove a piece of sushi in.

"No."

"Come on." Tats pauses in her chewing. "It's normal."

Sandra shakes her head and takes a bite of her sandwich.

"You can tell us," Tats prods.

"Maybe some people don't," I say. "Maybe they haven't discovered anybody interesting."

"I think you should walk around expecting to meet interesting people," Tats says, picking another roll up. "Like I don't mind, Janna, if you tell Sandra all the guys I've liked before."

"What? Why?" I scrunch the granola wrapper. I'm still hungry. "Why does that matter?"

"Because I'm not ashamed of being open to people. Who cares if it doesn't work out?" Tats puts two rolls on the discarded wrapper off her tray and pushes it to me. "If it doesn't happen with Matt, I know I'll find someone else."

"Thanks, but only one. You need lunch." I take a roll and push the other back to her.

She gets Sandra's eye and motions toward the sushi. Sandra shakes her head again and continues eating her sandwich. It's always turkey and lettuce.

"Sandra, if you ever fall for someone, let me know," Tats says, leaning over the table to whisper. "I'm helping Janna, and it's like the best. To make it *happen* between two people."

Sandra looks at me. I shrug. I don't want to tell her about something I'm not even sure of myself.

"It's nothing," I say. "Just a crush."

When Sandra looks back at her sandwich, I frown at Tats and shake my head.

"Anyway, I think I might grow up to become a professional matchmaker if acting doesn't work out," Tats says. She looks up and then smiles big, waving.

I turn around. Matt and his crew are walking by on their way out. He doesn't even glance this way. We're not on the same planet as him.

I look back at Tats. She's still smiling, wrapping her chopsticks with the saran wrap.

Her tray is in front of me, a roll on it.

Tats deserves someone awesome.

But someone accessible. Or at least on earth.

. . .

Tats pops her head out of the locker room into the gymnasium to check if it's true. When we entered, we heard the word "substitute" being tossed around.

"YES! A sub!" Tats confirms. "Last-day sub!"

I'm in front of the mirror winding my hijab on my head in bandanna fashion, to accommodate physical activity, when she sticks her hand out, palm up.

"Give me your hijab," she says. "He likes your hair. The guy likes your hair, and you're going to hide it from him?"

Obediently, I unravel the pashmina. I hold on to it for a while before giving it up. She takes it and walks over to our bags on the bench.

My hair isn't the greatest today, so I tie it up in a high ponytail, staring at my unsure expression.

Lauren walks by, pauses, and backtracks. She stands behind me, smiling at my reflection, before leaning in and whispering, "He's my cousin."

"Who?" My eyebrows, good actors, do their jobs, curling up curiously.

"Jeremy. You like him, don't you? I noticed in gym yesterday."

I don't turn around. I have to approach this with care if I don't want it to splatter all over my face.

"I don't really know him," I say.

Tats is walking over to us, a curious expression on her face, and I cringe. She's volatile. She loves that she thinks she's in control of my involvement with Jeremy, and she'll actually have it out with Lauren if she perceives interference. On the way to gym class, I told her what Thomas had said about them being cousins. Her response was a frown.

"Well, do you want to get to know him better?" Lauren asks, as her best friend Marjorie appears behind her. "I can arrange that."

"Thanks, I'll think about it," I say. "After exams maybe."

"Last-day-of-school party," Lauren says. "At my house, next Friday. Jeremy usually comes, if I beg him enough."

Marjorie smiles and bumps her shoulder into Lauren's.

"Thanks," I say again, ignoring Tats's mouth hanging open.

Tats crosses her arms after they leave. In the mirror, I see Marjorie whispering something, giggling. Lauren doesn't laugh but turns around abruptly.

"You too," she says, pointing at Tats. "You're invited too. Add me on Facebook to get the details."

Tats smiles and drops her crossed arms.

"That was awesome," she says as we walk out to the gym. "How'd you do that? That's her brother's party too. Matt will be there; he's best friends with her brother."

"I don't know why that just happened," I say.

"It doesn't matter! We are going." Tats does a dance. "Hey, maybe you should do your hair. Jeremy will be there."

"I don't think so. I'm okay with my scarf." I split my

ponytail in half and pull to tighten it. "Anyway, why'd she invite me? Us?"

"Come on—she obviously approves of you for Jeremy," Tats says. "Speaking of the guy, where is he?"

A tall woman with short hair and a wrinkly smile stands in the middle of the gym holding a clipboard.

"I don't get why she'd approve of me," I say. "She and her friends act like we don't exist most of the time."

Tats isn't listening because she's gone up to talk to the sub.

I sit on the floor with the other waiting girls and can't help noticing how Marjorie has joined some sort of whisper fest with Lauren, across from me.

"No sign of Jeremy or evidence he's supposed to help us with softball again, according to the sub," Tats says, crossing her legs to sit beside me.

Then, like he's heard, he peeks out from the weight room, and our eyes meet. He smiles and nods. I draw courage and smile back, doing a little wave before realizing Lauren has seen and is looking back at Jeremy. Marjorie is clenching her lips to stop laughing, shoulders shaking.

I drop my hand and nudge Tats with my knee. She leans back and says, "I see him."

"No, look at them, Lauren and them," I say. "And don't make it obvious."

That's like telling a cat not to pounce on a mouse. Tats whips her head and stares at them. By then, Marjorie is openly laughing. Only Lauren stays composed, with this sly smile on.

Like hell I'm going to that party. They're up to something, and I've been chosen to be a part of it, probably the butt of it.

As we run laps around the gym on the sub's orders, I stay far from Lauren's gang, jogging lightly. I notice the pause Lauren takes at the weight room, waving pointedly at Jeremy, who takes a step out to exchange a few words with her before she rejoins the jogging herd.

Beside me, Tats slows down as we near the weight room. She begins to walk, holding her sides as if she has a stitch in them, and I slow too. The sub's busy reading the clipboard and doesn't notice our approach to the weight room.

He's waiting at the entrance and comes out as we reach the doors. He looks past Tats to me, and I feel that clench that I used to feel thinking about him. But this time it's stronger and deeper. How would I even open my mouth to speak to him? Because I'm pretty sure only a croak would emerge, scaring him off. I look away to gain a moment and give me a chance to return to normalcy.

When I look back, ready to say hi, I notice he isn't alone in the weight room.

Farooq is staring back at me from beside the bench press. Looking at me, hijabless, taking me in with eyes wide open, surprised.

I take off like a shot, not looking back. I've never felt so naked in my life before.

I want to charge into the locker room and wrap myself in the biggest hijab I can find.

After school, I lie in bed, staring at the ceiling. The apartment was quiet when I let myself in earlier, and I could tell Muhammad wasn't home by his big shoes missing from the mat.

And then I noticed how clean the living room looked. There was a suitcase beside the armchair, a plastic sword—from Mr. Khoury's table—leaning against it. Most eerie, the Risk game was put away, back on top of the bookshelf.

I looked in the dining room, and there, too, was evidence of a change in the air. Muhammad's papers were gone from the table, and Mom's favorite rustic-candle formation was back to commanding the center space. I retraced my steps to the living room and unzipped a corner of the suitcase. Sure enough, it contained his stuff.

Is he going, I ask the ceiling, *to Amu's?*

Was I being mean to him? I went beyond the ceiling and asked God. *Is that why you're doing this to me, Allah? This drama in my life?*

I get up and walk to Mom's room.

It looks huge now. Mom's new twin bed appears tiny under the weight of a mature sheet set, the edges of the quilt comforter sweeping the floor. The headboard's against the wall facing the door, off center so that there's a sizable empty space near the window. The room's been swept out, and the sun streams on the half that's supposed to be mine.

The divider screens, folded against the wall, look at me.

I go lie on my bed again.

Dad. He'll know what to do.

I open e-mail on my phone and scroll to find his daily message. *Sharing guarantees success because you're acknowledging the importance of your network. Thus strengthening them, thus strengthening you.*

I click off and stare at the ceiling. Is it wrong to make a deal with God? I'll reorganize myself in the apartment if you reorganize my life?

I jump off the bed before I change my mind again.

I begin with my art desk. I move fast, dragging as opposed to lifting it. I take bundles of clothes by their hangers. It irritates me to see that Mom has cleared half her walk-in closet as if she *knew* I'd give in, but I shake it off, realizing there's more space in even half of this compared to my teeny hard-to-get-into sliding-door closet.

I don't take the mattress off to move my bed, just push and pull, a little this way and that. At one point I think the bed will be forever stuck in the door and I'll have to sleep in between privacy and not, but then I push a little while lifting up one of the wooden legs and the whole thing comes free. I drag it the rest of the way, ignoring the banged-up floor's protests, and place it under the window.

I want this done before Muhammad comes home and says

something to make me mad at him. And then mad at myself for deciding this.

Moving the green dresser is easy as it has wheels at its base. I put it next to my headboard, and it serves as a night table for my phone and lamp.

When it's done, I shelter my "room" with the screens.

It's okay in here. Sitting on the bed, I realize I get most of the light.

I check my phone and see it's time to pick up Mr. Ram.

Before I leave, I put Muhammad's suitcase in my old room, laying his toy sword on top. I wonder if I'm nice enough for Allah now.

"Janna, your mom told me you don't have school tomorrow. Would you be able to do your studying here? Stay with my father?" asks Mr. Ram's son, Deval. "Ravi's teacher asked if I could replace a sick parent on the field trip tomorrow."

"Sure." I wheel Mr. Ram out of the door, waving at Ravi, who's eating cut-up apples on the couch. He stays with his dad until his mom comes home from work and then with his mom while his dad goes to work. When do they ever see one another all at once?

"Mr. Ram, are you cold?" He's wearing a tweed jacket. His hat is houndstooth with a freckled brown feather in it. "You've been wearing more clothes than I do lately."

"The cold comes suddenly to me. Even though my son

tells me there's a heat wave." He laughs.

We exit the lobby and maneuver up the walkway. Ms. Kolbinsky waits where the sidewalk starts, brilliant in her yellow, black, and orange sheath dress. Her hair is fanned out around her face, a mixture of gray and misty brown. Sandra's beside her, drab in her jeans and gray T-shirt, long hair parted flat on her head, stringing down and covering the sides of her face.

Mr. Ram holds up his hand. "Who is this lovely lady with you, Ms. Kolbinsky? I see a beautiful resemblance."

"This is my granddaughter, Sandra, and look at what she has in her hand." Ms. Kolbinsky beams. Sandra waves the form, filled in with tiny writing. "I'm coming to Parcheesi today!"

I take out my phone and click a picture of Mr. Ram's silent laugh. Now I'm convinced he's in love with her, too.

Sandra folds the form up and hands it to me with a smile before walking back to her building.

I push the wheelchair, and Ms. Kolbinsky falls into step beside us.

I tolerate the giggling all the way to the community center. Sociological note to self: People never forget how to flirt.

Nuah walks Ms. Kolbinsky through the particulars of Seniors Games Club. From my usual table, while I wait for my laptop to start up, I watch him take her to the restroom area, the fire exits, and the snack counter. He's talking the whole time, waving his arms about.

As he's walking her back to where Mr. Ram and friends are waiting, he sees me watching him. I don't look away this time, so he does a salute toward my corner before proceeding to tell the old people looking eagerly up at him a joke about a talking muffin. They burst out laughing together.

What does he do, memorize a whole page of corny jokes every Wednesday night?

Ms. Kolbinsky thinks it's so funny that she hits the table, with tears in her eyes. Mr. Ram looks at her and shakes, mouth open. I can *never* stop my echo smile when I see him laugh.

So, he walks over to me. Nuah.

"You like muffin jokes? I got a whole page of them," he says.

"I knew it. You don't make them up," I say, looking at my agenda open on the table. It's on top of the declassified math exam.

"Oh, but I can. I can do improv right here," he says. "Give me a topic."

"Algebra," I say. "Ha."

"Okay, so what did six-*x* say to five-*x*?" he asks.

I shrug, doodling.

"What do you know, we're both children's sizes!" he says." "You know, as in clothing sizes for kids' clothes?"

I groan.

"Come on, give me a fair topic," he says. "Like horses. Or teeth. Oh, teeth, I can do a whole act on teeth."

I click my mechanical pencil. "Um, actually, I have a lot of studying to do. Maybe another time?"

"Yeah, sorry," he says, backing away. "The tortoise is going, going, gone."

He does this thing with his head where it almost tips right over to the side while he's watching me and backing away from the table.

Weird.

"Mr. Ram's really smart, but you must know that, huh?" he says, right before he turns the corner to head back to the front desk.

I nod. He disappears with a salute-wave again.

And then he's back. Holding his phone, its screen out to me.

Like I said before: weird.

"I have to show you this. Since you helped." It's a picture of a cute kid with his front teeth missing, wearing a snug kufi on his head. "My brother."

"You didn't end up choosing the fez?"

"Nah, my brother's not that dapper." He swipes the screen and turns the phone to me again. "And, I couldn't resist."

His brother, face scrunched up with concentration, swinging a golden plastic sword.

"So, Janna, you make a good arms dealer." Nuah closes his photo app.

"Told you I wasn't nice." I raise my eyebrows, looking up from the doodling I picked up again.

"Now I believe it. Almost," he says. "My mom's going nuts with that clanging noise. And my brother won't stop. He sleeps with the thing."

"Interesting, so does Muhammad."

He laughs. "We all bought one. But I bought one for my *little* brother. Muhammad and Farooq, they're another story."

I stop doodling. Why does the monster always show up?

"I have to get back to my studying." I move around my books, not looking at Nuah. "I've already wasted time."

I move my fingers on the track pad to wake my laptop.

"Sorry, outta here." He's gone.

Lauren's added me as a friend on Facebook. I click accept, telling myself I'm doing this only to check her pictures to see if Jeremy's in them. He's not.

I wonder if she'll notice if I unfriend her right away.

Instead, I open the questions on Amu's website. Next week is teen week, the time of month when Amu discusses topics of interest to young people on his website, and there's always a host of interesting questions that his blog posts generate.

Dear Imam, are we allowed to wear nail polish? (By the way, I'm a girl. I'm saying this because there are some STRANGE questions on your website. My dad doesn't even let me read it anymore. So I have to be sneaky and read it at school.)

What's the youngest a guy can get married? Not legally, I mean really.

Do you have to grow a beard if it turns out ugly? My brother's beard is ugly and I don't want him anywhere around me.

I only like to wear black hijabs and my mom says I'm depressed. She wants me to wear pink or orange or something bright like that so no one thinks I'm forced to wear hijab. I'm not, but I don't feel the need to prove it to anyone. Can you give me some research to show her she's wrong to dictate my hijab color?

That last question is interesting.

Still, I erase them all.

Dear Imam, what if you know something bad that someone's done, something against the laws of God, but no one else knows it, and people think that that person is really good and should get a position of responsibility in the community, like, say, leading prayers . . . what should the person who knows the truth do?

Dear Imam, what if you find that you've fallen for someone who is not Muslim?

I read over my questions, and, before doubts set in, I press send.

SAINTS AND MONSTERS

"Deval called and said you'd promised to be downstairs with Mr. Ram in ten minutes," says Mom the second I wake up. She's lying in bed reading, on the other side of the privacy screens, but of course she still knows my eyelids have fluttered open to Friday morning. Such are the woes of cramped living.

I wiggle out of my sleep T-shirt and put on an old tunic top that Manisha, Mr. Ram's daughter-in-law, brought me back from India. Slip on yesterday's jeans and hijab, both lying at the foot of the bed, and I'm ready, except for my teeth. As I head to the bathroom, I think about Nuah and his offer to tell me teeth jokes. I can't even think of one that would be funny. He must be easily amused.

Across from the bathroom, the door to my old room is ajar. Muhammad is lying on top of a sleeping bag spread on the floor. I tiptoe in and stand over his sprawled form. I'd forgotten he sleeps with his eyes partially open, whites showing. Eerie, yet oddly comforting, knowing he's got some semblance to my brother BSS—Before Saint Sarah.

He takes in a sudden sharp breath, jerks his left arm, and widens his eyes, pupils returning to life, strange sounds sputtering from his freshly unpouted mouth. "Egh gawph. Gharhakk."

He registers me and jerks his arm again. "Hey! What are you doing?"

"Just wondering how you do that."

"Do what?"

"Sleep like a blobfish. Eyes open, mouth puckered. Sarah will be thrilled, if you guys make it that far."

He flips over and hugs his pillow. "What time is it?"

"Late, for those employed. Like me." I turn to walk out. "Also, Gandhi has a message for you: 'Rise, traveler, the sky is light. Why do you sleep? It is not night.'"

"Thanks. For the room."

I stop in the doorway. "You can thank Dad for that."

Mr. Ram is set up in his favorite seat in the corner of the living room. I sit down on the sofa next to him and hold up my seerah book. He smiles.

"No, Mr. Ram, I'm not finishing it," I say. "There's a quiz competition tomorrow, and going through this will help me prepare for it. Anyway, I brought it for you to read while I study."

I lay the planner on his lap. It falls open to a caravan scene. There's a heart, animated with lines, floating in the last frame, when Khadija, the Prophet's first boss and first love, fifteen years older, sends a marriage proposal to him. They were happily married for twenty-five years before she passed away. Afterward, until *he* died, the Prophet couldn't say her name without tearing up. I copied his words about her into my seerah book, in lionet-gold marker: *She believed in me when no one else did . . . and she helped and comforted me when there was no one else to lend a helping hand.*

The Prophet had been an orphan from a young age so he really understood what it means to have no anchor. To be on your very own, maybe with problems no one can know or bear for you.

Mr. Ram settles his glasses snugly and grips the book. The smile remains on his face.

I'm reading history notes, thinking, *This is nice.* Me and Mr. Ram, reading together, surrounded by plants crammed into every available surface in the condo. *Thank you, Allah,* I mouth. Being nice to Muhammad appears to have been a good idea.

Mr. Ram interrupts my reverie, a shaking hand holding a page taut. "Do you know Rumi?" he asks.

"A bit," I say. "Mom has a book of his poems."

"Yes," he says. Then he stops. I wait and then go on reading about the creation of the United Nations.

He puts his hand on my arm.

"Do you know what Rumi said?" he asks. "What he said about love?"

"Um, no," I say.

"He thought love was confusing until he realized there's only one real love," Mr. Ram says. "Love of the divine. Through which you could love everything."

"Oh," I say, flipping a notebook page. "Okay."

"Here, let me give you this," he says, pulling himself upright in his overstuffed chair. "This is Rumi."

> *This is love: to fly towards a secret sky,*
> *to cause a hundred veils to fall each moment.*
> *First, to let go of life.*
> *In the end, to take a step without feet;*
> *to regard this world as invisible,*
> *and to disregard what appears to be the self.*

I ask him to recite it again slowly, while I copy it, to make him happy, to make him feel important again. He falls asleep almost immediately after he finishes the last line. I close the seerah book and take it from his lap.

I'm shuffling through my backpack to find my English notes when the house phone rings. The noise is so loud in the shady stillness of the plants and gentle huddled form of Mr. Ram that I'm ticked as I pick up.

"Janna?" It's Tats.

"Hello?" I whisper loudly. "Mr. Ram is sleeping. Shhh."

"What's with your cell phone?" Tats says.

"It's charging for the Chicago trip. But not with me," I say, annoyed at her blustery intrusion. "Who gave you this number?"

"Yo mama. Log on to Facebook."

"Why? I'm working."

"Working at your neighbor's while he's sleeping? That sounds illegal. Anyway, log on, Lauren's posted you."

I scramble to Deval's laptop, but it's password protected. "I can't; I don't have access here. What did she post?"

"It's you without hijab, in gym, I think from yesterday," Tats reports. "Don't worry—you look good."

"Did she tag me?" I ask, about to puke. "Untag me if she did."

"She did, but I can't because I'm not you," Tats says. "You want me to log in as you?"

"No, I'll do it. I can't believe this. I hate her."

"Why? She called it 'Hotness uncovered.' That's the title, so maybe she thinks it's okay to put it up. Everyone's commenting. I keep refreshing to keep track of it for you. Am I a good friend or what?"

"Thanks," I mumble. "Can you message her to take it off?"

"Me? Like she'd listen to me."

"Can you ask Jeremy to message her?" I say, desperate,

thinking of everyone from the mosque on my friends list who'd see it on their news feeds. "Please, Tats."

"I don't get it, but okay, I'll try," Tats says.

"You don't get it? What's not to get?" I whisper-yell, keeping an eye on Mr. Ram. "I don't want pictures of me without hijab on the Internet!"

"Sorry! I forgot! I just thought you looked good. I forgot it's something in your religion."

"How can you forget? It's been on my head since seventh grade!"

"You forget too. What about gym class? Janna, stop getting mad at me when you haven't figured it out yourself!" She's actually yelling. "AT LEAST I CALLED YOU ABOUT IT! BECAUSE I ACTUALLY CARE!"

I glance at Mr. Ram again, wondering if her shouts are reaching him through the receiver. His eyes are closed.

I take a deep breath. "Okay, thanks. Thanks a lot for telling me, Tats. I'm just getting worried, that's all."

"Chill, I'm keeping on top of it for you."

I hang up and chew my nails. Only thing to do now is count down until Deval gets back. Or go upstairs quickly for my laptop.

As I cover Mr. Ram with a blanket before I leave, I notice that he hasn't even changed out of his pajamas. It's almost lunchtime.

• • •

The apartment is empty, so I take my laptop to the dining table and position myself facing the front door to watch for Muhammad's potential reentry.

Opening Facebook has never been so scary. I close one eye and click.

There's a gruesome picture of me jogging by with my ponytail flying toward the camera. The intense look of concentration on my face tells me the photo was taken soon after I ran away from Farooq.

I untag myself, horrified that it's already received so many likes and comments.

Twenty-four people like the picture.

Sixteen comments.

I stop reading after the posts *hawt turd* and *sizlin brown stuff.*

Who are these people? I click on names and see faces I don't recognize.

I scroll through Lauren's list of friends. Some are vaguely familiar from the hallways at Fenway, but most don't ring a bell for me.

I open random profiles of those of her friends without privacy settings. Some of them appear to make it a habit to post compromising pictures of their friends. Is that why Lauren thought it was okay to post me like that?

A part of me wants to remove her as a friend, but the pragmatic side reminds me that then I'd never get to see what else she puts up.

I go back to her profile and read it over, trying to figure her out.

She's so poised in her selfies, like she's at Who's Who events, but the pictures she puts up of her friends make them look less than refined. There's one where Marjorie and another girl are laughing with their mouths open wide in unattractive poses while Lauren smiles serenely at the camera. Her hair is parted to the side, and the white of her diamond earring catches the light.

I look up at the mirrored hallway closet and try a Lauren smile. Mona Lisa in a pashmina stares back at me, and I feel spooked.

My charging cell phone rings in Mom's bedroom and I jump.

"Janna?" Mom shouts. "Where are you?"

"Mom, why are you yelling?"

"Deval just called me because he's been calling home and no one's answering!"

Mr. Ram. I forgot him.

"Mom, I came up to get something." I run to the door, glancing at the clock. How did an hour and a half pass?

"He said he left instructions for Mr. Ram's medicine and food!"

"I'm going down now!"

I fumble with the key as I lock the door. I hit the bulkhead that sticks out right by our door.

"I have to go—the phone won't work in the elevator." I

end the call. There's no way I'm waiting for an elevator, but I don't want Mom's input right now.

I run down the stairs, wondering if Mr. Ram is all right. He can't move without help. He'll be trapped in the overstuffed chair.

I hate Lauren.

My laptop. It was open to Lauren's profile and my unhijabbed picture. Muhammad would see it for sure.

I hesitate mid-step. Should I go back and close my laptop?

I take a breath and continue down the stairs, a prayer on my lips. After all, Allah knows about Facebook problems too.

He's awake. But he doesn't smile at me when I enter.

I follow Deval's instructions silently.

After I feed him, I put the seerah book in his lap once more. He doesn't open it. He just falls asleep again.

Sitting beside him, I don't move a muscle except to turn my English notes.

The plants don't offer shady stillness anymore. Instead, they make ominous shadows on the wall as the afternoon sun moves, bringing Deval home soon.

As soon as Deval enters, I try to slide past him in the doorway to the living room, but he stops me. "Janna, you could have just said no. They could have found another parent for the field trip."

His face, normally relaxed and jovial, is held taut by raised eyebrows. With his receding hairline, he looks eerie, like he's presiding over my sentencing.

I flinch in the witness stand. "I wanted to do it."

"Then where were you?"

"I went upstairs to get something."

"He's very frail."

"I needed something for school." I can't look at him anymore.

"Just let us know if you don't want to do this any longer. We'll find someone else."

"I want Janna." The blanket around Mr. Ram has fallen and reveals an unbuttoned pajama top. He is so skinny. And shaky.

Deval goes to the bathroom, from where Ravi is calling.

Mr. Ram points a trembling finger at the bookcases. "Janna, go to the shelf. That one. And get that folder for me."

I take a bulging manila folder to Mr. Ram.

"Can you take this to your teacher?" he asks, not taking the folder, but waving slowly at it. "It is my thesis. On Shakespeare."

"Okay." I hold the folder against my chest, imagining Ms. Keaton's reaction.

"I think she'll like it."

"I'm sorry, Mr. Ram. For leaving you like that."

"You were gone for thirty poems."

"I'm sorry."

"My son. Tell him that. Not to me, Miss Janna." He smiles.

"I even recited Mr. Silverstein's poem. That one that is our favorite. That is when you came."

I lean down to hug him. Deval enters, and I whisper sorry as I leave.

I take the laptop into Mom's room and check in. No new tagged pictures of hijabless me, but the comments have grown exponentially. Nothing from my mosque friends though. Dad's message is apt today: *While sharing may seem limitless, it ends where privacy begins. Privacy keeps the sacred safe.*

I'm about to click off when Fizz pops up on instant messaging with a *?*. Then: *OMG Janna, is that you??!!* I don't reply, and a new message window appears: *Why is there a haram picture of you online?*

Haram means "forbidden" in Arabic. Somebody must have captured a screenshot of my picture before I untagged myself.

I change my status to offline.

Something pops up in my friends' activity bar just then: *Fizz likes Farooq's status: "So sad Muslim girls are letting go of their modesty these days. A sign of the End Times."*

A faint bicycle horn sounds. It's from Muhammad's phone out in the hallway. I turn my laptop to shield my face that's exploding in unnamed emotions, each one rearing itself and layering on top of the others before I can express it. Something like rage, something like disbelief, something like shame, and something so intensely sad that the only way to release it would be to wail.

In the end, I sob quietly, not even letting a whimper out. Fizz likes what he has to say about me.

Her ideas of good and evil are split so clearly into one side or the other. In her mind, because of the posted pictures, I've taken a step to the other side. The evil one.

And for her, the monster is firmly on the good side.

I swallow and stop my tears. *Fizz likes what he has to say about me?*

She doesn't know about him. Because of his cloak of piety, he is untouchable.

Rage at the unfairness rears its head again. It ripples away from my previous thoughts: *No, he's not. If you don't let him be, he isn't untouchable.*

I start typing under his status *you are a despicable* . . . and then stop.

I don't want to be seen, or known, or discussed. I don't want to be part of holding him accountable. It means me, exposed again.

I erase my part by erasing my words, deleting backward, *despicable a are you.* I wish I could keep deleting into my life, deleting the Sunday the Monster came down into the basement.

This time I don't try to stop the tears.

The bicycle horn sounds again. In Mom's bedroom, right outside my privacy screens.

I gulp. "Go away."

"Quiz Bowl practice. At Sarah's house!"

"That's later." I hover my cursor over the unfriend button on Fizz's profile. I don't click it, even though the wetness blurring my sight is telling me to.

"That's now," Muhammad says. "I'm leaving. The chauffeur will meet you outside the lobby, your royal highness."

I close the laptop and look in the small ornate mirror that hangs by a ribbon on my bedpost. The area around my eyes looks inflamed, a typical outcome of crying when you have sensitive skin. People might comment, especially Saint Sarah, who makes it her business to pounce on evidences of grief, bereavement, any occurrence that mars the tra-la-la-la gaiety of everyday life. I wish I could stay home. But I'm pretty sure Saint Sarah would bring the whole team over here to visit me/practice if I called in sick.

I go over to Mom's side of the room and open the junk drawer in her dresser. She has an old pair of sunglasses that would appear fashionable yet do a good job disguising my condition. They're a prescription pair, but there isn't much to see at Quiz Bowl practice anyway.

The Meet Your Match flyer is gone.

I wear my hijab the fluffy way, so that certain essential folds fall forward, into my face. All in all, on inspection in the hall mirror, I look like a hijabi version of a paparazzi-avoiding actress. I'm trying to see what would happen if I totally shielded my face, bringing my hijab folds completely in, when I hear keys being fitted into the door.

Mom.

I whip off the sunglasses only to notice my eyes. I decide questions about me borrowing her sunglasses are easier to take than questions re my eyes, so I put them back on.

"And where are you going?" Mom asks after salaams. She has groceries in her hands. I grab two bags and head to the kitchen.

"Sain—Sarah Mahmoud's. For Quiz Bowl practice. Muhammad's taking me," I say. "I think there'll be pizza, so we won't need dinner."

She follows me to the door, so I turn and kiss salaams on her cheeks, to disarm her from further questions. I can almost feel the querying powers gathering in her forehead. *Why do you need to wear my sunglasses to Quiz Bowl practice? In a cocooned hijab?* I open the door quickly, turn to blow another kiss, head out, and run right into Jeremy's chest.

I step back. Tats is at his side.

Pulling on the door handle behind me, I swiftly move into the peephole's line of vision, in case Mom decides to check up on things.

"What are you guys doing here?" I ask. This is my first opportunity to talk to him, and this is what I think up?

I look at Tats and tilt my head to the right, where the bulkhead juts out. Our apartment doors are recessed, so I'm hoping they'll move along into the area of the hallway inaccessible from Mom's peeping, should she decide to take the paranoid-parent route.

Tats, being my friend of many years, gets my drift and begins walking. I let out a suspended breath and follow them.

The door opens behind us.

"Janna?" Mom says, stepping into the hallway and seeing the three of us. "You forgot your seerah book."

She holds it out, and I swiftly close the gap to get it, even though I have no need for it. "Thanks, Mom," I say.

"Hi, Tatyana," Mom says, forehead animated with curiosity. "You're going to the meeting too?"

"No, Ms. Yusuf, I just came to see if Janna wanted to go by the lake," says Tats. "I didn't know she had to go to the mosque."

"Oh," Mom says, appraising Jeremy. "And you are?"

"Jeremy," Jeremy says. "I go to school with Janna."

It's the first time I've heard him say my name. If it weren't in front of Mom, I would have taken a moment to savor the experience.

"Nice to meet you, Jeremy," Mom says. "I'm Janna's mom."

"Yeah. My mom," I say, fiddling with the ends of my scarf. Awkward. Awkward. Awkward.

My phone rings. I pick up, waving Mom back. Three long honks emit from the phone. Jeremy and Tats laugh, and Mom goes back inside.

"My dumb brother is waiting for me downstairs," I say.

We walk to the elevator in this silence that I want to fill with words that would erase the awkwardness. He is so close by, Tats in between us, and there's this question in the air: What are we going to do now?

Now, meaning now that we started this thing rolling.

"So, I guess it's a no to going to the lake then?" Tats asks. "There are a couple of others coming too."

"I have this meeting to go to," I say, glancing at Jeremy apologetically. He shrugs and gives me a cute crinkly-eye smile. I clutch my seerah book tighter.

"What's that?" he asks, nodding at the book.

"That's the book Janna made when she was a kid," Tats says, ever ready to help me out. "It's awesome. Like a comic book story of a guy's life."

She dislodges it from my arms and flips it open.

She's showing the life of the Prophet to Jeremy.

I'm stunned at the course of events that's brought the Prophet Muhammad and Jeremy into such close vicinity.

"Do you mind?" Jeremy asks, half reaching for the book.

A totally out-of-the-blue possessiveness toward my seerah book takes hold of me, and it must show in my face, because Jeremy drops his hand and shoves it back into his pocket as we step into the elevator.

Tats returns the book with an expression I rarely see her wearing: disapproval. Severe epic disapproval—such as moms and teachers do real well.

As soon as the elevator doors close, awkwardness descends again, this time with Dementor-like strength.

At any other time, I would've reveled in this daydream come to life: enclosed in twenty-seven square feet of space with Jeremy, with the possibility of being stuck between floors, as often happens in our building. Even with Tats there with us, it would've been a truly welcome scenario. Before.

Now? Now I'm aware of my seerah book and how I have it affixed to my chest and how Jeremy's eyes inadvertently keep wandering toward it once in a while, totally unlecherously, if you know what I mean.

Tats is counting floors aloud as they ping on the indicators above the elevator doors. She's probably occupying herself in order to refrain from reaming me out for not sharing my book with Jeremy.

"So," I say, my cheeks warming steadily toward temperatures I've never experienced before. "Are you guys ready for exams?"

Jeremy shrugs and my heart deflates. I can tell he's not impressed by *moi* thus far.

Tats shrugs as well and says, "Most of my classes have assignments instead of exams. I have one on Tuesday. But of course, *you* must be ready, huh?"

She gives Jeremy an exasperated eye roll and adds, "Jan's a nerd. She gets As without trying. It's sickening."

He looks unmoved, which makes me wonder about the state of his academic record. I shake my head to eject such a revoltingly responsible thought out of it. Jeez, I felt like Mom for a minute there.

"I'm not really ready," I say. "I'm going to cram this weekend. After Chicago."

"Oh yeah, Farooq told me you guys were going to Chi-town," Jeremy says, looking right into Mom's sunglasses.

I look back at him though he's fuzzy, appearing in focus then out of focus, in turns. My eye muscles are straining to work out the layout of his features. Mom must be near blind, because that's some prescription in these glasses. Finally, I settle my gaze on that beautiful forehead, an expanse of uninterrupted clarity.

"Yeah, we're leaving tomorrow morning," I say.

"Yeah, that's what he said," Jeremy says, still looking at me looking at his forehead.

"We're coming back Sunday afternoon," I say. "Maybe we can go by the lake then?"

"You guys can go," Tats says. "I'm going to be at my grandparents' cottage again. Dad's renovating it for them. We're coming back on Monday night."

"Sure," Jeremy says to me. "But I thought you had to study?"

"I'll study on the way there. And tonight," I say, immediately regretting my overeagerness.

"Then it's a date," Jeremy says.

"Ooooooh," Tats says, flicking my shoulder with hers.

"Oh," I say, apprehensive now. When I hear the word "date," I get scared. I feel like I've been thrown out of a plane without a parachute when Jeremy says it—even though he means it lightly. If I get it to be more like a group of friends hanging out, then it'll feel safer somehow. "Is anybody else going to be there on Sunday?"

"You mean, like we're hanging out today?"

"Yeah?" I say quietly.

He must think I'm weird.

"Sure," Jeremy says, nodding, like he understands. "That'll be cool."

And then he smiles at me again, and I swear my heart inflates into one huge red balloon.

The elevator doors open, and we go out the lobby doors in adorable silence, Tats squeezing my arm so that only I can feel her joy for me, Jeremy strolling slightly ahead, hands in his pockets and shoulders thrown back, relaxed. I wave good-bye to them as I get into Muhammad's car. He's texting something while snorting in laughter, but I have no interest in knowing his business. "Hurry, everyone's there already. Sarah said to come right in—door's unlocked."

It feels beyond a crush now. Jeremy understood me without me saying anything weird like *I'm a Muslim girl, and I'm scared to meet with you.* He was okay without me explaining myself. Whoa, this is stirring something up in me, breezy and swift. I feel unanchored and it feels good.

That huge red balloon that's my heart? It's floating somewhere in the sky—no parachute needed. Unleashed.

• • •

Walking into Saint Sarah's house is like walking into a tomb. There's this hush that comes over Muhammad and me as we step lightly through the white hallway toward the door at the end that leads to the basement. Pristine white tiles, glowy white walls, with no pictures or decorations to mar the sobriety.

"This is so interesting," I whisper. "I feel like we're visiting the Mausoleum at Halicarnassus or something."

I sense a slight flicker of something from my fuzzy peripheral vision. Saint Sarah's parents are sitting in the dining room off the hallway. There are coffee mugs and an Arabic newspaper open on the table in front of them. Her father holds up a corner of the paper, and, from the way he peers at me, I can tell he heard my comment.

"Assalamu alaikum warahmathullahi wabarakathu," Muhammad says, moving his bulky body into a please-the-in-laws-to-be pose, very similar to how a praying mantis may appear approaching the most sacred of altars.

"Walaikum musalam," Saint Sarah's dad says, keeping the greeting of peace short and only sorta sweet.

He looks back at me while lifting his coffee cup to his lips, gaze stern.

"This is my sister, Janna," Muhammad says, bowing lower. "She is in tenth grade."

"Hm," Saint Sarah's mom says. "I know you from the

mosque. You always pray in the back, you and your friends. Am I right?"

OMG, was she thinking of the times Fizz and I used to whisper to each other in prayer when our foreheads were on the ground and we thought no one was watching us? We used to get into so much trouble when the older women caught us.

Muhammad turns to me, raising his eyebrows taut in an effort to prod me to answer without thumping me on my back, as he would have done at home.

Wait. She couldn't have been thinking of me and Fizz whispering. Saint Sarah's family moved here two years ago, when Fizz and I had learned to actually pray during prayers.

"Yes," I say, smiling. "I'm usually in the back of the prayer hall."

"Hm," she says.

"What is this that Sarah is saying, that your father has invited the quiz team to stay with him in Chicago?" her dad asks, semiglaring at Muhammad. "Why is this? Why this new thing? What is it about?"

"Oh, yes. My father thought that since the Quiz Bowl may be late in finishing, it would be nice to have a place to stay instead of returning so late on Saturday," Muhammad says. "The girls would be downstairs and the guys would be upstairs, so it would be quite proper."

"Hm," her mom says.

"We have family in Chicago," her dad says. "We used to

live there, you know. So Sarah will be staying with her cousin."

"Oh," Muhammad says, his praying mantis position collapsing slightly. "Thank you for allowing her to stay in Chicago. She'll get the rest she needs before driving back."

"Of course we would think of that. We are her parents," her mom says. "Hm."

"And you, this sister," her dad says, looking at me over his coffee rim while snapping the newspaper. "You are also in this quiz game?"

Is it my insecure imagination or does Saint Sarah's mom have a look of disbelief on her face?

"Yes, she is! She is awesome, Mom and Dad!" Saint Sarah says, materializing suddenly (and stealthily, I might add) to wrap an arm around my stiff shoulders. "This girl knows so much about our beloved Prophet Muhammad, peace be upon him!"

She's wearing something frothy, with pink and yellow bouquets painted over it. Her hijab has a large rosy silk peony pinned to the side of it.

This is what Muhammad gets treated to every time he visits? This vision of the feminine mystique?

Saint Sarah's dad nods and resumes reading his newspaper. Her mom keeps staring at me though, like she knows about me and Jeremy in the elevator, so I quickly join Muhammad and Saint Sarah as they head down the basement steps. We follow Saint Sarah's gauzy dress trailing down the carpeted (white) stairs.

• • •

The whole team is downstairs. Sausun is curled up on the only single chair, so I end up sitting between Saint Sarah and Aliya on the sofa. Muhammad and Nuah hang out on the floor, relaxed. From the way he and my college brother are high-fiving and carrying on every time they're in sync with something—shouting out answers, cracking jokes, or providing commentary—it's like Muhammad's found his long lost twin brother.

As for us girls, we have nothing in common.

Sausun: tall, thin, languid, bored, yet easily irritated, especially by pleasantness of any kind; has immensely set-apart, huge, dark-lined hazel eyes, like a manga character; memorized the whole Qur'an in Arabic at a young age; born to a loaded Saudi father and a beautiful South African–Indian mother; speaks Arabic and Urdu in addition to English.

If she did end up covering her face, it would be like saying to the world *You cretins and peasants are only permitted to see my eyes. Which, lo and behold, wouldn't you know it, happen to be my most striking feature.*

Aliya: a jolly, wholesome, triangular-scarf-wearing, kind soul; with standard-issue big glasses that have survived all the phases possible for their existence, from the only choice in eyewear to a staple of geekdom to the latest cool accessory; possessing a motherly yet giggly nature, sometimes laughing at the wrong times while saying the wrong things to the wrong people (i.e., she and Sausun did not hit it off); born a big sister, always hustling ahead to smooth the way for others; complete lack of evil tendencies or stealth behavior sometimes makes her boring (but dependable in the times when your own depravity has caught up with you).

Saint Sarah: Miss Muslim Universe.

That's why, with this fact that we're extremely unlike one another, it's weird that we get into a groove, a rhythm, practicing for the competition. Saint Sarah sits, barking questions that she's collected from previous Quiz Bowls, her silk flower turning with her head to gaze at the person she's asked or aimed her quizzing at. Sausun, rocking back and forth with her arms wrapped around her knees and a frown on her face as if she's experiencing menstrual cramps right in front of everyone, clips her Qur'anic answers in staccato. Aliya sits with her hands raised in prayer, responding to her dua questions by reciting a long prayer of an answer, followed up by a full belly laugh.

The guys animate their answers with fist pumping and jumped-up bro hugs and take-thats and all manner of behaviors that make it seem like we're participating in football practice and not a dry Quiz Bowl.

Me? I jolt, then mumble my answers. Jolting, because I'm spending a lot of time thinking about Sunday at the lake. As I wait for my questions from Saint Sarah, I can't stop myself from turning to the last page of my seerah book. I slide the sunglasses up on my head and doodle a picture of Jeremy and me standing with our feet in water. Birds fly above us, and they look like they have hearts as wings. Cheesy but necessary.

I carefully write in Sunday's date and underline it three times. I add a special memo in a cute cloud: *meet J at the lake.*

I look up to answer my final question, and that's when I notice something at the end of the long rec room, now that my vision has recalibrated itself.

The monster is on a low beanbag chair in the corner, using a laptop.

On the way home, the most I get out of Muhammad as to why Farooq was there the whole time is that he's helping Saint Sarah with the logistics of our Quiz Bowl participation.

Logistics? Like it's difficult to drive three hours to Chicago, answer some questions, and drive back? I clear Farooq out of my head and think about Sunday again.

Mom's sleeping when I get back, so I take my exam notes to the dining table. I'm prepared to sacrifice my sleep for a long night of studying. For Sunday.

Before I start with the declassified math exam, I check if Amu has sent answers to my questions.

There's an e-mail from him, but, weirdly, it's an answer for another question. A question that never even came through my filtering.

Janna, a gentleman keeps e-mailing me this same question every two weeks and I fear if I do not address it, I may be held accountable by our Creator. Please edit this so we can add it to next week's posting.

Dear Imam, can Muslims grow (medicinal) marijuana? My neighbor wants to start something with me—don't worry, it's not going to be at my place but his—and I'm all for helping people. Besides, God grew it here on earth, right? Just want your opinion before I invest.

Answer: Thank you for your interest in being of aid to people. It is a noble outlook on life, especially if undertaken without the expectation of a return, investment or otherwise. I take it you have perused the laws of your state? A Muslim is a follower of laws—the laws of God and the laws of the society he or she lives in. Thus, if one is not permitted to grow such a crop on private premises by law, such pharmaceutical farming initiatives are forbidden. Furthermore, in our religion, the laws of God ask us to not come near anything which alters our senses, as a Muslim must be mindful of Allah's creation at all times. However noble your intentions may be, I find it at odds with your investment interests. And yes, God did grow it. But he also grew poison ivy. And Allah knows best.

I laugh. I can't wait for his answers to my questions.

MONSTER, SAINTS, AND MISFITS

I'm in a car driven to Chicago by the monster.

He was the fourth person, the one Aliya said was coming along to keep Nuah company. Her "devout" cousin.

I'm sitting in the back, trying to ignore his glances in the rearview. I made sure to not sit behind him. He made sure to adjust the rearview mirror.

I am not going to open my mouth the whole way over. I am going to disappear.

Can I text Aliya to shut up with her pointless chattering next to me? And Nuah, with his dumb jokes? And Farooq, with his continued insistence on existing?

Feigning sleep, I curl down into my lap to escape those eyes in the mirror.

I pretend to be nudged awake by Aliya in front of this blank building. Blank, meaning there are no windows, signage, or any indication that things, other than nothingness, go on inside.

By the looks of the surroundings, we're in an industrial area. Cheery.

I actually brighten up a bit at this. The less this Quiz Bowl is made into a big deal, the faster I can skedaddle out of here, I surmise. This inference is quickly shattered when we get inside the building, and I realize we've entered through the back door of a local community cable station, STUDIO WKTN, RIGHT HERE, RIGHT NOW. That's what the lettering along the walls tells us. Aliya gets giddy and goes charging ahead. I hang back, taking laboriously slow steps as Farooq is right behind Aliya, and the last thing I want to do is give him a thrill by colliding into him. Nuah is behind me, being Mr. Nice Guy and not passing me but moderating his pace.

We end our walk in a burst of black and bright: black stage, black furniture, black fixings lit up by lights from all directions and vantage points. A studio, with a small audience sitting across from us as we enter. Who would want to watch us get nitty-gritty with Islamic facts?

Muhammad cheers when he sees us. Saint Sarah waves us over with blue T-shirts in her hands. There are other teams huddled offstage, on the floor.

"Assalamu alaikum, we're the blue team," Saint Sarah says. "Wear these."

I note with satisfaction that she doesn't hand a T-shirt to Farooq and that he's disappeared from our midst.

"Where's Sausun?" I ask, loosening up now that the

monster is gone. I hold up the enormous one-size-fits-all shirt that's the color of Cookie Monster. There's no way Sausun would wear this.

"Right here," Sausun says. "Right in your face."

I look up to see a tall woman in a black gown, face covered, by Saint Sarah's side. On first glance previously, I'd dismissed this personage as someone's mom.

She actually did it. She's wearing niqab—well, beyond that, because her eyes are covered too by an almost sheer black fabric.

Does this mean she *doesn't* have to wear a big blue T-shirt?

I wiggle some fingers at her in hello but feel more distant from her than ever before, if that's possible.

For the rest of the time, while Saint Sarah preps us with the information the studio people gave her, I keep peeking at Sausun. She looks so . . . so . . . so elegantly aloof? Are these the words to describe the vibe she gives off? Like someone who doesn't give a crap about anything, even things like a stalker guy in your mind's comfort zone or the potential for an annoyingly perky person to become your sister-in-law in merely two more chaperoned sessions.

Basically, she looks like she's excused herself from the proceedings of life's unnecessariness.

At the same time, she looks like an in-your-face ghost or someone cloaked in a very obvious invisibility cloak. Powerful stuff.

I slip the blue shirt on top of my clothes and follow the team onto the stage. We get assigned one of the six tables, staggered slightly diagonally so that we can sort of see the other teams. The host and judges are on the floor in front of the stage, with their backs to the audience. They look serious, with suits on or sporting sharp ties against neatly buttoned-up shirts.

We get dusted by the makeup people. It's telling that Saint Sarah does not need any *additional* makeup, and I glance over to see if Muhammad has duly noted this. But he's engaged in some sort of intense handshake thing with Nuah and misses the opportunity.

My niggling admiration for Sausun blossoms as she casually waves away the makeup people, like some ninja diva.

Saint Sarah goes to huddle with the other team captains. I notice her hands are free. Her clipboard. It's lying facedown on the table in front of Sausun.

I pull my chair close to Sausun. "Sarah forgot her *clipboard*."

She glances at it and then flicks it over. We peer closer.

It's a hand-drawn table of the weekend, including Friday. The column on the left lists top, bottom, hijab, shoes, purse, and accessories, and the next three columns are filled in with her outfit details. Details, as in pink-necklace-with-dangly-crystals details.

Sausun shakes her head and flips the clipboard back. "Wow. That was refreshing."

• • •

Round one starts with questions on Islamic history. Muhammad braves that one pretty well against the reds from Michigan, the yellows from Ohio, the purples from Minnesota, the oranges from Iowa, and the greens from Indiana. We vault to third place after he correctly identifies a picture of the oldest surviving mosque in America: Cedar Rapids, Iowa, early 1900s. The oranges groan in unison at this fact about their home state.

Then Sausun takes on the Qur'an questions and catapults us to first. She's really cool to watch. Her voice seems to materialize out of nowhere, reciting verses with precision and rhythm. I think it really throws the other teams off to be challenged by a faceless competitor. I give Sausun a low five at the end of her round. Saint Sarah hugs her so hard that she leaves shimmering eye shadow on Sausun's veil.

Nuah's turn. Islamic laws.

"What are the primary objectives of Islamic laws? The primary objectives of Islamic laws? Islamic laws? Objectives?" The host is a kindly older man. He's got a thick Arabic accent so he makes sure to repeat the important parts of his questions several times, with twinkling eyes and encouraging nods of his head. His beard is Santa white.

Nuah buzzes in. He gets a fist bump from Muhammad as he leans in to the microphone. "Mercy, justice, education, and God-consciousness."

"Excellent. Good." The host shuffles his cards. "And what are the five categories of protections enshrined in the laws? Five categories of protections? Enshrined in Islamic laws? Islamic laws?"

One of the girls from the red team buzzes in. The three girls on their team have red hijabs on, and I wonder if they were informed about their team color ahead of time. Not that it would have changed anything for me. Black scarf all the way.

"Faith, life, inheritance, family, and lineage?" The red-headed girl sits back, unsure, as the host begins shaking his head in the middle of her response.

Nuah's already buzzing in. The green light goes on above our team to indicate it's our turn to answer.

"Life, intellect, faith, lineage, and property." The white beard's nodding as Nuah finishes.

From then on, Nuah's on an untouchable streak. He cleans up the next three questions and completes round four, keeping us in first place.

At the start of a short intermission, when Aliya and Sausun go for a restroom break, he turns to me in the next seat over. "Seerah's next. Virtual fist bump?"

He holds up a fist, and I pretend to bump it in the air. I can't help laughing. Unrelated Muslims of the opposite gender aren't supposed to touch each other, so his gesture's funny.

Nuah is looking at me laughing, his head tilted in that odd way of his, the wooden prayer beads hanging around his neck askew. "Aha, I knew it. There're a lot of smiles in there somewhere."

"What's that supposed to mean?"

"Nothing. Just that it's nice seeing people smile."

"I smile."

"A lot?"

"When I need to."

"I get it. It's on a needs basis. Very economical." He's got a big smile as he says this.

"It would be kind of freaky to have this huge smile pasted on all the time." I arrange a freaky smile on my face, crossing my eyes to add to the effect.

He laughs. "Uh-oh. I'll have to reevaluate my policy of walking around with a smile now. If that's what I look like."

"Well, ask yourself: Do people ever move away from you slowly as you enter a room? Do they glance at each other ever so carefully as they back away?"

"I don't know. Do they?" He's looking at me quizzically, a smile still on his face. "At the community center. When you first saw me. April sixteenth."

I stop and pretend to think. Why does he think I noticed him on April sixteenth?

"Was that your first day of work there?"

"No, I started on April first."

"So why would I have seen you on April sixteenth?"

"Oops. My bad. I mean that first Thursday in April then. Or whenever you first saw me. Maybe at the mosque. Whenever." He's looking away now, tilting his chair back.

Muhammad leans over from the other side of Nuah. "Jan, if you need to review your notes, now's the time to do it. Look at that girl there."

A petite girl with long curly hair, drowning in a yellow T-shirt, is consulting a seerah book. A published one. *The* authoritative one. Sticky notes protrude from the book's pages, and she closes it once in a while to mutter things to herself before checking the book again.

"Where's your seerah book?" Muhammad asks.

"I left it at home."

"Nice."

"Don't worry. I'm sure I can keep us in first place."

Saint Sarah comes over to the front of our table from where she was huddled with the Quiz Bowl organizers. "Okay, we're in the final round. After the seerah and dua rounds, only the top two teams will compete for the finals."

She doubles forward and hugs me, squishing me against her perfumed self. "You're awesome, Janna. I know you'll be amazing. And thanks for coming through for us at this busy time for you."

After she leaves, I turn to Muhammad, noticing Nuah's empty spot as I do so. "Is there glittery eye shadow on my scarf?"

"Round five: seerah." The host looks at the three teams, Michigan, Ohio, and us, in turn, eyes twinkling. Red, yellow, and blue.

"Question one: Why did the Prophet Muhammad's mother choose his name for him? Why did the mother choose his name? The Prophet's name? Why?"

I hit the buzzer.

Farooq moves into view from the audience as I open my mouth. His phone is aimed squarely at me, taking a photo or video. I blink into it for a few seconds.

"Yes, blue team?" The host is encouraging me with kindly nods.

I forget the question. The word "why" reverberates in my head. *Why? Why? Why?* "Why" what?

The green light turns off above our table.

Curly yellow girl buzzes in. "While she was pregnant, Amina, the Prophet's mother, had a dream with an angel calling her newborn Ahmad, which is a variation of Muhammad."

"Yellows, one point.

"Question two: Who in the Prophet's family owned a leather-goods business? Who owned a leather-goods business? Leather-goods business? Who?

"Question three: What key military strategy did the Prophet take his wife's advice on? Key military strategy advised by his wife? His wife? What strategy?

"Question four: From where did the Prophet ascend to heaven on the Miraj? Prophet ascend to heaven? On the Miraj? From where?

"Blues, you have not buzzed in for any more seerah

questions." The host is looking right at me. "If you don't get this last question, you'll be eliminated from the finals, and Indiana will get your spot.

"Question five: When was the first written constitution, the constitution of Medina, written? When was the first written constitution written? The constitution of Medina? When was it written?"

Who? What? Where? When? The questions bounce around my head as I stare into the host's face.

I can tell that the monster is still filming me.

I sit back. Curly yellow buzzes in. Her team explodes with hoots as they take first place.

The Indiana greens stand up and cheer, clamoring back onstage. The audience, our home-state audience even cheers.

The only silence comes from our table.

As our team streams offstage, I excuse myself on the pretense of needing the bathroom. I go down a hall beside the studio audience steps, this hallway dingier than the one we entered the studio through, and open the first door I see. It's a cleaning supply closet. There's a ceramic garden gnome hanging out on the shelf beside a container of pink liquid, and he watches me spread the Cookie Monster T-shirt on the floor before taking a seat on it.

I lean against the wall, tipping my head back to stare at the stains on the ceiling.

What would it feel like to glide by the monster, all in

black, like Sausun? I'd give him no access to me, or my expressions, even my body language, if I wore a huge, tentlike outfit. I could be giving him the finger the whole time, and he wouldn't even know it.

But what I can't get is why I don't even want him to know it.

Why does it feel like I'm wound up, my hands and mouth, by some binding I can't see?

I dip my head down and rest it on top of knees that are pulled tight to my chest. My eyes close. Maybe I'll wake up tomorrow, and everyone will have forgotten I lost for the team.

I wake to the beep of a text from Muhammad: Where are you? We're leaving to get something to eat.

The time: 8:12 p.m. The date: still Saturday.

Coming. Can I join your car?

After a minute: That's a no. Sausun refuses to ride in a "stunted car like Aliya's." Something about long legs and necks.

I ride downtown curled in half again.

"Janna's really tired," Aliya says in a soothing voice to the guys as she strokes my head.

"Must be exams," Nuah says.

"Yeah," says the monster. "Exams."

I pretend to need to be nudged awake again, this time in front of Baba's Pizza and Pasta. The others rush in and I hang back, leaning against the bricks outside the restaurant.

Saint Sarah's car pulls up and coughs out Sausun. Muhammad emerges minutes later and strides over to me.

"Remember your offer to chaperone a few more meets?"

I shrug. I'm not in the mood to dispute his misuse of the word "offer."

"Well, a couple of streets over, on Randolph, there's this really nice Vietnamese restaurant," he says. "Will you come with us?"

I nod, open to anything that will take me away from the hulking crudeness known as Farooq, currently inside Baba's.

"Thanks," Muhammad says. "And don't worry about the Quiz Bowl."

I shrug and walk a few steps ahead to prevent him from seeing the wetness pooling in my eyes.

I knew why the Prophet's mom had chosen his name for him. I knew about his ascension to heaven. I knew exact instances when he'd consulted his wife about military strategy. I knew who in his family had a leather business.

I would have gotten us into the Quiz Bowl finals.

I cry into the wind that blows off Lake Street, hoping I'm headed in the right direction, hoping they didn't mean to drive to the restaurant. I want to cry and not attack my eyes to stop the tears. Somehow this cry feels deserved.

By the time they catch up with me, I'm composed and looking up at the "L" train tracks running above us.

We walk silently until Muhammad indicates a turn.

"There," Muhammad says. "It's nice, isn't it?"

The restaurant patio is a composition of dark and light wood. Minimalist, lots of clean lines, good for my state of mind.

"Muhammad?" I ask. "Do you mind if I sit at another table? You guys can talk, and I can make some exam notes."

"Sure," Muhammad says. "Sarah?"

"No problem," Saint Sarah says, leading the way into the restaurant. "You get cracking on those exams, and we'll promise to be super good."

I eat shrimp and sweet potato cakes and write words on blank lined paper: "fade," "extinguish," "evaporate," "niqabize." The ways to disappear.

I don't need to pretend to make notes. They're so into each other, they ignore my presence. I do my Islamic duty of glancing at them periodically to make sure they aren't reaching for each other's hands or playing footsies. Alas, no such drama.

The highlight comes as we're leaving, when Saint Sarah tells us about the text she received informing her that the others had squeezed into Aliya's car, even Sausun's legs and neck, and gone on to Dad's house in the suburbs. It will be only us three in the car. Sigh of relief.

We're walking by the patio when someone calls out, *"Sarah?"*

"Oh my gosh," Saint Sarah whispers on turning around.

It's this girl with trim hair and neat, high bangs. Her lips are red, and she wears no other makeup. She stands up, revealing a black fifties-style dress with crisp white collars. The guy beside her, wearing huge red-rimmed aviators, stays seated.

"Never thought I'd see you here," the girl says, coming over to us. "How *are* you?"

Her voice is husky and carries over the other diners.

"I'm great," Saint Sarah says. "And you?"

"Fantastic," the girl says. "Malcolm is with us too. He's in the restroom."

"Oh, really?" Saint Sarah says, moving a step closer to Muhammad. "What's going on with you?"

"Just working," the girl says, glancing up at the restaurant doors. "At an art museum, a small one. When did you start wearing the head scarf?"

I snap to attention. Saint Sarah started the hijab recently?

She, our study circle leader, pauses and says, "Two years ago. After I moved."

"Awesome," the girl says. "It looks good on you. Colorful. Oh, here's Malcolm."

A tall, thin young man exits the restaurant and turns toward the patio steps. He looks the total opposite of Muhammad. My brother's fashion sensibilities run more into the support-your-sports-team end of the aesthetics spectrum, whereas this guy is wearing a faded concert T-shirt under a fashionably loud plaid jacket and fitted, distressed jeans. Muhammad's hair is short and boring, whereas this guy's is up-and-coming, straight-up rakish. An impressive forehead lies below the hairdo. And beneath *that,* a five o'clock shadow finely mists his strong jawline, just so.

Cute.

"Malcolm, look who's here," the girl calls out. "It's Sarah."

Malcolm does an abrupt dramatic stop when he sees her. At first I can't tell if it's put on or actually authentic, but when he resumes walking, overly casual, hands in his pockets, arms stiffened, it's evident his initial reaction *had* been real. He stops by the girl with red lips and observes Saint Sarah. It's an openly searching look, and I would've blushed if I'd been her.

"Whoa, Sarah," he says quietly. "What's up?"

Saint Sarah, uncharacteristically mute, smiles half her wattage and weaves an arm through mine.

"Just finishing up school," she says. "This is my friend, Janna, and her brother, Muhammad, my fiancé. Guys, this is Malcolm and Trish, old friends."

Trish takes Muhammad in for the first time as he steps forward to shake hands with Malcolm, pumping enthusiastically like a goofball politician. I'm still contemplating the ramifications of Saint Sarah's reference to Muhammad as her *fiancé* so I don't make any moves toward friendliness.

"Congratulations," Trish says. "Wow, that's zany. Getting married so young."

Saint Sarah laughs high and fake, and I become intrigued

with these "friends" from her past. Especially since Malcolm keeps staring at Sarah like she has an extra eye or something. Muhammad takes no notice, probably reveling in being called her fiancé.

"Oops, look at the time," Saint Sarah says. "We've got to drive to Inverness. Catch up later?"

"Where are you staying in Inverness?" Trish asks.

Muhammad steps in and clarifies. "My sister and I are staying there, but Sarah will be with her cousin in the city."

"Oh, at Noura's?" Trish asks. "Maybe we'll stop by then."

Saint Sarah smiles and leans in for a hug with Trish. Malcolm moves in as well, but Saint Sarah turns away and strides off.

Muhammad and I have to hustle to catch up with her after we bid adieu to her friends.

"Old friends," Saint Sarah mutters. "No biggie."

"That Malcolm guy? He acted quite weird," I say. "Don't you think so, Muhammad?"

"No, not really," Muhammad says. "Sarah, you'll have to come in and meet my dad now that we're, you know, engaged."

"Oh," Saint Sarah says. "Right. About that . . ."

"We'll need to get a ring," Muhammad says. "How about during the week coming up?"

"Um," Saint Sarah mumbles. "Maybe."

"Aren't you going to congratulate us?" Muhammad asks, thumping me on the back.

"Don't tell anyone yet, because, it's not, you know, finalized," whispers Saint Sarah, as though the man talking to himself across the street is going to put an announcement in the *New York Times* if he hears.

"Yeah," Muhammad says. "We'll tell our families first."

I don't say a word because I'd taken a few glances back and seen Malcolm and Trish remaining standing at the edge of the patio, talking, eyes fixed on us.

Something's fishy, and, like the last time, on the first date of my brother's that I chaperoned, I'm stung with pity for my brother. He couldn't seem to see the kernel of the matter: Saint Sarah and Malcolm have a history.

I hang back and let them walk ahead. For a couple that has apparently just got engaged, they sure are atypical. Muhammad's the one getting giddy with the wedding prep, while she stays silent.

I'm getting an intuition about maybe-not-so-saintly Sarah's sordid past. I vow to investigate and put my findings to good use.

On the ride over to Dad's, I try in vain to bait her ("Malcolm looks a lot like Liam Hemsworth, don't you think, Sarah?" and "He looked at you like he's known you for a long, long time, eh, Sarah?"), but she doesn't bite ("Liam Hemsworth? Really? You think so?" and "Did it look like he's known me for that long? Well, he does wear glasses and he didn't have them on. Probably explains his eye trouble."). She's concentrating on the road like she's taking a driver's exam. Muhammad is counting things off on his fingers, things to do re the engagement, and doesn't pay attention to us.

Sarah does realize I'm quick on the uptake though and, after a while, begins to take control of the situation by opining on diverse topics totally unrelated to 1) guys, 2) engagements or weddings, and 3) friends.

I fall asleep and have to be nudged awake, truthfully this time, after she parks the car on Dad's circular driveway.

I run up to the front door thinking about baby Luke, my laddoo. Dad opens it with a smile, his arms out for a hug.

He's wearing his weekend outfit of crisp button-down shirt and khakis. The way you know it's leisure wear is that the shirt collars are lifted up, not curled over a tie.

His wife, Linda, holding the laddoo, is coming down the massive staircase. She hugs me, hands over Luke, and directs the maid to take my backpack to the basement. Linda's another one who has a constant smile on, a high, gummy one. I smile back at her out of habit. And because of the laddoo.

He's seriously chubby, with a dense roundness that's solid and real. His eyes take a while to register me, but once they do, he giggles and scratches my face in boisterous greeting. Linda tells me that Logan is already asleep.

I sit, bouncing Luke on my knees, in the formal living room while Dad and Linda listen to Muhammad's elaborate introduction of Sarah.

I learn quite a few things listening to him. Firstly, Sarah

wants to do her PhD. Secondly, my brother's choosy about what he says. Like, he never tells Dad about Sarah's Islamicity. About how she moved to Eastspring and took over the mosque's youth committee. How she quotes Qur'an and sayings of the Prophet in a cheery voice whenever she can, like in the middle of conversations, like when you least expect it. He never tells Dad that as a daughter-in-law she'll be a thorn in his secular side.

Instead, he tells Dad about her career aspirations and how she doesn't want kids until she's become a professor. He makes her seem like a totally modern gal.

Sarah sits with her legs crossed, holding a glass of water with two hands, listening and occasionally interjecting to downplay the hype.

The laddoo screws up his face and throws up on me as Dad begins asking questions about Sarah's parents.

"Here, let me take him. You get cleaned up," Linda says, scooping up the laddoo and thrusting a box of tissues at me. "It's my fault. I should have told you he'd just eaten."

I stand up, blotting at the mess on the front of my shirt. "It's okay. It's lucky I brought extra clothes."

"Why don't you get cleaned up in the bathroom downstairs? Your friends are already there."

She takes the laddoo back upstairs. I open the door to the basement, hoping I don't reek too much of baby vomit. Stepping onto the dark landing, I feel for the light switch, but they turn on a second after the door closes behind me.

He puts a finger to his lips and his other hand out to still me, but I flinch.

He slips the hand to the doorknob, holding it tight.

"I just want to talk to you," he whispers. "Just talk."

And not attack me?

"Why are you avoiding me?" he asks. "I can tell, you know."

I look down, thinking of my stupidity in slipping my phone into my backpack pocket before I fell asleep in the car. Now it's downstairs.

I don't even want to give him my gaze.

"That thing before, what I did, I'll admit it, it was a mistake," he says, voice low. "But you admit something too. You wanted me, before you got this thing for Jeremy. Which is so wrong. A non-Muslim guy. Admit it."

I back into the wall and then realize my mistake too late. It gives him the idea to step closer and prop one hand up against the wall, blocking me from the stairs.

"Showing off your hair to him?" he says. "He's playing you. He wanted us, me and you, set up, not you and him. He got caught up in it, he told me."

I want to scream because he's now less than a foot away from me. But everything is twisted in me—what he's saying, what he did before, what my dad would think of me. What Muhammad would do. I can't even find my voice among my emotions.

"You're playing with fire, this thing with Jeremy," he says, coming closer, lowering his head. "You think it's so easy to do what you want?"

He draws his hand away from the doorknob and—

The door opens and Nuah is on the other side. Farooq turns to him, taking a step back, and I flee down the stairs.

"Is everything okay?" Nuah calls. "Bro, why are you here? You said you were going down to get water."

I run to the nearest open door and close it, my heart hammering like it's fled down hundreds of flights of stairs. Leaning my forehead against the door, I work on stilling my breathing. That only results in me sobbing, shoulders quaking.

"I can tell you're *not* crying because we got trashed at the Quiz Bowl, in front of our own supportive home-state audience," a voice says.

I turn and see Sausun, lounging in a tank top and huge track pants with a laptop on her flat stomach, on one of the twin beds in the room. Her hair is glossy black and hangs to her waist. There are candy wrappers littered around her on the bed.

I open the door to go. The last person I need to see right now is a know-it-all grim reaper.

"Wait it out in here," Sausun calls. "You want Sarah to pounce on you? Or Aliya to laugh at you?"

"Sarah's going to her cousin's," I say. "And Aliya's an early sleeper."

"I heard her shuffling around right before you got in here," Sausun says, selecting a piece of candy from a bulging paper bag that says SWEET NOTHIN' on it. "Just lie on that bed and calm down a bit. I won't be nosy. I'm YouTubing anyway."

I look at the other bed. It's up against the wall opposite the door, and I'll be able to turn away from Sausun, so I get in.

It's like Nuah was waiting outside the door, how he opened it as soon as Farooq let go of the knob. What if he hadn't? What was Farooq planning on doing? Why couldn't I stop him? The last question is pounding in my head, threatening to send me over the edge into losing control of my emotions again, so I dig my face into the pillow, trying to force myself to think of something else.

As I'm clearing my mind, quieting it, I become aware of the sounds coming from Sausun's computer. She's shrieking with laughter at times. The girl must be crazy, I decide, before turning over and arching myself to peek at her screen.

It shows two girls in niqab, vlogging, accompanied by really simple, ugly white doodles and words scratched on top of almost every image. It's not easy to take my eyes off of the YouTubers' antics, which include going to a haunted roller-coaster-ride attendant to ask for a job haunting the place. The words *I'm afraid to see their resumes* float above the attendant's head.

"Who's being nosy now?" Sausun says, not taking her eyes

off the screen. She holds out a small, clear bag of licorice candy.

I lean over, take the bag, and pick out a couple of pieces, hanging off the bed, a strange compulsion forcing me to stare at the screen.

"Who are they?" I ask, chewing slowly. "They're weird."

"They're the Niqabi Ninjas," Sausun says. "You've never heard of them?"

I shake my head as the Niqabi Ninjas hand out big smiley stickers at some corner in New York. Only a few people take them, and those who don't get a sad-faced doodle drawn, digitally, on the back of their heads as they get away.

"Why are they doing this?" I say. "Are they making fun of people?"

"They want people to not be scared of niqabis, girls who cover their faces," Sausun says. "So they try to lighten people up. Give them another image of niqabi girls."

She sits up and slides off the bed, holding the laptop high. Placing it on the carpet, she pats a spot beside her and puts the candy bag between us.

We watch the back episodes of the vlogging Niqabi Ninjas. I eat candy and slowly, bit by bit, tell her about Farooq.

Sausun listens without once looking at me, just lowering the volume on the vlogs and handing me a big red jawbreaker when I break down again. I take the candy and roll it around in my hands until it mixes with my tears and runs red over my palms. That gets me to stop crying.

I throw the jawbreaker into the fake soil of a fake tropical plant by the window and turn my blubbery self to Sausun.

She clicks off YouTube and closes her laptop.

"Are you looking at me for some easy solution?" she asks, rustling in the bag until she finds a pack of bubble gum. "Because you do know there's a reason you're hiding here crying about it, right?"

I nod, even though I have no clue as to why I'm hiding here crying about it. That's what I can't figure out, why it feels so hard to scream it.

She unwraps a cube of gum, flicks it into her mouth, and says, "*Although*, you can do what I do when I get mad at things I can't change. Burn the suckers."

She rips off a portion of the candy bag and hands it to me. "To wipe your hands on."

I comply. "What do you mean 'burn the suckers'?"

"I read it somewhere. You write the thing out that you can't deal with, the unmentionable, write what you want to do and then burn the pages. Slowly." She smacks her gum. "I fed a fireplace once with seventeen pages about a man who needed to be mutilated. I described the torture lovingly."

"Why'd he need to be mutilated?" I say.

"Because he married my sister and then married two other women on different continents without telling her," she says. "My sister doesn't roll like that. He knew that beforehand."

"Did she leave him?" I ask. "I hope she left him."

"No, she's in Saudi," she says. "He left her there. With a baby and a huge empty house. She's part Saudi so she's bound by their laws. Can't leave without the deadbeat."

"So why's he an unmentionable?" I say. "Tell the world about the bastard!"

She looks at me and blows a bubble. It becomes quite large, menacingly so, before it pops. She picks it off her face and rolls it into a ripped piece of the candy bag.

"You have no idea about the world, do you?" she says. "I mean, I could ask you, Why'd you keep quiet about your thing? Tell the world about the bastard yourself."

I don't like her dismissive tone. It's too close to the Sausun I know, so I get up off the floor, stretch, and go to the door, opening it cautiously. My backpack's at the foot of the stairs, and the light from the room is enough to reveal no one waiting to pounce. I grab my bag and bolt back into the room. I decide to stay in here tonight, bunking with Sausun, rather than be in a room by myself, with Farooq merely two staircases away. I'd never attempt to stay in my bedroom, on the same floor where the guys are sleeping.

I plunk on my chosen bed and take my laptop out. No new picture postings on Facebook. Only a bunch of messages from Fizz that I don't touch.

I'm so glad she didn't come to Chicago.

Sausun takes her blanket off and spreads it on the floor. "Prayer?"

Nodding, I close my laptop and rummage through my backpack for my pajamas.

I change and make wudu in the en suite bathroom, cleaning myself slowly, thinking about talking to Allah. When I get back to the room, Sausun's in her black gown and scarf.

We perform the night prayer in unison, with Sausun leading. She stays a long time with her forehead on the ground, the time we can say our personal prayers to God, so after I finish mine, I add one for her sister in Saudi Arabia.

After prayer, Sausun gets into bed and watches me for a while as I put away my laptop, before turning over to face the wall on her side of the room.

"I'll trade places with you on the drive back to Eastspring tomorrow," she says. "If you want, that is."

My shoulders and neck instantly relax, surprising me. I didn't know I was wound up until I go slack with relief on hearing her words.

"Thanks," I say, looking at her back with an immense sense of gratitude I haven't felt toward anyone in a long time. "And I'm taking your advice. I'm going to write it out."

She turns back to me and says, "Yeah, but that's the least you can do. The meekest thing. If that perv had tried to hurt me, believe me, I wouldn't be just writing it out."

I stay quiet because my idea is to actually write it out, online, and not burn it. No one would know who wrote it. No one in my world. To post it would feel like some sort of justice. Like posting details of a crime on a wanted poster.

It isn't my fault no criminal would ever get caught.

MISFITS

I stay in the basement, rewatching the funnier Niqabi Ninjas episodes, while Sausun does her gig upstairs at breakfast, convincing Aliya and her carpool crew that she needs to leave right away so *they* need to leave right away, now that she's officially part of their lot. When she comes down to get her bag, she flips up her niqab and gives me a grim smile.

"It worked," she says. "But Farooq knows. He wouldn't look me in the face, the perv."

"Um, hello? That's because you have no face?" I say, elation flickering in me at the news I will be nowhere near the monster for the rest of the day.

"And, also, Nuah is coming with you guys," she says, ignoring my giddiness and letting her face covering drop again. "He switched too."

I slide my legs off the bed and watch her gather her things and pick up candy litter. It's weird that I'd told her something

I don't even allow myself to think much about. Is it true, what someone said, that it's a million times easier to tell a stranger your deepest secret than a person who cares for you? Like those confessions people write on postcards and mail to that guy who collects them. Mine would be short and blunt. It would tell all but not reveal all. *My best friend's adored cousin tried to rape me and now thinks it's a mistake but still wants me to admit I wanted him in the first place.*

But really, I'd told Sausun way more than my anonymous postcard. So maybe she isn't exactly some stranger. Maybe I'd sensed she actually does care.

I mean, this is not the Sausun I thought I knew. Well, sort of knew. At the mosque, it was always a salaam wave from afar. Fizz thought she was too intense, so we kept our distance.

"You staying down here till we leave?" Sausun heads to the door. "Aliya will start making noises if you don't come up to say salaam—you know that."

"Tell her I have girl problems," I say, feigning cramps.

"Meanwhile, you have douche-bag-guy problems." Sausun pauses in the doorway to look at me. "You know, when I first saw you around the mosque, I thought you were the lone rebel type, with your artsy clothes and stuff."

"And?" I say, holding back what I'm about to do, which is give her a good-bye hug.

"And you're just not," she says. "You're weak."

"Okay," I say. "Who wants to be a *lone* rebel anyway?"

"I don't know," Sausun says. "All I know is that sometimes I wonder if I'll get presented with someone kicking up dirt in my life like in yours. Or like what's happening to my sister. Because, you know what I'd do? I'd grind the guy into the ground. Enjoy every moment of it."

I don't say anything. She waves salaam without looking at me and exits.

Maybe she's some stranger after all.

After hearing them leave, and giving myself an extra half hour in case they needed to come back to get something, I emerge from my self-banishment in the basement to find an empty breakfast room full of breakfast. It's crazy stocked with everything from waffles to mini Spanish omelets to samosas and halal sausages, kept hot in those silver warmers. I pile a plate and sit down to eat at the empty table.

A burst of laughter enters from somewhere to the right and above. It's Muhammad's snorts and someone else's hoots mixed with Dad's big belly laugh. I get up, balancing my plate carefully as I negotiate the winding staircase. I follow the noise to Dad's study/entertainment room.

"There she is," Dad says, opening his arms wide.

I set my plate on a sideboard and go over to hug him. Nuah and Muhammad are sprawled across the two huge leather megasofas, laughing again at something on the screen behind me. To his credit, Nuah gets up and kicks Muhammad's legs off to join him, which gives me a spot on the now vacant sofa. I turn to get my plate and take it over.

It's me. They're laughing at *me*, BD. Before divorce, when I was young and naive.

An eight-year-old me is blown up on the home theater screen, holding up my nose piglike at the camera while pointing at thirteen-year-old Muhammad eating a huge bag of chips. The camera then follows me upstairs, in our old house, to show the viewers my neat room in contrast to Muhammad's mess. I'm doing a little jig in my room when Muhammad sticks his head in and says, "But what about this?" He bounds in and opens my closet. Things spill onto the floor—clothes, stuffed animals, school artwork, junk. Kid-me growls, picks up a pink stuffed octopus, and attacks Muhammad with it. "Don't. Touch. My. Closet!" Muhammad stands still in a yoga tree pose while getting whacked. "I am peace. Peace is me," he chants over and over as I pick up more weapons to deal with him.

I search Dad with a questioning look. Why is he showing this stuff? To Nuah? Who's enjoying it way too much?

"Remember?" Dad says. "How we used to film the *Janna Yusuf Show* every Sunday? This episode we called 'Clean vs. Muhammad.' Sometimes I still put it on and watch it. The boys love it. If they weren't at swimming, they'd be in here laughing with us, even little Luke."

I'm not laughing, Dad, I want to say. Then a thought crosses my mind.

"Did you show this to anyone else?" I ask.

"Some of your other friends saw some before they left. Your friend Farooq practically camped in here last night, watching DVD after DVD with me," Dad says proudly. "You're a hoot to watch, sweetie."

I pick up my plate and walk out, mumbling something about getting more food.

I go back down to the basement.

I wait for Sarah on the porch steps, the lone rebel way, with a packed backpack at my side and an iPhone plugged into my brain, pumping in the right playlist for this moment in time. Angry, sad, punch-him-where-it-hurts-most-but-don't-'cause-you-don't-want-to-touch-him, only-crush-his-dirty-little-heart playlist.

The woman across the street waves at me while directing some guy gardening for her, but I ignore the random act. She probably sees a kindly babushka doll when she looks at me, sitting in my hijab. Well, that's okay, because I see overfried hair and strange taste in fashion.

See, that's the thing. I don't get why it's easy to up-yours someone I don't even know, maybe someone who's even nice. But Farooq? He freezes my anger. My justified anger.

Ya Allah, help me. I'm descending. I can't speak the truth like I'm supposed to. Help me.

A second backpack joins mine on the steps, and I know

who it belongs to without looking up. Only one person would carry around a Teenage Mutant Ninja Turtle backpack proudly. The kind that looks like a turtle shell.

Well, besides my brother.

"Oh man, your dad loaded our plates again so much that I can't move," Nuah says. He doubles over in feigned pain before stretching his bent arms back, as though getting ready for some basketball shots.

I notice he happily waves preemptively at the woman "gardening," and she flails her arms back at the happiness of it all. Well, yeah, he doesn't have some person in his life trapping his ability to simply be.

"Did you guys feast like this growing up?" Nuah asks.

I tilt my head at him so he can notice my do-not-disturb earbuds. Then I scroll up the volume.

"Is that 'Walking Contradiction' by Green Day I hear?" he asks, louder, so loud the woman across the street waves again.

"What?" I say, flinging the buds out of my ears. "I thought you guys were having so much fun watching the *Janna Yusuf Show*. Wait, no, it must be time to do some weird yoga on the front lawn while waving at Ms. I'm-rich-now-so-I-will-order-around-this-Hispanic-guy-doing-my-grass-while-waving-at-the-nice-loaded-brown-people-across-the-street-and-guess-what-I-still-do-my-own-hair-from-a-box-ain't-I-economical?"

Nuah does this look I've never seen on anyone, so I hold up my phone and snap a picture of it.

"Wait a minute," he says. "I know what's happening with you."

"Yeah? What's happening with me?" I ask, using an editing app to clone, enlarge, flip, skew, and totally mutate his picture until he looks like some bizarre freakoid. Now I know why Flannery used the line *She looked at nice young men as if she could smell their stupidity.*

"You're mad 'cause we lost," Nuah says, leaning back on the sole tree in Dad's front yard, a birch, not even trying to peer over at my ongoing voodoo job on his photo. "The Quiz Bowl. It stings. You're upset. Hence the Green Day."

I snort really rudely and throw my phone on the steps.

What is wrong with this guy? *Go away, go away, go away,* I think over and over again. Then I say it.

"Go away," I say, looking up at his face looking down at me, with that same expression he had on before. It's the expression you make when you're shocked at something but pretending you've got a handle on it. "Away, far away. It's like you guys can't hear people who say things. I don't want you around, okay? Good-bye, loser."

"Okay," he says.

He picks up his backpack and leaves. Back into the house, turtle shell clinging to taut shoulders.

That was so bad, it feels good.

Sarah drops us at the mosque back in Eastspring, where Muhammad's car is parked. While Muhammad hangs around, leaning into Sarah's driver's-side window, I bolt to his car to get away from their waltzing talk—him, pumped up about their impending marriage, thrusting discussion topics at her; her, nimbly sidestepping every major commitment.

My phone vibrates as I slump into the seat.

Nuah. Who was in the car the whole way back from Chicago and didn't say a word to me the entire time.

I know why you're mad.

I look up and see him walking to his car, head bent over his phone.

My traditional self would have ignored such an intrusion, but something kick-ass woke in me when I saw the Teenage Mutant Ninja Turtle backpack walking away this morning, actually walking away from me when I told it to. I want to wreak something.

Do you have a problem other than a total lack of maturity and intelligence?

It's that dude Farooq.

Go play with your turtles.

He's bothering you.

Did I ask your opinion on anything? No, cause you're like 4 years old.

Right?

I glance at his car, hoping he'll look my way and see my scowl. But he's at the steering wheel, intensely staring at his phone, oblivious to my shut-the-hell-up face.

I'm about to turn my phone off but can't resist one last message. And fyi, only hot guys look good in necklaces.

Muhammad gets into the car, and I shut the phone off. As Nuah drives by, my brother waves, but there's no wave back because Nuah's eyes are straight ahead.

I, astounded at my power, finally smile. I can't wait to get home and get ready to meet Jeremy at the lake.

Mom, who is totally absorbed in her own state of affairs most of the time, decides to pick this day of all days to "reconnect" with me.

She starts with questions about the Quiz Bowl and then hops to Chicago and then home-runs to gossip gathering about Dad and his brood. Though Muhammad is available and willing to entertain her with a fully mimed performance of the whole weekend, saving his surprise status change as the last juicy tidbit of his recount, Mom persists in following me while I head to the bedroom to dump my stuff.

I grunt replies. I mean, what can you say to "Did Linda cook Indian food or white food or Greek food?" except "Food, just food"?

I close my/her bedroom door on her after I grunt, "Sweaty, must change."

Where were you, Mom, when I came home from Fizz's house a few weeks ago and curled into bed without taking off my shoes or hijab because no one told me Muslim boys could also be pervs?

Oh yeah, you were with your friends, having another girls' night out.

And then I see my seerah book lying on my bed, open to the last page.

A sketch of two people at the lake and a date, today's, underlined three times.

OMG, Mom totally knows. She'll never let me out of the house.

But not overtly, because she promised me privacy. Such a lie.

"Janna, I made your favorite, salmon cakes," Mom calls from too close to the door, her breathing, uneven and stressed, belying her chipper words. "And I got us season four of *Downton Abbey*, Mary on her own. We got a long night, so I got a big tub of Ben and Jerry's Half Baked."

I need help. I need Fizz.

Can you call me right now? On the home line?

I wait for a text back but instead get the sweet sound of our phone ringing. Muhammad raps on the door, yelling, "Fizz to Janna, come in, come in."

I open the door and grab the phone, ignoring Mom standing in the hallway.

"Fizz, can I come over?" I whisper.

"Sure, but I'll be home in about an hour; I'm still teaching Sunday school," Fizz whispers back before yelling, "Adam, sit down! You don't need to wash your shoulders before prayer.

Can someone else come up here and demonstrate washing up before salat?"

"That's okay—I'll be there after two anyway," I say. "Thanks, see ya."

"Okay, give me a full replay of Chicago when you come. Aliya's version wasn't impressive. Plus, why are you ignoring my messages on Facebook? What's up with your nonhijab pics? Is someone shaming you?" Fizz says.

"I'll talk to you later. Promise."

I place the seerah book under the bed and slide out of my jeans and top. I already planned my outfit on the way home this morning: my white ultrathin sweatshirt, the one with the witty sayings written in an owl shape, layered over a pink shirt with my favorite jeans and pink jelly flats. And black hijab.

After changing, I throw some lip gloss and mascara into my sling purse. The lobby mirrors are perfect for adding last-minute makeup.

I open the door and breeze by Mom. She hasn't moved from her spot in the hallway, and though Muhammad has reached the pivotal point of Sarah "declaring" her commitment to him, it isn't him she's staring at.

I turn at the last second, at the door, as if in afterthought.

"Oh, Mom, Fizz wants me to come over for help with something," I say. "So assalamu alaikum."

"But Fizz teaches at the mosque and it's not done yet," Mom says, coming closer to me.

"But it is at the mosque," I lie supremely. "I'm going there now. To help."

"I can drive you," Mom says, stepping forward to reach her purse hanging on the hooks by the front door. "Auntie Fatima asked me to try to come by to pack the care packages for Syria. That's why Fizz probably needs you. We can work together."

"No, I need to stop by the stationery store to get stuff for studying anyway. I'll go."

"That's on the way; I can take you," says Mom, sliding her purse up to her shoulders.

And then, thank Allah, Sarah saves me. She rings up from the lobby, saying she wants to come up to drop some stuff we forgot in her car. In the noise of Muhammad insisting that she be asked to stay for lunch and Mom scrambling to find something to serve her (*What about salmon cakes and Ben & Jerry's, Mom?*), I slip out.

For sure the sun has to shine the rest of the afternoon: I don't even see Sarah on the way down, even with our elevator situation. I put on makeup hassle free in the lobby.

The wind that's ever present outside our lobby doors due to the way the buildings are clustered feels special when it hits my face and blows back my hijab a bit. Some of my bangs loosen and fall across my forehead. The wind skips behind me, nudging me forward down the walk and then away from the main road, toward the older homes, his neighborhood, right beside the lake.

I refuse to glance back. Mom's bedroom looks out right onto the path, and I know the face that would be staring at me from the window would be filled with utter disappointment. While I'm filled with utter hope.

How do you know if an experience is going to become a memory while you're actually in it? Like, as I come closer to the picnic table next to where Jeremy stands, with the lake shimmering behind him, I can feel the nostalgia already creeping in for this scene to repeat again and again, even though it hasn't even officially begun yet.

Me, walking toward the guy I've been thinking about since April. Him, waiting with a smile on his face.

I adjust my hijab and turn to snap a picture of the formation of rocks edging the walkway. To quell things.

When I turn back, I see the rest of them. Besides Jeremy, who's turned around to face the water, there are a few others. So he came through on his promise of making it a group thing. How had I not seen them before?

Three guys and two girls, older than me. I suddenly wish Tats were here. She would run up to them and start chatting.

I meander over, pretending to be really interested in the ground leading up to the group. I take a lot of pictures of the trail.

I would have bumped into the picnic table had J's feet not shown up in my phone's screen.

"Hi," he says.

I do a wiggle-wave with my fingers, realizing two of his friends, the girls, are looking at me.

"Nice view," I say, trying hard to look at the lake and not his face.

"Yeah," he says, looking at me and not the lake.

He backs up and gets up on the picnic table, his feet resting on the bench, elbows propped on his knees. Facing me.

His friends are now clustering close to the water, and someone's taking a bottle out of a backpack. I pretend not to see. I have nowhere to look but Jeremy's face.

"So, do you come here a lot?" I say.

He laughs and I cringe. How did I blurt out the cheesiest pickup line in existence?

"Actually I do," he says. "It's almost in my front yard. See, that's my house up there."

He gestures up a hill on my right, and I immediately turn and look at it, without needing much of his directing. The house that I'd looked at through Google Earth countless times.

"A lakeside house," I say. "Nice."

"Yeah, you can come up after," he says. "My dad's barbecuing."

"I'm kind of a vegetarian," I say.

"You mean you eat halal?" he asks, laughing again. "Not to worry, we have halal hot dogs. I've got Muslim friends."

"That's cool," I say.

"Want to see something that is *actually* cool?" He gets off the bench and walks toward a group of trees. I follow, glad to get away from his friends.

We stop at a tree with a small burlap sack hanging off a branch. He takes it down and opens it up. Birdseed.

"Watch," he says.

He holds out a pile of seeds in the palm of his hand and makes a bird noise. A *real*-sounding one.

Pretty soon a few tiny birds begin assembling on the branches overhead. One hops down from branch to branch in a zigzag fashion, watching me carefully. I stand still, and it lands on Jeremy's palm, pecking at the seed while giving me sidelong glances. I wonder if it's female.

"Want to try?" he asks. "They're chickadees. Very friendly."

I hold out my palm, and he tips in the seeds remaining in his hand. I don't know if he's being careful not to touch me or if my hand stiffens involuntarily, but there's no contact. I make the mistake of looking up at him at that moment. He looks back, and there's so much that passes between us that I feel exposed.

He calls out his bird sound, and a chickadee finds its way into my palm, grazing my skin with its light claws. It's so thrilling that I laugh and it flies away.

"They'll even come over to the picnic table," Jeremy says, walking back to our previous spot.

I drop the seeds on the table, flicking off the ones sticking to my clammy palm. Jeremy's about to call out again when we hear a whistle. An older man in a white apron stands waving a spatula on the lawn of the house with the turquoise door.

"Hey, food's ready," Jeremy says to his friends.

As they begin walking to the house, Jeremy works on smoothing out the birdseed on the table.

"Here, you might want to take a picture of that," he says, revealing his handiwork. "For the love of chickadees, you know."

I position my phone and click, the skin on my face prickling with heat. The seeds have been shaped into a heart.

As we amble up the hill, he's quiet and I am too, wondering what to say next.

"Good, Farooq is here," Jeremy says, pointing at a Honda parked in front of his house. "You know him, right?"

"Yeah," I say, freezing.

"He hangs out at my place a lot. His house is the next street over."

"Which reminds me, I promised his cousin I'd be at her house right about now."

"Really? Now?" he asks, pausing on the sidewalk. "At least have a bite first. Food's hot."

"No, I can't," I say. "Sorry."

Down the side of the house, by the fence, Farooq is standing beside Jeremy's dad at the barbecue. He hasn't seen me yet, but in a matter of seconds he will.

I take off down the street, not even waving good-bye to the sweetest guy I've met so far in my life.

Of course I get to Fizz's early, even with the slow Sunday bus service. Everyone is at the mosque, so I slip into the backyard and head to her dad's hammock.

I need to sprawl on this thing to think about getting rid of Farooq's presence in my life for good.

What can I do that's legally permissible? Nothing. I'll have to be a Silent Sufferer, like those women Mom watches documentaries about. She showed me one woman's lined face as she toiled in the fields, two kids attached to her legs, while her husband hung out at the tea shop with his friends. Mom said, *Look at that beauty—now* that *is a strong woman, keeping on while the going is rough.* She admires stuff like that. Mom told me that her mother, my Teta, had lost four children in Egypt to various things, some even at young ages, and yet no one saw the toll it took on her.

Anyway, why are all the Silent Sufferers women? Silently suffering men are not looked up to in any way, as far as I can tell. I mean, even Gandhi, Mr. Ram's favorite go-to for quotes, the man of peace, was not like that.

Come to think about it, Mom isn't even like that. She didn't suffer in silence with Dad. She jumped to action and dumped him. She acted like Sausun said she would if somebody kicked up dirt in her life.

I'm not Mom. I'm not Sausun. I'm this girl who wants to be left alone.

Thinking so hard makes me fall asleep in the hammock.

I wake up to a low, laughing voice. Fizz's dad. "There you are! Your mother is in the house saying you were abducted by a boy at the lake."

I'm groggy, and what he's saying doesn't register.

"Your mother came to volunteer at the mosque and asked for you. No one knew where you were so she's very worried. Auntie Fatima and the girls are comforting her in the house right now."

I walk to the back door. Is she freaked out in an angry or a devastated way? I hope the latter. She'd be happier to see me.

Her face instantly registers anger when she sees me. She clutches my sleeve and leads me out to the car, like I'm a juvenile delinquent she arrested. The twins are laughing behind their hands, and Fizz mouths, *What boy at the lake?*

Thank you, Mom, I seethe to myself. *Do you want me to be a woman of action or, really, just your ideal Silent Sufferer?* I conclude that she wants the latter from me as I bear her lecturing.

Fizz calls me after dinner, while Mom watches *Downton Abbey* by herself.

"I don't know what to say," she begins.

"Okay?" I say. Her tone sounds like Mom's in the car.

"You kept everything from me? Like every single thing?" she says.

"Can I know what you're talking about?" I say, throwing my Chicago clothes into the laundry hamper while scouting for new hiding places for my agendas and notebooks.

"I'm talking about this," she says. "There, look at your video messages."

I draw the phone away from my ear and open the new-message indicator.

It's me and Jeremy by the trees, this afternoon. I'm looking up at him with this really fawning expression while he feeds the chickadee. Then he gives me the seeds, and we look at each other. I didn't know that I smiled afterward, but apparently I did and it looks sort of cheesy.

"Where did you get this?" I say, replacing the phone to my ear.

"Janna, I don't know what you're up to, and I don't like that you're just hiding this whole thing from me," Fizz says. "Am I a friend or not?"

"Who sent you this?" I say, slowing my voice as I realize there's only one person who could have done this. Motive and opportunity.

"Farooq, who had the decency to tell me," she says. "You know they're like best friends, right?"

"I don't care!" I scream. "He's an asshole! A disgusting creep!"

"What is wrong with you?" she screams back. "You're talking about an innocent guy . . . he's got nothing to do with what you're doing behind everyone's backs. You're actually stepping away from Islam, and you get mad at the guy who's helping you back to it? Janna, you've changed so much!"

"He's a pig and I hate him!" I say, crying now.

"He's a hafiz of the Qur'an. Watch your mouth," she says. "I don't want to talk to you. I can't believe you're saying all this just to protect your relationship or whatever with this non-Muslim guy? Someone you know nothing about?"

"You don't know anything about your cousin," I say, aware that she can't probably understand anything I'm saying because I'm blubbering so hard. "He's a . . . a . . ."

She hangs up on me.

A new-message notification pops up on my screen instantly. It's Muhammad, who probably heard me screaming from his bedroom next door.

Everything okay?

"A 'No' uttered from the deepest conviction is better than a 'Yes' merely uttered to please, or worse, to avoid trouble." That's what Gandhi said. Mr. Ram told me.

I'm coming.

He opens the door and shuts it behind him quietly before moving a portion of the privacy screens back.

"What's going on?" he says.

Can I just go to bed? I text. He sits on Mom's bed to read his phone.

You and Fizz fight?

M, I'm tired. I'm sure mom told you about the drama.

That's it?

Yeah, that's it.

You sure?

Yeah, and that guys suck.

Except Gandhi and Mr. Ram?

Zzzzzz

He leaves the room but is back as I'm settling into a long night of sleeplessness. He's holding his phone out for me to see.

"Farooq sent me this," Muhammad says. "Why?"

It's the video of me and Jeremy by the lake.

The creep is ruining me.

Anger like I've never experienced before, tsunami-size, crashes within.

MONSTERS

My history exam is at nine o'clock. I think I'm ready. War is bad and there were many. Misunderstandings account for most of them. Clear communication between affected parties would have saved countless lives. Describe each war thus, citing dates and locations, and earn an A, as Oliver pointed out.

Avoid thinking about Farooq and the Nazis and the world is all good.

I skip eating breakfast, as Mom fell asleep on the couch. Kitchen sounds would have woken her, and I don't want to face the calm after the storm. With Mom, that means a guilt-laden experience with many allusions to her struggles as a single mom. I turn the key in the lock without fanfare, intent on making it out of the building without being sighted.

The elevator doors open in the lobby to reveal Sandra and Ms. Kolbinsky, who's holding a plate of samosas.

"Hey." I hold the doors apart for them. "Where are you two off to?"

"I will visit Mr. Ram. I made these for him. Here, there's some for you, too." Ms. Kolbinsky peels back a bit of saran wrap and eases a few samosas out. "Try it. They are very spicy."

I accept one and bite into it. The pastry covering offers muted flavor before the spiced potatoes explode in taste, tangy and hot. "Mmmm, oh my God, they're so good! You made these?"

"Yes! I'm a cook, always cooking. You'll like more?" She's unwrapping more of the saran, but I put out a hand to stop her.

"I have an exam, gotta go. But . . . so do you?" I turn to Sandra, who's already tucked into a corner of the elevator.

"I'm just taking my grandma up."

"See you then. Tell Mr. Ram I said hi."

I let go of the doors. Before they close, I glimpse Sandra's face changing as she turns to her grandma. It becomes unguarded, tender, like she's eleven years old again.

Like when she returned two weeks late into the beginning of the school year in sixth grade. She took a seat and turned a sweet grin to me. "You're new? I'm Sandra. Just got off the plane from Florida, visiting my dad. I live with my mom."

A little spark lit in me when I heard that. "Me too. I live with my mom too. My dad's working in Chicago."

She was my first friend in Eastspring, before Tats and I latched on to each other at the exclusion of everyone else. And before the art teacher made the class do an extensive study of

Frida Kahlo at the end of eighth grade, and Pradeep muttered that Frida's mustache was nothing like someone else's in our class. A group of guys coughed "Sandra" discreetly every time Frida's self-portraits were projected onto the screen. Sandra's sweetness began drying up and disappeared completely once mustache stickers made their way onto her locker door every week.

I take a seat beside the fake banana tree in the lobby to wait for her.

My phone beeps. Mom.

Why didn't you eat breakfast? I bought waffles for you, the big ones from Parades. They were in the freezer.

I swallow. Those are my favorite—thick and crispy on the outside. And the inside? A heaven of fluff. Slathered with buttery syrup, it's the best breakfast.

I'm not hungry.

You have an exam. Come back up, you still have time.

I got a samosa from Ms. Kolbinsky.

What? Ok, do what you want. Salaams.

I scroll through my messages.

And fyi, only hot guys look good in necklaces. I can't believe I wrote that to Nuah. I delete it and the previous texts that took me to that crazy point.

Salaams Nuah. It's Janna. I press send and wait for a bit. I just want to apologize for the texts I sent yesterday.

I wait. Is he driving or something?

Remember I told you I WASN'T nice? See it's true.

Maybe he's already in class.

Anyway, just wanted to say SORRY. I fill the text field after that with sad sorry emojis and press send.

Maybe he's taking an exam.

"I told Mr. Ram you said hi, and he gave me these for you." Sandra hands me a paper shopping bag.

I look inside. Three books. I let the bag swing at my side as we walk out of the building. "Thanks. Was he happy to see your grandma?"

"Does dressing up in a tuxedo mean you're happy? Gran was blushing and pretending it was because the samosas were so spicy." She smiles into the sun. I'm on her right side and can't see the birthmark, as it doesn't extend that far across. She has a flawless profile.

Anyway, why is the birthmark a flaw?

It's strange that something she was born with, that's of no choice of hers, is now the sole thing that defines her in the eyes of others. She lets it define her for herself, too.

"Sandra, why do you take it?"

She turns to me. "What?"

"Why do you take how they treat you?"

"I don't get what you're saying." She quickens her pace.

"I mean why did you become quiet just because of the people who pick on you?"

"I didn't. I'm a quiet person."

"Not from what I remember."

"Janna, you don't really know me."

"I did know you."

"When we were little. People change when they're older." She bends her head, and hair falls into her face.

"That much? When I knew you, you were sunny. Remember? We had nicknames for each other, and Tats said you should be Sunny because you were always seeing the bright side of things."

She slows her pace and shrugs. "So maybe things happened to show me there's more to the world than being happy all the time."

"Well, remember I was called Merdy? Which was a code for Nerdy. Consonant before the letter *N* was *M*? We thought we were so smart." I lift up the books from Mr. Ram. "Guess what? I'm still Merdy."

She laughs. "Yeah, but that's different. Are you telling me you're the exact same person you were two or three years ago?"

I think about that one. "No. But am I that different? As in the opposite of what I was like before? No."

Is this what Mr. Ram was talking about? Your "kernel" not changing?

She stops. "So what're you saying? Just change?"

"Be yourself?"

"And the myself in sixth grade is the real myself?"

"Wow, that's deep. Okay, new nickname for you: Deep."

"And new one for you: Oprah."

"Sizzle!" I weave my arm through hers, and she stiffens for a moment before relaxing. "You're a sizzler."

"A deep sizzler? Sounds like a steak."

"If you're the Deep Sizzler, and I'm the Oprah Special, maybe a kind of salad, what does that make Tats on the menu?"

"Something mushy, gushy."

"A dessert."

"Tiramisu. Mushy, gushy, and dramatically good."

"That's good. It matches her hair. Let's call her that when she comes back tomorrow. She's at her grandparent's cottage. She'll be like 'Tiramisu?'"

"I don't have an exam tomorrow so maybe Wednesday."

"She's done after tomorrow."

"Oh."

"Come over on the weekend. We'll do something."

"Maybe."

"Come on, I can't go a whole summer without being sizzled!"

She laughs again but stops when she sights Fenway High.

Right before I go into school, I check my messages. None from Nuah.

Fizz posted a picture of the quiz team in Chicago on Instagram. It's onstage but I'm not in it, so it must have been when I was in the supply closet.

The monster is in it.

Thanks for repping Illinois, Fizz wrote. Lots of likes. There's a comment from N_ABDULLAH: *It was cool but practice was better!*

I click on N_ABDULLAH. It's Nuah. His most recent picture is of his brother sleeping with the sword. He posted it two minutes ago.

Maybe he's ignoring my messages.

I breeze through the exam. It's a recounting of three self-selected conflicts from the timeline of wars we as a class had agreed upon. I knew Mr. Pape would be hippie about finals. I cram the accounts full of pathos, casualty counts, and dry commentary on the illogical thought processes of warmongers. I hand it in early and wait in the hall for Sandra to finish.

The fourth person to exit the classroom while I'm waiting against a bank of lockers is Lauren. I'm about to avert my eyes when I remember my talk with Sandra this morning. Hypocritical.

"Hey, Lauren?" I straighten up. "Um, I didn't like the picture you put up of me on Facebook?"

She stops walking. Turning around, she places one foot at a right angle to the other, as in ballet position, and clasps her hands. The strap of her messenger bag slides off her shoulder and collects where her hands are pooled. Is that an encouragement pose, like, *Go on; keep talking; I'm listening*?

"Like, I'm not supposed to show my hair to guys who aren't in my family?" I gesture to the hallway as though it stands for the male gender.

"But you don't wear it in gym. Jeremy's not in your family." Her voice is smooth. Controlled sarcasm, a well-practiced art form.

"That was by mistake?"

"I saw the hair stuff *Tit*yana brought, so I just assumed you were taking off your scarf from now on or something." She hasn't moved, and the people coming out of history simply stream around her.

"Do you mind if you don't post any more pictures of me? On Facebook?"

Sandra comes out of class and stands by me, looking at Lauren with curiosity. Lauren doesn't take her in but lifts her bag up onto her shoulder and unclasps her hands.

"Don't worry. I won't." She pirouettes and leaves.

I don't like the way she said that. Smooth and controlled.

With Sandra at my side, I head to the cafeteria to pick up Soon-Lee for our study session. She's sitting on Thomas's lap.

"I'm ready. Bye, Thomas." Soon-Lee pushes her glasses up, and they kiss on the lips, lingering until Thomas's friend from the next table yells, "Get a room!"

We walk to the library, and I cringe, thinking of getting into a state like that with Jeremy. Never.

"Soon-Lee, this is Sandra. She's also studying for her math exam."

Soon-Lee smiles at her. Sandra looks ahead.

"So did you study?" Soon-Lee fixes her hair, pumping it up in the back with her fingers. She's got awesome hair: voluminous where it needs to be and sleek where it needs to sit subdued.

"On Friday. And only the parts we never learned with Mason."

"That's what I did too." She gives me a fist bump.

We sit near the windows overlooking the parking lot. Beside me, Sandra takes out her math textbook, lays it on the table, and then packs it away in her bag again. She gets up.

"I have to go. I forgot I'm supposed to pick up my grandma."

She goes through the book stacks, in the opposite direction from where we came. Setting my laptop on the table, I look at Soon-Lee quizzically.

Robby and Pradeep are taking seats three tables away, behind Soon-Lee.

"Is she okay?" Soon-Lee's taking out her notes. "She seems kind of down."

"Imagine years of Robby and Pradeep on your back. And others picking up on it."

"Why?"

"Her birthmark. They call her Mustache."

"That's cruel."

"Yeah. She's nice, too." I open my e-mail. "Let's do something. To those guys."

"What? Beat them with a book of manners?"

"My dad's message for today: *Imagine your competitors are hay. They'll stay if you let them. Mow over them, roll them up, take charge of them by the superiority of the engine that drives your business. Drive that tractor.*"

"We aren't a business. By the way, what does your dad do?"

"He's in the business of annihilating all Indian sweet makers in the world. He's already cornered the North American market."

"Sweet."

"His stuff is amazing. Melt in your mouth."

"So what does that have to do with your friend and the losers on her case?"

"Let's mow over them." I watch Robby pretend to aim a pencil at me. Such an immature fool.

"I don't have the time with this exam and all." Soon-Lee looks up at me. She turns to look behind her just as the pencil ricochets off the back of her chair. "I was wondering why your eyes were narrowing like that."

She picks up the pencil and cracks it in half. "Okay, I wish I had that tractor now."

"Remember how we started freshman year with four girls in enriched math? Now it's only the two of us. Because of them and their comments. And the heckling when you get something right that none of the boys did."

Soon-Lee leans over the table. "What if we mess with them? Let them think the exam is different?"

"What do you mean?"

"What if we tell them that Mason found out they've got the exam and he changed it." Soon-Lee raises her eyebrows and smiles. "That'll throw them off."

"But they'll wonder why we're trying to help them." I'm sitting back, keeping my eyes on Robby. Pradeep's busy watching something on his laptop, earphones on, but he's the mastermind who makes Robby dance to his tune.

"Chill, I know how to do this. I've got three brothers." She gets up and sweeps the broken halves of the pencil off the table, into her left palm. "You stay. You've got a give-away face."

She walks over, deposits the pencil bits on their table, and puts her hands on her hips. Pradeep ignores her, plugged into headphones, but Robby's eyes are on her as Soon-Lee nods at their strewn papers. She relaxes her arms as she listens to him and then begins to laugh. She walks away, continuing her laughter.

"So *that's* why Mason said he's gotta change the exam . . . ," she says loudly as she gets closer to me.

Robby's out of his seat and by our table. "What're you talking about?"

Soon-Lee ignores him. "Remember, Janna? How we heard him saying to McConnell that he's got to make a new exam now that some kids accessed the site? He's talking about these goons."

"How would he know?" Robby looks at Soon-Lee, then at me, as she opens her textbook, situated carefully over our copy of the exam. I nod toward the checkout area and shrug my shoulders.

He glances at Ms. Lionel at the library desk, and she looks up at that moment, her face in its typical pose: angled, with one eyebrow raised in perpetual curiosity.

He goes back to their table and yanks the headphones off Pradeep's head.

Soon-Lee draws a tractor on the top margin of her notes. I lean over and scribble Dad's e-mail address under her tractor. She grabs her phone and adds it into her e-mail app. I hide my smile, turning to the window. Jeremy's walking to school from the parking lot. Farooq's by his side.

Ugh. How are those two even friends?

"Ah, there's your boy." Soon-Lee watches my face.

"He's not mine."

"Lauren's cousin. How quaint." She picks up her iPad. "You'd be moving on up. *Do you want to?* is the question."

"He's not tight with her. Anyway, there's nothing happening between us."

"Her homeys are onto you." She's scrolling on Facebook.

"I'm friends with Marjorie, and she put up like eight pictures of you. Well, not of you, you're just majorly photo bombing them."

She hands me the iPad. Marjorie and Lauren, in the hallway at school, with me in the background, face scrunched tight, eyes closed but mouth open wide mid-word or screech, judging from my expression. From behind Marjorie, the back of Tats's head is visible. What was I saying to her? It looks painful. And ugly.

I hover on my face. It's tagged "J.Y." and a click reveals a ghost account.

I scroll through the other J.Y. pictures on Marjorie's account. The more gruesome the photo, the more likes it's garnered. There's one in gym, a nice-hair day matched with a mutilated face, framed by a Marjorie selfie. The pictures were posted this weekend.

"So, why would Missus Marj be posting photo bombs of you?"

"How would I know?" I look at Marjorie's friends list. Sure enough, Jeremy's on it.

"Come on. There must be a reason."

"Maybe they're telling me to back away from Jeremy." There's no way I'm going to that party on Friday.

"That's a weird way to do it. Without you aware of it." Soon-Lee resumes writing notes. "That bunch are as crazy as the goonies behind us. Pringles is what I call them."

"Why?"

"I don't know. It just came to me. But when I thought it over, because my mind is extremely logical, I figured out it must be because they're pr-etty—or at least the guy population thinks so—but they're also flaky, like chips."

"I don't think Lauren's flaky. She's got one of the best grades in history."

"I don't mean flaky as in not smart. Marjorie's in my English class. She's cleaning up there. I mean soulless."

"Soulless."

"Yeah, no awareness, no substance."

I think over what she's saying. Maybe there's some truth to it. I did move onto Lauren's radar on account of not taking part in picking on Sandra. That's soulless. Or, as Mr. Ram would say, devoid of fruit. Or would it be devoid of a kernel?

Sandra moved onto everyone's radar because of a mark on her face. Well, because a few guys decided to home in on it. Because the art teacher chose Frida Kahlo as a topic of study?

If Sandra had worn a niqab, no one would've even known. If I wore a niqab, the Pringles wouldn't get any pictures of me.

"Maybe I should just cover my face."

"Like a ninja?"

"No, like a niqabi." I google it and show her the image results.

"Um, no."

"Can you imagine them trying to get a pic of me then?" I laugh. "*I'd* be in control of my image."

"But you'd also be gagging yourself. That's a steep price to pay for avoiding getting bad pictures of you."

"Hello? How would I be gagging myself? My mouth would still work, you know. Plus most girls who cover their faces do it because they want to be the ones to decide who gets to see them."

Soon-Lee pauses from writing to consider that. "Well, when you think of it that way, it sounds kind of powerful. Like no one can sum up your identity without permission. Your real identity, I mean."

I look up Niqabi Ninjas, clicking on the latest vlog, titled "Doormats and Other Losers." "Check these girls out. They're badass."

The video is of one of the niqabi girls this time, and she's sitting there talking to the camera. I'm about to close it to show Soon-Lee a real episode when I hear the niqabi say, ". . . back from a weekend in Chicago."

I pause and rewind to the beginning, turning the iPad to myself. The intro blares out again, a mix of drumming and a man's deep voice saying something in Arabic.

"Here, take these—you watch. I've got an exam tomorrow." Soon-Lee flings earbuds to me.

"Okay, so I just came back from a weekend in Chicago. And I'm pissed. The weather? No, that was great. Thanks for asking. Yeah, and in terms of that, all those people asking for a FAQ video, that's still in the works. My partner's supposed to be on it, but instead she's studying for the MCAT. Where are her priorities, huh? Anyway, this is going to be a short one. Just wanted to rant about doormats. I'm looking at you if you're a loser who thinks it's okay for someone, another being, to click the mute button on you. I was going to look up the definition of doormat so I can make this all deeply philosophically linked, but who cares at the end of the day? It pisses me off if you're crying about your life, acting like someone took the reins out of your hands, when you're here in the land of scream-whatever-you-want. Loser. That's what you are. If you've got the means to fix your life and no man-made laws stopping you, then it's your God-given right, scratch that, God-given *duty* to face your assaulter, stalker, whatever and squash him. Don't snivel in the basement of your dad's million-dollar home that you can't do anything. Sorry, that took a bit of a personal turn, but pretend I took artistic liberty there. *Any resemblance to actual events or locales or persons, living or dead, is entirely coincidental blah blah blah.* Okay, rant over, will expand on this in another video when Ruki takes her head out of books long enough to ninja-it with me again. Salaams, see ya and stomp on."

A shot of her Doc Martens ends the scene.

I close the browser and place the iPad next to Soon-Lee's textbook.

I pack my books. It's my turn to leave with a lame excuse. "I forgot I had to do something for my mom."

• • •

I call her. She picks up but doesn't say anything. I wait too because Mom's just come into the bedroom from the shower, and the first word poised to come out of my mouth would have had her up in arms.

"I'm guessing you saw the latest vlog and you're not too impressed. Whereas I'm impressed you're actually subscribing to me. See, I see you in my channel's new subscribers list from yesterday: janjan123," Sausun says.

"You're a bee with an itch," I say the minute Mom goes into the closet to change. "You lied. You pretended the vlogs were by someone else. You wanted me to spill my secrets."

"Why? Did I use your secrets? Did I tell anyone the perv tried to—"

"You never told me it was you!"

"You didn't ask. I wear niqab, don't I?"

"Yeah, but so do thousands of other girls. You're a major bitch."

"Janna! What are you saying?" Mom peers through the privacy screens. Like, so respectful of my privacy. "We don't use language like that around here!"

I hang up and run to the bathroom, steamy and cloistering. I call the bitch back.

"Major bitch speaking. How may I help you?"

"I hate you and never want to see you again."

"Okay. No problem."

"You played with me. You broke my trust."

"Not guilty on both counts."

"Why'd you have to talk about me? What am I to your stupid vlogs?"

"It was a rant. I let myself spew. Give me a break, no one will know it's about janjan123."

"You owe me for using me as fodder for your rant."

"Okay, now you're speaking my language. What do you want? Money? Don't say drugs because I don't have any."

"Get him."

In the silence, I unwind my scarf and smooth my hair.

"Though it's intriguing, it's also disproportional. You're asking of me more than I did to you."

"Life's not fair. Get him to back off."

"Me? Who am I to him? He'll blow me off."

"Make him a star on your stupid show." I stop talking because I'm getting this idea.

"Oh yes, he'd come running to do that."

"What if he didn't know he was on the show? That he was being film stalked?"

"And then what?"

"And then we get him."

"We? Oh, I like this idea now." She laughs.

I didn't realize I'd added the "we" in there. "I mean you, you get him."

"I'm in if you're in. That means you get to take Ruki's place. Ruki's my other half, but she's busy studying to get into med school so she'd be willing to give you her coveted spot. You can even borrow her abaya and niqab."

"I don't want to be on video."

"No one will know it's you. That's the beauty of it. Besides, aren't you already on video? You're practically viral in the Muslim community, thanks to your 'friend.' He passed the Bollywood feature of you with a boy under a tree to everyone on the quiz team."

Sarah saw it?

Nuah saw it.

Is that why he isn't responding to my texts?

"I can't be in it. Just do a show on him. And nothing to do with me."

"I'll think about it. I'm not into filmmaking for hire."

"Think of it as what you owe me for using me."

"Are you saying there's no truth to what I said? If so, you're blind."

"Bye."

After Mom leaves for work, I sit my laptop on her bed and look up the doormat vlog again. Gone.

I call Sausun. "You took it off YouTube."

"The guilt, the terrible, gullible guilt ate up my insides."

"I still hate you for what you did."

"Good. See all that anger that's fueling the hate? Take it and aim it at the right target."

"You."

"Whatevah. Why are you calling me?"

"Did you think up something?"

"Yes, it's a blockbuster, coming to a theater near you, called *Deal with Your Own Crap*."

Muhammad opens the door, talking into the house phone stuck between his ear and shoulder. "She's right here."

He holds out the phone. "Sarah wants to talk to you."

I indicate my own conversation.

"Jan's on the phone right now but will call you back. Pronto." He nods at me and leaves.

I wonder what Sarah wants. Dirt on the video Farooq's passing around? "I gotta go."

"Don't call me again unless it's to say you're participating in fixing your own problems. Why should I help someone who refuses to help themselves?" Her voice has lost the flippant quality. Now it's plain mean.

I end the call and look up Sarah's number. I reach voice mail. "Assalamu alaikum, Sarah, it's Janna. You wanted to talk to me? Give me a call."

Muhammad opens the door again. "Are you calling her on the other line? Here."

He unsticks the phone from his ear and stretches it out to me. He waits, leaning on the doorframe with both hands in his pockets.

I muffle the phone. "Are you part of the conversation?"

He nods.

"Assalamu alaikum, Janna! Respond to me as I tell you because if I know your brother, he's hovering around there somewhere. Say 'walaikum musalam.'"

"Walaikum musalam?"

"Okay, so your brother is really worried about you and this video that Farooq's been sending people. He asked me to talk to you and figure out what's going on. But I know that's not really going to happen. Now say 'nothing much.'"

"Nothing much?"

"So my idea is that you say yes or no to me. And 'sorta' if you want me to know it's none of my business."

"Sorta."

"You catch on quick. Are you in any trouble?"

"No. I mean sorta."

"Do you need help of any kind? That could mean support through talking or hanging out. Whatever."

"No."

"Is someone bothering you?"

"Yes. I mean sorta."

"Is it the guy in the video?"

"No."

"Is it the guy who took the video?"

"Sorta."

"Do you want to eat cupcakes with me at Soliloquy's?"

"No."

"Ouch. Okay."

"I mean, I have exams to study for."

"I know. It's just hard over the phone."

"I'm not a cupcake person."

"That's because you haven't been to Soliloquy's. How about we meet and I talk. About Malcolm. Now please don't say 'Malcolm?' really loud. It'll be good for both of us to meet up."

"Why?"

"Because I need to get something off my chest. You sit there and listen and eat cupcakes. Mindlessness, that's what you need now."

I think about it. Maybe it would be a healthy diversion: inhaling sugar while listening to someone's sordid past.

"Okay."

"Give the phone to Muhammad, and I'll get him to drive you on his way to the gym."

Soliloquy's is the polar opposite of the modern restaurant where Sarah first met Muhammad and me. There's enough chintz in here to kill modernity. And it's not just one type of floweriness. The armchairs around the low tables are upholstered in different prints, as are the heavy draperies at the windows and each wall segment surrounding the diners. The ceiling is painted in more ornamental flourishes.

"Look at the cups and plates," Sarah whispers as we wait

in line to place our orders. A waiter walks by with a tray filled with diverse flowery china.

"My grandma would love it in here," I whisper back. "She'd feel at home."

"Most of the crowd here is young. It's about the irony." Sarah indicates a young woman in black with blue hair, snuggling into a yellow chair while gazing at her phone. In front of her sits a steaming cup of tea and a huge pink-frosted cupcake. I want to take a picture.

We score a table by the window. The chintzy chair is nice and roomy, and I don't resist pulling my legs up into it. There are even wings at the sides that welcome my head to rest into them.

"Yes, he does look like Liam Hemsworth." Sarah arranges the cutlery and salt and pepper shakers. "We dated for almost two years. Beginning of first year to end of second year of college."

"He's really cute."

"Yeah, and he really knows it."

"Is that why you broke up?"

"No, I broke up because I found another love."

"Some other guy?"

"No. I began helping out with this group that does PR for unfashionable causes. Like organizations that help young unwed mothers find career paths, community rehab programs for ex-prisoners, stuff like that. That's when I was studying marketing."

"Liam, he didn't like that?"

"No, no. Malcolm didn't mind. He's kind, a giver too. It's only that I began drifting away. I found out I love making things happen. In a big way. And he wasn't into it as much as I was. So we fell apart."

The waiter appears with a teapot, two cups, and four cupcakes. Two mocha almond fudge for Sarah and a cherry cream and key lime for me. Exam fuel.

Sarah pours me a cup of tea. "It's chai tea."

I laugh. "My dad always laughs when people say that."

"Why?"

"Because the word 'chai' means tea. Just tea. So it's like people are saying tea tea."

"But what's this kind of tea called? The one with spices?"

"Masala chai. Or masala tea. Masala means spices."

"That's good to know. So when I make spicy tea for your dad, I'll say masala chai, like a good daughter-in-law." She finishes stirring her tea and places the teaspoon into the saucer.

"About that, are you really going to marry Muhammad?"

"I want to. But I hope he's okay with waiting until I finish my PhD."

"Why?"

"I'm so driven when I'm doing something that I'll ignore him until I'm done with my doctorate. That's what I meant about Malcolm and me drifting apart."

"But how were your parents okay with you dating? Didn't they think it was haram?"

"They weren't into religion back then. I got them into it. Third year of college, before we moved here, I started volunteering to do PR for a Muslim group doing street advocacy." She takes a huge bite. I'm impressed.

"So you got into Islam."

"In a super big way. I love it. It lets me be driven."

I taste the key lime. The frosting is heavenly. "Mmm. This is not a kiddy cupcake."

"Told you so."

"Can I ask you something? Without you getting offended?"

"Sure." She's finished a cup of tea already and is pouring her second.

"Is it your drivenness that makes you want to be in charge of everything?"

She pauses mid-sip. She looks a lot like her father when she does that. "Hmm, maybe. Why, do I look like a control freak?"

"No, just like you like everything perfect."

"That's the definition of a control freak."

"Okay then."

She laughs and sets her cup down. "Is that why you avoid me?"

"I don't know what you're talking about."

"Janna Yusuf, you're funny and so right. Maybe I sometimes mistake control freaking for being driven."

"Anyway, now I know you're not so perfect. You dated Liam Hemsworth. Haram, haram, haram."

"No one is perfect except God. When I say driven, I mean striving. You can always strive to make life better. For you, for others. For the planet. Whatever."

"You're saying that with a gigantic frosting mustache."

"Don't turn now but look at who else has one."

The woman in black with blue hair is talking into the phone, a pink frosting line under her nose.

We laugh.

I take a picture of Sarah with my phone. Maybe, just maybe, it'll replace the old picture in my head.

On the drive back, Muhammad's quiet. It's eerie, so I fill the void with cupcake facts. "Sorry I didn't get you one. But I didn't want to undo your gym visit, plus you know what they say about dudes with beards eating cupcakes."

He doesn't respond.

I say, "Okay, I don't know what they say about beards and cupcakes. But I thought for sure you'd know."

"So did you tell Sarah about it?"

"About what?"

"This thing Farooq's sending out."

"No."

"Janna, why can't you tell me about it? What's happening?" He pulls over to the side of the road and shuts off the car.

"Muhammad, it's nothing. I'll handle it."

"It's nothing? I tell you my stuff. You're helping me with

one of the most important things in life—getting married." He turns to me and waits.

I close my eyes. I don't want to tell him. I don't want his sympathy or anger or it'll-be-okays. It won't change a thing.

"Why do you shut Mom and me out? If you don't want to talk to me, at least talk to her."

I open my eyes. His voice is breaking.

"You act like Mom is some enemy. I know you think she ruined things by leaving Dad." He looks away and turns the key in the ignition. "But she didn't."

"She did. She moved out. She talks about patience and forbearance being part of Islam, but she didn't put up with anything in her life!" I'm yelling and crying at the same time.

"Janna, there was nothing to leave. Dad was already gone."

"No, you're lying, he married Linda after!"

"I'm not going to get into it."

"You hate Dad!"

"No, I just love Mom, too," he says quietly. We're pulling into the parking garage.

My phone rings. Tats. I'm done talking to Muhammad so I pick up.

"Just got in! OMG, Dad took forever with the cottage. What happened with Jeremy yesterday?"

"Can't talk now. Roof tomorrow after my math exam? At eleven?"

"Okay. Did you meet with him?"

"Yes."

"Awesome. Why can't you talk now? And what's wrong with your voice?"

"I have to cram for my math exam. I've had a weird, busy day. Talk to you tomorrow."

"Okay, but don't change that you agreed to go to the party on Friday! If you do, I won't talk to you. Ever."

"Whatever, Tats. Like that's the most important thing."

"It's the only thing for me right now. Marjorie even added me on Facebook."

"We'll talk tomorrow. Bye."

She'll drag me to that party.

SAINTS

The math exam is nothing like the one Soon-Lee and I studied. We glance at each other before she twists the ends of her hair and gets started and before I flop down on my desk. The exam is only on the stuff we studied in class. None of the new work outlined in "A Course Review" appears. None of what I studied intensively until three a.m. is on it.

I do the best I can, reaching into the recesses of my mind to remember old formulas, and then spend the rest of the period calculating the lowest mark I can get on this exam without throwing my math grade for the term out the window. In another universe, the calculations I do to figure this out would be worthy of some academic merit.

I feel like roaring when Mr. Mason releases us. He has a strict policy on no one leaving until everyone is done, so we have to wait until the clock strikes eleven and Soon-Lee puts her pen down.

"What were you working on until the bitter end?" I'm incredulous at her prowess.

"That last trigonometric function wasn't as easy as it looked."

"I'm going to fail. All I studied was the new stuff." I avoid a group of freshmen, rushing by clutching armloads of books, fright covering their faces. I look behind, and sure enough, they're entering Mr. Mason's room for their exam. It's the freshman enriched math group. I wish I could stop one of them and give them sage advice about the future and bootlegged exams.

"I hope you don't fail. Then I'll be the only girl in the program next year."

"You studied everything?" I pause by the stairway doors that lead to the third floor and the teacher's old storage room. "You did, didn't you?"

"I did. I didn't want to take a risk."

"Well, we go our separate ways here. I hope it's not forever."

She leans in and gives me a hug. "Janna, I love you. Thanks for being my study pal. We'll meet up in the summer. And I'm sure I'll see you in enriched math in the fall."

"If not, we'll meet to deal with the goonies."

She walks away and turns. "And the Pringles. Don't forget about tackling them."

And the monster. Don't forget about tackling the monster, a small voice adds.

• • •

I open the door and start climbing. Technically I'm going up, but inside, I'm going downhill. I can't take a failing grade on top of what's happening in my life. It's not supposed to be like this. School is supposed to be the best part.

When I open the roof hatch, the place is empty. Tats hasn't arrived yet.

I take off my backpack and lie down. The sun is almost directly above, and I let it heat my face.

What if I pretend to have fallen asleep? Then I won't have to talk to Tats. And rehash everything.

I take out my phone and check Dad's message. *Your competitors don't know what you're made of. They don't know what you're capable of. They don't need to know. Strike when you're ready. Let them know your power.*

That sounds scary. If Muhammad saw this, he'd go on and on about how ruthless Dad is.

Am I like Dad? Or even like Mom? She kicked butt when she needed to.

The only thing I know is I refuse to be one of Mom's idolized Silent Sufferers.

My phone pings: Thy apologies, plural, accepted.

It's a text from Nuah.

I sit up. At least you got to know the real me: mean.

I don't buy that. There's nice in there.

I look in the distance, at the chain-link fence bordering the parking lot.

Something tells me you see nice everywhere. Even serial killers.

Whoa, that's a big leap. From Janna to Charles Manson.

Okay, maybe my kernel can sometimes be nice.

Kernel?

Yeah, Mr. Ram talks in fruit allegories.

I can tell this is going to be deep.

Some people have nice-looking husks with nothing inside. Some people have dried husks but there's fruit and even a nice kernel in there.

Ah, knew Mr. Ram was spiritual. Spiritual AND smart, good combo there.

I decide to be brave. Nuah's seen me and Jeremy together in the video, and I need to know what he thinks about it. Did you see the video?

There's no reply. Then, The cat on the skateboard? Hilarious.

I pause. Yes, lol. Also yes to the question you texted on Sunday.

Hence he sent the video.

Yes.

Need help?

No. Anyways, I'm busy with exams.

Duas for you.

Thanks & salaams. I add a turtle emoji with a thumbs-up.

I lie down. The phone pings. It's a video of a skateboarding cat. I watch it over and over. It's the best thing I've ever seen.

When Tats finally arrives, I *am* almost asleep.

She settles in and demands a recount of Sunday at the lake. I mumble a synopsis and then ask if I can be silent to tan.

She nods and begins a conversation with herself about me.

Tats 1: "Okay, so we're a hundred percent sure he likes you."

Tats 2: "No, make that two hundred percent, because any guy who shows a girl his nerdy side right away is, like, double sure she's the one. I mean, birds?"

Tats 1: "Yeah, but actually, he *is* sort of ultra geeky. You can tell that right away. He's on the tech crew, hello?"

Tats 2: "But actually again, he's on the baseball team too. So that makes him only half-nerdy."

Tats 1: "Which is fifty percent nerdy."

Tats 2: "So, two hundred percent into you, fifty percent nerdy, I guess that equals one hundred and fifty percent worthy."

Me: "Please, I had a super-fail experience with my math exam. Please cut the math. Please."

Tats 1: "Okay, basically, we need to figure out how to keep him into you. Which is hard because you can't do anything to keep him into you. Like date. Or kiss the guy."

Tats 2: "But, you can play hard to get. Like the *hardest* to get in the world. That could be your thing."

Tats 1: "But too hard to get can turn him totally off. I mean, the truth is, Janna, is he even going to *get* you at the end of it all?"

We're silent, pondering this profound question. I mean, I don't know if Tats is silent because she's pondering it, but she does stop the monologue to stare intensely at me. Like I have the answer to the purpose of life or something.

So I add my own soliloquy to throw her off my back. "To be got or not to be got? That is the question."

Tats: "No, I'm serious; where does this all go? You are going to go out with him, right? If he asks you out for real?"

I sit up, pick up my backpack, and say, "Yeah, yeah, whatever, time for English."

"This is serious, Janna. A guy's life is at stake."

I look at her. Is this the way I looked at things before? Just this past weekend, in fact? It's almost crazy.

"A guy's *life*?" I say. "Really?"

"Love life," she says. "Really."

I open the door and descend the secret stairwell. Pausing to put my ear to the door on the odd chance a teacher has come up to look for a textbook from the 1970s, I whisper, "Tats, relax. I'm into saving lives. If it really matters to him that much, I will not hesitate to lend a hand to keep him alive."

Tats claps her hands at my benevolence, as I open the door. To five guys.

Who begin to furtively put away their stashes of illegal substances until they see that it's us nobodies.

"Hey, guys," Tats says breezily. "Keep it clean up there, will ya?"

She holds the door open for them. They go up wordlessly.

This is why I love the girl. She knows how to stay calm and carry on.

It almost makes me tell her about Farooq.

Almost. The 60 percent reason that I hold back has to do with something I'm 100 percent sure of: I can't handle people thinking I come from a messed-up community. I'd rather close the hamper lid on that one.

Tats walks me to English, which is not good, because she gets to see how there is no English.

"Oops, I forgot. Ms. Keaton said it was a study period," I say, feigning a look of dawning remembrance. "So let's study. In the library."

"No, change of plans, because guess who's coming this way? Looking bored? Looking to hang with us?" Tats says, waving at someone behind me.

I turn, adjusting my hijab instinctively into what I think is the most flattering shape for my face: a flop-to-the-side look. (It's a science, making the exact folds and lay of the hijab cloth to suit your type of face.)

Jeremy is walking, no, striding toward us. I lean against a row of lockers, smiling.

"Hey," Tats says, motioning him over. "What's up?"

He waves and walks by, turning around to move away from us, backward.

"Nothing," he says. "Just gotta help Coach with some equipment inventory."

He's gone. Without even one glance at me.

"Huh?" Tats says. "What was that about?" She turns to peer at me. "Is there something you're not telling me about Sunday?"

"No!" I say, this time not feigning confusion, but exuding it authentically.

"He acted like you didn't exist," Tats says. "Let's go to the equipment room."

"No," I say again. "I'm going to study."

"Don't be such a nerd," Tats says. "Come on!"

She pulls me forward, and for some reason we find ourselves almost running after Jeremy. Who isn't in the equipment room but on the stairwell landing, with two other guys, just sitting there. Tats, the brash thing, starts running down the stairs toward him, apparently unaware that she's huffing. I hang back, realizing how crazed we must look.

"Jeremy, what's going on?" Tats puffs, right in front of his friends.

He gets up and comes up the stairs a bit to draw her away from humiliation. Because she doesn't notice, but his friends are laughing and not even hiding it. I back out through the doors, letting them shut heavily and move to lean my head against the side windows from where I can watch the drama without anyone seeing me.

Jeremy looks tight, his arms stiff against the sides of his body, but he's doing most of the talking. Tats has her arms crossed, listening intently to him, and as I watch her, my embarrassment at her behavior slowly dissipates.

She's really into this. Trying to make what she thinks of as happiness for me. But is it happiness for me? Am I going to go through with letting Jeremy and me be together in the end? I haven't really thought that far. But now, watching his lips move and his body tighten up further as time ticks by, the mother of all rhetorical questions whams me with such force that I almost bang my forehead on the glass. *Why is everything neater in my head than in real life? What is real life anyway?*

I pivot abruptly and walk to the library, because I know for sure my English exam is real Real Life.

Tats joins me at a study carrel as I'm reviewing arguments against humanizing Caliban. Although I see Mr. Ram's point that Shakespeare wrote him with the specter of an almost racist form of Otherness in mind, he reminds me too much of Farooq, so I'm all for caging the dude up.

"Are you sitting down for this?" Tats asks my seated form. Her face is livid.

I slump down.

"Apparently, there's this guy, Farooq, who says you and him are together," Tats says, carefully watching my face. "This guy is good friends with Jeremy, so now he says he doesn't feel right. . . . Okay, who is Farooq?"

I stare at her, willing her to stop.

"So, there *is* something you're not telling me!" Tats says. "Jan, I thought we didn't do that? Keep stuff from each other?"

"Tats, can you just shut up? I need to study. I can't fail another exam."

"But who is he?" she says, leaning forward, really expecting me to launch into an essay explaining who the Caliban in my life is.

I close my books, slam them into my backpack, and drag it with me out of the library. Tats doesn't follow, and I wonder how real she is in my life because I don't care that she sits there, shooting me a steady, evil glare.

At the rate I'm going, I'll have no friends left by Friday.

I make it to the condo lobby before collapsing into a faux-leather couch. With my English notes perched on the armrest, I pick up where I left off: the depravity of Caliban.

I don't realize I've fallen asleep until lights flashing across the lobby wake me. An ambulance is parked out front. It's not a common occurrence, but I don't give it much thought until I see Mr. Ram's daughter-in-law coming out of the doors to the stairwell. She waits, looking toward the elevators, her hands clenched.

I go over to stand beside her. "Is everything okay?"

She looks at me briefly and shakes her head before watching the elevators again.

"Mr. Ram?" I ask. She nods and then clutches my arm suddenly.

The elevator doors open, and ambulance attendants come out wheeling Mr. Ram, laid out, with an oxygen mask on his face. My stomach flops.

Mr. Ram goes by soundlessly, his son and daughter-in-law, now sobbing quietly, following. I go to the lobby doors, wanting to climb into the ambulance with them.

But the ambulance drives away.

Something breaks in me, and I start to heave, tears running down my face.

Mr. Ram can't go.

I lie sprawled on my bed. Muhammad backed away when I let myself in earlier and he got a glimpse of my face, so I have a bit of respite. Plus, I wedged Mom's dresser against the door for double protection.

Lying motionless, I stare at the water stain on the ceiling for so long that it takes on more and more details that make it look like Farooq.

I shake my head and fish my phone out of my backpack. Scrolling down, I find his number in my messages folder.

I wonder briefly if he's at school, but still, I let it ring. I'll have to be brave enough to leave a message if no one answers.

"Assalamu alaikum?" Nuah asks. "Janna?"

I nod, afraid to speak.

"What's up?" he says, the surrounding noise of many voices fading. "I can hear you better now. I'm not in the hall anymore."

"Mr. Ram, he's not well. They took him away in an ambulance."

"Oh. Do you know which hospital?"

"No," I say.

"Let me call and check. Call you right back?"

"Okay."

I hang up and fish under my bed for a piece of blue poster board. I move the dresser back to its place, go into Muhammad's room, and put the blue board against the window. When Tats first moved into Fairchild Towers, we used to communicate through window colors. Blue meant "All is lost; come over now." Even though I can't talk to Tats, I want her to see this. I want her to know something—I mean a lot of things—is not right.

I go back to my room without shutting the door. I need to be ready to go when Nuah calls. The hospital wouldn't be too far so I can bike it. I look around the room for something to take with me. Mom's Rumi poems. Maybe I can read him some.

My seerah book lying on the dresser catches my eye. He'll probably like that, but I haven't added anything new to it since I was twelve.

I hop on my bed and cross my legs, cradling the book in my lap. I reach for my gel pens in a basket on the window ledge and spread them out. I choose a dusty brown and draw a valley by a high hill. I want to write about the Prophet's farewell sermon. *Hurt no one so that no one may hurt you.*

I'm not aware of how much time has gone by until Muhammad knocks on the door that's ajar.

"Janna?" He peers in. "Nuah is here."

I look up, and the opening in the door widens, Nuah's face appearing behind Muhammad's shoulder.

I get off the bed and walk with them to the living room, holding the seerah book.

"I can go right now," I say. "To the hospital. Which one is it?"

"Janna, he passed away," Nuah says. "I spoke to his family."

I nod.

"Inna lillahi wa inna ilayhi rajioon," Muhammad says. "To God we belong and to him we return."

I repeat the words Muslims say when someone dies and then walk back to my room. The mess on my bed leads me to Mom's bed, where I promptly fall asleep.

I wake up to Tats scraping and flicking her dried nail polish, sitting beside me on Mom's bed.

"I heard about your friend," she says, pausing her handiwork to look at me.

I flip over and let my left arm hang off the side of the bed.

"Sorry to hear," she says. "Do you want me to bring you

something to eat? There's a guy eating chow mein with your brother in the kitchen."

Nuah's still here?

"I'm okay," I say. "I didn't get much sleep last night."

"I'll get you something."

The bed creaks as she hops off.

I get up and catch my reflection in the mirror. My hijab's askew with tufts of hair escaping around both ears. I unwind the hijab and fling it across to my bed and then lie back down, spread-eagle.

I'm kind of fed up and exhausted with the last few days: with Farooq, with my friends, with Mr. Ram gone without any prior warning.

I mean, he gave me that file, that ancient file, a few days ago and told me to be sure to tell my English teacher about it. And I nodded, pretending I would, but really thinking *as if!* I can remember almost nothing of what he said to me before this exchange.

But he said so much, so how could that be?

What's in my head now is his face, especially his tightly-held-lips face, when he'd listen or watch me but not say anything. That face of his would freak me out because he had this way of knowing I didn't mean everything I said I'd do when he'd ask me to read something or write about something or do something or talk to someone about something. I'd drop my eyes when he got that face. Without looking up, I knew his eyes would have grown more knowing as I sputtered along filling the spaces with empty pronouncements. I didn't care about things as much as he did, and he knew it.

I close my eyes because they begin stinging. I realize this awful thing: Mr. Ram was the adult I had the most consistent communication with for the last few years, mainly because even though I kept talking crap and he knew it, he let me be. He just listened.

And when he spoke, he always gave me something good. I know this for sure, because I always left him feeling good.

Tats comes in holding two plates. She sets them on Mom's dresser and, after a quick glance at my face, perches on the bed gingerly.

She begins scraping her nails again.

I sit up and wipe my face with my sleeves.

"Let's get out of here to eat," I say, wrapping my scarf on really horribly. "Mom hates food in her bedroom."

I refrain from looking at my blotchy self in the mirror.

Tats grabs the plates and walks ahead. She stops in the middle of the hallway and whispers, "By the way, is that guy in the kitchen Farooq?"

I shake my head and make a face as we enter the kitchen. Nuah looks up from the breakfast table and immediately stands, chopsticks in the air.

I don't know why, but I reach for my scarf, almost instinctively, to fix it up.

Nuah indicates his chair, and I go toward it as Tats takes Muhammad's empty seat and sets down our plates. We eat quietly, but something's growing loud in me. It's reaching into every part of me, and I let it be.

I let the ocean of anger be.

Mom comes home shortly thereafter and sits with us in the living room, listening to Nuah. Mr. Ram had a stroke, the kind that shuts everything down. The funeral services are being arranged, but Nuah told us it would be cremation followed by a family-and-friends gathering. Deval would let us know the details soon.

Mom goes into action, heading to the kitchen to rummage in the cupboards for something to cook for Mr. Ram's family.

"Vegetarians, they're vegetarians," I mumble. Muhammad leans over and rests a hand on my arm. That just makes the tears spill.

Nuah stands and says he has to leave, that he'd let Mr. Ram's friends at the community center know. I nod. *Thursdays without Seniors Game Club?*

I say salaams to Nuah and good-bye to Tats and lie on the couch with my eyes wide open. The smell of chickpea sauce begins to meander into the living room, and I spring up.

I watch Mom stirring the pot, still in her work clothes. Missiles of brown sauce bits launch out of the bubbling pot and land on her white shirt. She wipes the spatters away absentmindedly before scattering a teaspoon of salt into the chickpeas.

It dawns on me: Mom's never been glam because she makes no time for extras. Only for taking care of the things that need to be taken care of.

So why does she want to become this other person Auntie Maysa thinks she should be? To *meet her match*?

I'd rather have her be the Mom she's always been.

I drape my arms around her shoulders and rest my head on the nearest one. It's been a long time since I've given her a hug on my own, and, after a moment of tensed surprise, she turns to me and hugs me back.

"Can I take the food over to Mr. Ram's family?" I mumble into her scarf.

"Yeah, that's a good idea. I'll come, of course." She turns back to lower the heat and cover the pot. "I'll change; just let it burble here. If you smell something burning, take it off the burner. Let it sit."

That's Mom's idea of cooking: Let it burble but don't let it burn and let it sit. Her food is edible but not the kind you relish.

I feel bad saying this about her cooking because I know she doesn't have much time and that she does the throw-everything-in-a-pot method due to that, but right now, it feels too similar to what's happening inside me.

Burbling bits of stuff about to burn.

• • •

I call Sausun. "What do I have to do to be in?"

"Good choice."

"What's your plan?"

"Don't worry your pretty head about it. Just wait for instructions."

"Promise me I'll be undercover."

"No one will know it's you. I'll call you later. Let me get to work."

MISFITS

I wake up to two messages.

Dad's: *True achievement is birthed by failure. Even public failure, for then you're guaranteed a greater audience for your eventual rising. Let your detractors watch as you arise anew.*

Sausun's: *Initiated contact with enemy combatant. If he confirms, are you okay for convening at 5 tomorrow? At the Book Nook?*

I have twenty minutes to change and get to school. I call Sausun as I fling things on. "What's the plan? I need to know before participating."

"So I called him and said I've got some more information on the video he sent. Something to do with you. I asked him to meet me tomorrow in the coffee shop at the Book Nook at six."

"And?"

"And we'll film him. And reveal his crimes to his face. Capture his reaction. Put it on YouTube. Finis."

"Who'll do the revealing?"

"I think it should be you, but if you want, I can participate. The beauty of it is he won't know it's you. You'll be incognito."

"I'll think about it."

"No, the only thing you'll think about is if the time is okay with you. I got the wheels in motion. You asked and I delivered."

"A good friend of mine just passed away. I'm not feeling my best."

"I'm sorry to hear that. Take care. I've gotta get going."

I finish the exam and wait. It was pretty straightforward, like Ms. Keaton described, so I'm relieved.

After everyone leaves and she's putting the exam booklets into her bag, I approach her with my open backpack.

"Ms. Keaton? I'm sorry to interrupt, but a friend of mine wanted you to read this." I hold out the file folder with two hands. "It's his view of some of Shakespeare's plays."

She opens the file, and we both look at the title page, "The Other in Shakespeare's Works: A Critical Reading by Vinesh Ram."

"Thank you. I'll try to get at it this summer. Maybe some of it will come in handy when I teach Shakespeare again." She puts the file in her bag.

I pause and turn to her at the door. "He passed away yesterday, so I wanted to make sure I gave it to you."

"I'm sorry for your loss." She joins me, and we walk out together. "Were you very close?"

"I took care of him once a week. He was elderly. He loved reading."

"Why don't you write about him then? It really helps you when you're grieving to do that. Capture the best points about him."

"Maybe I should." I wonder if I should say it, what I'm thinking. Then, because it's the last day of English and there's nothing left to do, I let myself blurt, "But I've known him for four years, and I feel like I never paid real attention to him. I'm ashamed that I don't know much about him."

"Ah, here's where I can give you your favorite writer's advice: 'I write to discover what I know.' Flannery O'Connor."

I smile. "She always knows what to say. Thanks, Ms. Keaton. Have a good summer."

"You have a wonderful summer. See you in September." She gives me a wave by the staff room door, Mr. Ram's file in her bag.

I log on to Facebook and click through the notifications letting me know I've been tagged and then untag myself methodically. There are sixteen new ones, from one or another of the Pringles, and that doesn't count the J.Y. account. Don't they have a Tiffany sale to go to or something?

I unfriend Lauren and create a new page: "Mr. Ram, You'll Be Missed."

Scrolling through my camera, I find Mr. Ram's Belly-Laugh smile and upload it. His first Facebook picture.

Mr. Ram was a dedicated person—that means he didn't let go of the things that were important to him. He was dedicated to Seniors Games Club every week. He got dressed up to go. Everyone knew he was serious about spending time with his friends, that's how dressed up he was.

He was dedicated to people. Even though he was a serious person, with a lot on his mind, he made sure to let you know he remembered you. Always. He smiled at jokes even if they were only sort of funny. He remembered that it was a person *who was telling the joke, so he smiled for that person.*

He was dedicated to reading good books, even if they were from another generation or didn't make complete sense to him. He read the first Harry Potter when he was ninety years old because someone told him it was good. He would have read the rest of the series if that someone had been able to find the large-type versions in the library for him. * *He smiled one of his loudest smiles ever at the Shel Silverstein poem about a pet snowball. But his favorite Shel Silverstein poem was "The Little Boy and the Old Man."*

Like the old man in the poem, he was dedicated to someone too, dedicated to helping her find out what the really important things for her were. What she *should be dedicated to. She misses him but was happy to have had someone like him in her life. Thank you, Mr. Ram, for the warmth of your hand.*

**Someone still regrets that they didn't find the rest of the HP books for him.*

I send friend requests to Mr. Ram's son, his wife, and Nuah and invite everyone already on my friends list to Mr. Ram's page.

Tats writes on the wall first: *Mr. Ram was a good friend to my best friend, rest in peace, xoxo.*

Muhammad: *To God we belong and to Him we return. Thanks for putting this up, sis.*

Then news: *Nuah Abdullah has accepted your friend request.*

I cringe, only now remembering that he's going to be able to see all the tagged crazy pictures of me put up by the Pringles.

I click on Nuah's profile. In his album I find a photo of him on hajj with his hair shaved, as is typical of pilgrims. I feel awful noticing his forehead, but I do. It's an okay forehead, well balanced with his smile.

Notification: *Nuah Abdullah wrote on your page, Mr. Ram, You'll Be Missed.*

Nuah: *It's true, Mr. Ram was dedicated to people. He had a lot of friends at the community center and he made them by honoring them. That's rare. Thanks Janna for doing this and please pass on that the funeral will take place on June 25 at 4 p.m.*

That's the day of Lauren's party. Now I have the perfect excuse for not going with Tats.

I walk across the street to Tats's building. The elevators here are normal, and within a minute I'm at her front door.

Her brother Alex lets me in and then goes back to playing a video game on the couch.

I find Tats in her room, looking at Matt's Facebook page. She gives a start when she sees me.

"You just made a page for Mr. Ram. How are you here?"

"I'm fast. Thanks for posting." I sit on her bed. "About the party."

"You promised." Tats twirls to me in her chair. Her hair is tied up in a huge severe and shiny bun. No tendrils of hair escape it. Her hair secret, a bottle of almond oil, stands on her dresser.

"Mr. Ram's funeral is on the same day."

"Oh."

"Sorry." I shrug my shoulders.

She turns her chair and checks something on her laptop. "But it's at four o'clock."

She faces me again. "Lauren's thing is at eight. Can't we do both?"

"How can I be in party mood and funeral mood at the same time?"

"Can you at least think about it? Otherwise I'll join you for the funeral and then go on my own to the party."

I panic at that. I can't imagine Tats at the mercy of the Pringles. They'll eat her alive, and she'll think she's having fun.

"Okay, give me time to think about it."

She turns back to Facebook. "So, Nuah? Yesterday at your place? How do you know him?"

"He's this guy who works at the community center I take Mr. Ram to. *Used* to take him to."

"Does he like you?"

"No. What do you mean?" I peer over her shoulder. She's added him as a friend, and apparently he's accepted because she's scrolling through his profile.

"He's really Muslim, huh?" She pauses at the hajj pictures. "You like him, don't you?"

"No. I mean, he's a nice guy."

"Better than this Farooq guy Jeremy told me about?"

I cross my arms. "Tats, Farooq is a pervert. He tried to . . . I can't tell you."

"What?" She's off her chair and in front of me. "What did he do? Who is this guy?"

"He's the cousin of an ex-friend of mine. I can't talk about it now."

"Why does Jeremy think you guys are going out?"

"I don't know. Can we drop it?" I get up and move to the door. "I'm dealing with it. Just know that."

"Will you call me if you want to talk?" She follows me to the front door. "This is going to bother me."

I turn to her. She's such a great friend. I lean over and hug her. "You're right about Nuah."

"What part?"

"The really Muslim part," I say, not telling her I also mean the other part: *You like him, don't you?* I wave at her from down the hall.

Fizz and Aliya are waiting in the condo with Muhammad when I get back. I look at Fizz. She looks away.

Aliya speaks first. "We heard about Mr. Ram and wanted to give our condolences."

Muhammad comes out of the kitchen with drinks.

"Thanks." I sit down on the armchair and keep my gaze on Fizz. I want to talk to her. Alone. But that would mean leaving Aliya with Muhammad. I take a breath. "You guys want to see my new room?"

They stand and follow me to Mom's room. I close the door behind them.

"Your cousin tried to rape me on the day the twins had their Qur'an party. Yes, Farooq." I look unflinchingly at Fizz's face, but my lips close up after saying his name. If I go on, it won't be clearly.

"Bullshit." Fizz has finally raised her eyes to mine. "I thought you'd make up something like that. To cover what you're up to with this guy."

Anger floods over my grief at having to talk about this. It blankets and quells me, and I regain my steady voice. "I'm up to nothing. True, I fell for Jeremy. But that's all that's happened. It's not a crime. On the other hand, your cousin is a criminal."

"Let's get out of here, Aliya." She reaches for the door. "This bitch here is trying ruin Farooq's good name."

I put my hand on the doorknob and hold tight. I push in and turn the handle to lock it.

"Your cousin ruined himself. And you enable it with your stupid belief that just because he memorized the Qur'an he's untouchable. The Qur'an is a book of messages. And he didn't get one of the main ones in it: respect."

"Janna, you're saying something serious. How can we believe you?" Aliya's face is flustered, vacillating between concern and disbelief.

"Aliya . . ." I pause, swallowing the urge to break down on seeing glimpses of care in her eyes. "Why would I make up something I can't even bear myself?"

I let go of the door and sink to the floor, spent. Fizz unlocks the handle, yanks the door open, and walks out. Aliya places an arm on my shoulder before following her.

Flannery: *The truth does not change according to our ability to stomach it.*

Muhammad knocks on the privacy screens.

"Yes?"

"Can I open this? Mom told me to get you to eat."

"Go ahead. I'm just reading." Flannery's "Revelation" is open on my lap. I'm at the part where Mary Grace throws a textbook at an insufferable self-righteous woman at the doctor's office. The textbook is aptly titled *Human Development.*

Muhammad holds out a plate. Waffles, with buttery syrup.

He has a plate for himself, too. I point to the chair at my desk.

"Technically, this is my room. So Mom's rule about eating in her bedroom doesn't apply here," I say, sawing a piece of thick waffle with the tiny fork Muhammad brought me. It's Mom's special pickle fork, two pronged.

"I have a feeling she'd make an exception in this case." Muhammad picks his waffle up like a pizza slice. It's slathered in Nutella. "But yeah, her land rights only extend as far as the screens."

"Hmm, maybe you *should* have gone into law."

"How are you doing? Tell me, really." He swivels the chair and takes a bite of his waffle.

"All right, I guess. He was old, ninety-three. And even if he wasn't, I know it's not up to humans to decide when we die," I say. "It's up to God."

"Ameen."

"The only thing that bothers me is I don't feel like I absorbed everything he tried to tell me. I wish I'd paid more attention to him."

"Janna, he loved you. Anytime I'd see him, he'd tell me about Miss Janna."

"I loved him, too."

"That means you paid attention to him."

"I don't know. You know how when you really want to get to know someone, how you make it a point to hang on to their every word?" I isolate a piece of waffle and sink my fork in. When I lift, it falls off the fork. "Like Sarah. You're so into her, right?"

"Of course. Hopefully, she'll be my wifey soon." He stops chewing and quickly adds, "Insha'Allah!" God willing.

"By the way, I think you made a good choice," I say, concentrating on cutting a suitable size of waffle for the pickle fork. Ah, so one waffle square fits the ratio of prongs to dough. I have a feeling Soon-Lee would have figured this out before me. "Sarah. She's okay, I mean."

Muhammad smiles. "I knew you'd like her if you got to know her."

"I don't really know her. It's like when Dad asked, *Is she down-to-earth?* And I found out she was."

"So what were you saying about knowing someone? About Mr. Ram?"

"Yeah, so like when I met Tats and she was so fun, I wanted to know everything about her. I think I *know* everything about her now." I put the tiny piece of waffle speared on my fork down. "But that wasn't the case with Mr. Ram. He was kind of just there."

"You guys were so different: generationally, culturally, so many ways. You wouldn't have wanted to hang on to every word. Being kind of just there for each other was amazing."

"I guess. I just want more time with him." I put the waffle square in my mouth and chew so that I don't cry.

"Just remember him and remember your times with him. It will come to you in bits. Mr. Ram moments." Muhammad puts his plate on the desk. "Remember when Rafiq died? That's what it was like. Things we'd done together would show up at the weirdest times. Or something he'd said. Even when I'm watching a movie. A Rafiq moment."

Rafiq was Muhammad's best friend when he was a kid. He died in a car accident when he was twelve. I can't imagine what Muhammad must have felt. His best friend.

I nod. It doesn't make complete sense, but at least he's trying to help me. "Are you going to the funeral with me and Mom?"

"On Saturday? Yeah."

"No, it's Friday."

"That's the Hindu rites. It's family only for that. Saturday for everyone else."

I check my phone. Nuah's modified his message on Mr. Ram's Facebook page: *Sorry, Mr. Ram's family wants me to clarify that the gathering for friends is on Saturday at the community center, three p.m.*

Muhammad takes a mini pack of halal gummy bears out of the pocket of his shorts. He places it on my desk. "Dessert. Got it at the open house for you."

• • •

A flurry of text messages.

Me: About tomorrow.

Tats: Janna! I can't stop thinking about you. Did this guy try to hurt you?

Me: Yes.

Tats: OMG!

Me: I can't talk about it right now.

Tats: I'll come over. You need someone.

Me: No. I'm dealing.

Tats: Police?

Me: Eventually.

Tats: Can I help you?

Me: You already have.

Tats: By the way, I like the Muslim guy. For you I mean.

Me: By the way, I'll come with you to the party for a bit.

Tats: You sure?

Me: Yes.

MONSTER AND MAYHEM

Nuah texts me at three fifty from Seniors Games Club. He was just getting the handshake. Mr. Ram.

☹ Is Ms. Kolbinsky there?

Yes. Her granddaughter brought her.

Say hi to them for me. And tell Sandra a joke about horse teeth. For me.

Will do.

Also, I'm having a Mr. Ram moment.

Yeah?

Sometimes people who appear great can be the real deal. The husk, the fruit, and the kernel align.

Yup, that was Mr. Ram for you. The real deal.

I mean not just him. I pause. Should I say it? A wave of courage buoys me: Thanks Nuah. For aligning.

Ah. And, aha, there you go, being nice. ☺

• • •

I open Amu's e-mail.

Dear Imam, what if you know something bad that someone's done, something against the laws of God, but no one else knows it, and people think that person is really good and should get a position of responsibility in the community, like, say, leading prayers . . . what should the person who knows the truth do?

Answer: Thank you for your important question. The person who knows the truth should act ethically and alert the people in charge that they are making a grievous error by entrusting a position of responsibility on a person unworthy of such a trust. It becomes a compulsory act on the one who knows to ensure that this entrusting does not occur. Of course this is granting that the person knows the evidence with surety. Otherwise, it would be a merciless and, indeed, a heinous action, as it would entail ruining a reputation and misleading a community. I pray this person takes the right step and comes forward should such a situation described in the question exist. And Allah knows best.

I pause scrolling. *Evidence.*

Amu thinks it's like a theft or something. Some kind of action where there's a scene of the crime, a sequence of events with anomalies or gaps you can see, and empirical proof laid out on a white-clothed table.

Evidence that can be examined, to determine "surety."

Here, I'm the only one who knows the evidence with surety. Other than him, of course.

And Rambo, Fizz's cat.

Does this mean I have to come forward and *prove* that he's a monster? Describe what happened when I can't even make sense of how it happened? Each step of the description would be reliving it.

It would be me laid out on that white table, to be examined, to determine surety.

If only Rambo, independent and impartial, could talk.

Because I'm not strong enough to tell Amu.

Dear Imam, what if you find that you've fallen for someone who is not Muslim?

Answer: Thank you for your relevant question. Living in a diverse society such as ours, this is bound to occur as we interact with each other on equitable and ethical terms (hopefully) in the large melting cauldron called America. As the cauldron swirls, we may notice the very admirable features and impeccable characters of many of the non-Muslim peoples that are bobbing alongside us. (Janna, does this sound too much like I'm describing the bobbing-for-apples pot I saw at the harvest fair with you when you were six? And, I tremble here, does this analogy seem LOQUACIOUS? Forgive me if so and adjust as you see fit.) The question we must ask ourselves at this point—a very tricky question to ask at a time of being intrigued by someone—is: Will this person hold dear the same things that I will in life? Will it be as important to them to observe Ramadan properly, bundling up in the winter months to head to the mosque in the evenings when there is work in the mornings; will they cherish the times and sanctity of prayers for my family as I will; will they observe the ritual cleansing acts so important to a Muslim; and so on. Perhaps the most important question one would need to ask of oneself is, Do I *hold dear these things? If so, a reevaluation of the attraction and the potential for realistic fruition may be in order. If not, Allah is the most aware of your situation and the one to turn to, being the best of all guides. I can offer no other advice than this. And Allah knows best.*

We meet at the Book Nook at five because Sausun says it's going to take at least an hour to "get into character." She hustles me into a bathroom and locks us into a wheelchair accessible stall, extra wide.

"If you fidget with your abaya and niqab, he'll know you're not the real thing. Which means he won't be convinced enough to get scared of you, which, knowing you, will get *you* scared and then, wham, you'll blow your *cover*. Pun intended." She unfolds a black cloak—an abaya. "Sorry, this is kind of long. Ruki's almost a foot taller than you."

"So, because I won't be able to see a hundred percent through my niqab, I'll probably trip on this thing and fall?"

"No, because a niqab doesn't mean you can't see. Actually, your sense of sight is accentuated, sort of like the way a blind person's sense of hearing becomes sharper. Your eyes are all you've got so . . ."

I look at her doubtfully as she holds open the abaya for me.

"Relax. You're not wearing the type I have on, no eye screen. Your eyes will get total freedom."

Just not my nose and mouth. Well, my mouth *is* going to get the freedom to tell him off, even if it's in a muffled way.

I finish buttoning up the abaya and wait as Sausun does some complicated thing with the head scarf portion of the outfit.

"I'm folding this so it's not as long and won't drape onto your arms. That way you can actually move your arms to lift up the bottom of the abaya, because, man, that's one looong dress."

She winds the scarf around my head and secures it with pins. Then she takes out the final piece of my outfit: the face veil or niqab, a small rectangular piece of black fabric with ties extending on either side. I feel a welling inside me, like a case of hyperventilating is about to unleash itself.

"I'm claustrophobic. Severely," I pant.

Sausun stops moving, the niqab dangling from her hand by one of the ties. "Do you want to do this or not?"

I don't say anything and stare at the niqab swinging slightly.

"Do you? Do you want him to keep thinking he's got you in control, like he's going to dictate how you act, how free you are, just because you won't give in to him? Do you want to put a stop to one more perverted scum acting all holy or not? There are too many in the world—come on already."

I pretend it isn't tears that drop onto the black fabric of the niqab as I bring it to my face. I join the ties at the back of my head myself before looking up. The first thing I see out of my niqabbed face is Sausun's eyes, wet, before she lowers her mesh eye screen on top of them.

We're two sad and angry women, about to wreak vengeance on one unsuspecting monster. I lead the way out of the bathroom stall.

The first thing I notice about wearing the niqab is that you have to like your own breath. Lunch was a handful of sour cream and onion chips, so I'm not having much fun. The walking candy store helps out by handing me two Wint O Green Life Savers from her bulging laptop case as she opens it to set up her equipment. Her eye screen is flipped back so she can work. We're in the coffee shop area of the store, with mellow French music playing.

"For the first part, where you're stalking him, use your phone cam. I can clean it up after," Sausun says. "I'll be here. You've got to get him into view of my laptop cam before doing your spiel. We need to get a frontal view on tape."

I avert my gaze from a girl paying at the counter who looks vaguely familiar. Was she in my English class?

"Janna. Nobody knows it's you. Even your mom."

"I have expressive eyebrows. They have a life of their own." I wiggle them to make my case. "I should have grown them out or something."

"No offense but your eyebrows are nothing special." Sausun finishes positioning her laptop. "I'm going to go stand where you need to be standing with the asshole. To give you an idea of where to get him cornered."

I sit in her chair and look at the image on the screen. I click record as Sausun comes into view, doing a twirl near the bookcases that say BARGAIN FINDS. A man in teeny shorts steps back from her, holding his coffee away. She curtsies and makes an after-you motion with her hands. Teeny-shorts man frowns and strides off, holding his coffee aloft.

Sausun walks back, with a lot more people looking at her now. She takes her chair from me.

"You can have a bit more space to play with, but try to stay tight. I won't be able to keep moving my laptop to track you guys."

"That guy is staring over here," I say, sucking then blowing out minty air for my personal pleasure. "The one in the baseball cap."

"Wouldn't you look at two identically dressed people? Just to work it out in your head? That's why he's staring."

"Yeah but not for-e-ver." I will myself to stare back.

He drops his gaze. Wow, what power!

I turn to a woman at the next table who's been taking glances here and there. I wonder if my eyes show that I'm actually doing a smiling sort of stare. She looks away.

"Having fun?" Sausun watches me, eyes crinkled.

"Are you smiling? I think I can tell now." I smile back.

"Hey, I thought of something. What about the music?"

"You mean what about the Edith Piaf playing? I think it would be a great soundtrack for what you're going to do." Now she's definitely smiling. "Very ironic."

"No one will hear me. On video."

"That's why you'll wear this mic under your abaya." She hands me a small silver rectangle with a clip on one side. "It's Bluetooth connected to my laptop."

I take the mic and rotate it in my hand. "If I don't go through with it, will you be mad?"

"No, 'cause you *will* go through with it." She scoots to another chair, one facing only me and the corner behind me. Lifting her niqab right up to her forehead and then flipping it back, she speaks. "Here's why you need to do this: It's not only for you. It's for me, too."

Her face is intense, with eyes open wide and mouth tight. "I'm planning something to help my sister. Something big so she can come back here to the States, with her son. Something that will blow up big in the media, in my bastard-in-law's face. So you doing this is my trial run. It's the first strike in the war against fake-holy shits."

I nod. She lets her niqab drop, then the eye screen.

Dad: *You'll fail. And maybe you'll fail and fail and fail again. But then each fall will teach you how to make a new wing. Your rise will be on that many more wings.*

I initially position myself near the doors, by the summer travel books display. But the entrance security guard is not doing a good job surveying me discreetly, and I'm afraid he'll start tracking me tracking Farooq, so I grab a book and move into the closest aisle.

Maybe a black cloak and face covering isn't exactly the best disguise. Maybe in Saudi Arabia but not here.

I open a book on Istanbul and read about the Harem at the Topkapi Palace. A labyrinth of three hundred rooms housing, no, make that *caging*, the wives and concubines of the sultan. I feel nauseated, thinking of Sausun's sister.

At the height of Ottoman power, one thousand women were kept in the Harem is what I'm reading when Farooq comes in. I put the book on a shelf and straighten up, feeling as though I've been released from something.

I turn on my phone cam and step behind him. He pauses when he gets a few yards from the coffee shop and picks up a book from a table that has a sign saying SUMMER GRILLING. He isn't reading but looking at the coffee drinkers in the shop. I can tell the moment he spots Sausun because he tilts his head and peers closer at his book.

A burst of bravado washes over me.

I go around to the bookshelves opposite to where he's pretending to read. Holding up my phone, I fit the camera lens in a gap in the books at my eye level. I zoom in and fix on his face.

The face I've been hiding from is on my screen. It's wide with squinty eyes and a slack jawline.

I record for a bit and then step back out as he begins to move toward the coffee shop, book in hand, *Guys 'n' Grills.*

Sausun looks up as he steps into the shop. She nods. He must think it's at him because he nods back at her. But it's my cue that he's in front of the BARGAIN FINDS sign. I move out from behind him and look him in the face for the first time.

His eyes widen considerably.

Will he know it's me? I stop moving, the bravado retreating on seeing the hand holding the book. I feel it under my shirt again, and my insides seize against the memory.

I can't do this. It's like letting him have access to me again.

"Excuse *me*, sister," he says, waving me away with his book, like I'm *ugh.*

Sister?

"I'm NOT your sister. NOT in your family, NOT your sister in Islam. I have NOTHING to do with you 'cause you're a big, empty HUSK of NOTHINGNESS! Trying to get in my pants, oh Mr. I-memorized-the-whole-Qur'an-so-I'm-untouchable? This guy is a pervert! An attempted rapist! This guy here!"

Who am I, screaming uncontrollably now and blocking him as he tries to get away? I'm me and Sausun's sister and the thousand women locked in the Harem. I look at Sausun, whose eyes are probably crinkled, and I wiggle my eyebrows at her. The security guard comes up and is reaching out for me, but I dodge him, which gives Farooq the opportunity to escape through the nearest doors.

I'm not done. No way.

I chase him with my abaya held up high over my jeaned legs with both my hands, the black cloth bunched around my hips. I don't know how far the mic can go with capturing sound, but I hope it gets most of my ranting.

"You're a disease! A cancer! Herpes! An oozing slime fest! HOW DARE YOU ACT ALL HOLY? YOU DON'T KNOW HOLY! HOLY IS RESPECTING GIRLS! I AM NOT *UGH*! NOT WORTHLESS! I'M A GIRL! A GIRL!"

He's at an intersection with a red light. Part of me wishes he'd get hit by a car, but another part doesn't want to see him coddled by paramedics.

I pause in my yelling. What if he stops and turns? What if he takes me on instead of running?

Then, I decide, I'll take him on too.

I shake off *all* the feeling of ickiness he creates in me, every bit, and it rolls off like it's oily gunk. And then I stop. A few feet away from him, as his right foot is stepping off the curb and his head is looking both ways to make a run for it, I stop because it's gone.

The disgust I feel *at me* is gone. The gunk of self-blame dissolves to leave just me standing there.

Only when he gets across the street does he turn to look back.

And he sees me. Me, Janna Yusuf, because I lift up my face covering.

He runs.

Sausun comes out and joins me on the sidewalk. We watch his retreating back. He's slowed his running to a getaway gait.

It's almost pitiful.

"I feel amazing," I say.

"There's no way I can upload that," she says.

"Are you telling me it was a fail?"

"A spectacular fail."

"But I faced him, Sausun. I'm not scared of him anymore." I tighten the grip on the abaya still gathered around my hips and look at her. "I can't believe it. I'm not scared."

"Yeah, but we didn't get anything that I can use to build a story. There's no *evidence*."

Ugh. I hate that word.

But there's something happening inside me. It's like what Sausun described in the basement of Dad's house, this feeling of wanting to grind the monster into the ground. Is this what strength's like?

"It feels good right now," I say. "It feels like if I see him again, I'm strong enough to death-stare him."

"That's great, but where does that leave us? Or take us?" She turns to me. "He's still a predator. You blew up on him, but he's going to find the next girl, or maybe there are already other girls—did you ever think that? Without a record of something, we can't put a stop to him."

I look away from her. He's gone now. I can't see him, literally or figuratively. I want to enjoy this moment, exult in it, but then there's Sausun.

"Can't you just let me be strong?" I drop the abaya and it falls around my feet in folds. I'm tired of her. Everything's bigger in her mind. It's not just about the now but about her sister, about other girls. "I haven't felt like this in a long time. Maybe I've never felt this strong *ever*, and now you're telling me it's not enough."

"I'm telling you to wield that strength. Sure, enjoy it, but don't let it wear off without using it." She walks back to the bookstore doors.

She's such a disappointment.

Because it's like she's always disappointed in me.

MISFITS AND SAINTS

Mom's earrings go with the shirt I've chosen for the party. But, to make them stand out, I'd have to switch up my scarf style.

I try draping it the way Sarah demonstrated on the date night I chaperoned: one end of the scarf wrapped around my neck and the other hitched up near my ears to reveal an ear-ring.

Maybe I'm doing something wrong, but it doesn't look the way it did at the restaurant. Both ends of the scarf stick out at odd angles, like hair that won't settle down. Bad-hair day is nothing compared to bad-hijab day.

I take the earrings off. They're beautiful: a filigreed pattern, like those Persian designs on mosques, supporting sapphire stones. I wonder where Dad bought them.

Maybe Dad wouldn't like it that Mom gave them to me.

The earrings are BD. When they loved each other.

Does Mom miss that? I mean, having someone love her like that?

I wrap my scarf the regular way and return the earrings to Mom's jewelry box. She has a shirt that matches them too.

Tats goes ahead of me, pushing the front door, already ajar, open with her hip. There are about ten people in the living room on our left, and she turns to them and waves. One of the guys starts laughing. "Wrong party," he says, pointing at me.

I fight the urge to leave and instead follow Tats to the kitchen at the end of the massive foyer. "One More Night" is pumping into the hall from a room on the right.

A huge island stands in the center of the kitchen, stocked with food and drinks. Simone is leaning on the counter watching an improbably tall guy pouring himself a drink. The bottle he's holding has fancy writing on it. Alcohol?

"Hey," Tats says, grinning at Simone. "How's it going?"

"Okay." Simone nods at me. "Janna, you're here. A drink?"

"I'll have a Coke. The regular kind," I add quickly as Tall Guy smiles.

"With some rum?" Tall Guy opens a Coke.

"I don't drink," I say, reaching for the can before he pours it.

"But I do," Tats says. "Make mine good."

Tall Guy laughs. Simone moves away with her drink, and I go to the window, drawn by the lights outside.

I can make out Lauren through the part in the drapes.

She's sitting back on a lawn chair beside a really good-looking guy who's on the edge of a swinging seat. He's talking to her, but she's not turned to him. It looks like she's watching the people in the pool.

I lean closer and draw away the curtain. Marjorie is sitting at the edge of the pool, laughing as someone tries to pull her in. There are a few people who've already been dunked, sitting or lying on the grass, drying. I look back at Lauren, who's getting up even though the guy beside her is still talking. She glances up at the house, her gaze lingering on the door, out of which more people are spilling into the yard. Then she's looking at the kitchen window and catches my eyes. I drop the curtain, certain my intense staring drew her gaze, in a psychic kind of way.

Tats is sipping a drink, making a face. She hands it back, and Tall Guy adds something to it. She tries another tiny sip, hands it back again. He adds two splashes from two different bottles. She makes a gagging sound. "You stink. Just give me a cooler."

He laughs and calls her a wimp.

Tats comes over to join me on the window seat just as Marjorie shows up at the kitchen door.

"Hi, guys!" She is wearing a blue strapless top and denim shorts. "Come out! There are *people* waiting for you!" She widens her eyes at me.

"Really? Like who?" Tats sounds genuinely curious. "Like Jeremy?"

"Who else?" Marjorie says.

"But I thought he was over Janna," Tats says. "Didn't you guys know?"

Marjorie appears unsure and then looks at the window. "Lauren also wants to introduce you to people, okay?"

I knew it. It's a setup. I look at Tats, who's parting the curtains. Do I have to keep a promise if it's stupid?

I stand up. I have to leave. Tats pulls me back down.

Marjorie waits. Tats gets up and starts going, but Marjorie's standing there, looking at me.

"Janna's going to stay behind for now, but I'm coming," Tats says, pulling on Marjorie's arm. "I'm here to party, not drink pop in the kitchen."

I watch them leave. There's a group of people waiting for drinks beside Tall Guy, and he's making comments on everyone's choices. I hope no one looks my way. I can't fake friendly to a bunch of people whom I know only from their Facebook pictures beside their comments about me. Mr. Sizlin Brown Stuff is having a beer with something in it that'll make his brain fart, according to Tall Guy. Ms. Hawt Turd is getting a Shirley Temple Black.

I turn to the window and, without moving the curtain, watch through the sliver of a gap.

Tats is right in front of Lauren. She's moving her hands and laughing, pointing at the pool, then at the people on the grass. I can tell she's being loud, as two guys sit up from their prone positions to watch her. A huddle of girls giggle to one another, looking her up and down, as if she's not dressed exactly the same as them. Lauren is staring at her with a don't-touch-me expression on her face.

God, I wish Tats would learn to tell social cues already! She's making a needless fool of herself.

Marjorie positions herself behind Tats, copying her movements in mime form, exaggerating their crass factor. That's it, I'm going out there to get Tats and drag her home. I owe her that at least.

But then Lauren is leaning in and listening. Tats points at the window, and I move, a fraction too late, as I catch Lauren's gaze again before shielding myself behind the drapes. What in the world is Tats saying? *My best friend over there wants to come out, but she's scared to be out here after you guys ran a Facebook campaign against her? Could you guys pretty please promise not to hurt her feelings so she can come out and enjoy your party? Pretty please with a cherry wine cooler on top?*

I can imagine her like that.

It's only Tall Guy and me now in the room. I sip my Coke slowly, watching him pour himself another drink.

"Never tasted anything before?" He's looking down as if talking to his plastic cup. "Even a sip from your parents?"

"My parents don't drink," I say. "Well, my mom doesn't."

"You're missing out." He looks at me before taking a gulp.

"Or. I'm. Not," I say. I turn back to the window to stop

him from talking. Even through the chink, I can tell Lauren is not out there anymore, and neither is Tats nor Marjorie. The drying people are spread out, though it looks like a couple ended up in the pool again. I open the drapes the whole way and peer to see out to the edges, near the fence. No one there.

Tats ditched me.

I start to panic and look around the kitchen. There's a door behind Tall Guy, near the counter. It's a side door. I can make a run for it and then text Tats from across the street to see what's going on. I wouldn't leave her. I'd wait, just away from this place.

While I'm thinking this, a group of guys come into the kitchen. Jeremy's one of them.

I try to turn back to the window, but he's seen me already.

"Hi," he says, from near the counter.

I wave back.

He turns around and that's it.

I feel strange: relieved in two ways. That he dropped everything and that he's here, in the room. I feel safer.

"Jeremy," I say, the first time I've said his name.

He looks at me, then comes over, holding a Coke too. I move over on the window seat until there's a wide space for him to choose a spot from. He chooses wisely, with a nice distance between us.

"I need to leave the party, but I can't, not without Tats. But I don't want to look for her around the house." I turn the tab of my pop can. "I don't really know anyone here."

"You want me to help you look?" he asks. I nod.

We get up and move out of the kitchen. There are more people in the foyer now, but Tats is not there, so we pass through to the den and connected dining room. The music is loud here, but I shout over it because I remember something. "Where would Matt be?"

"He's in the living room. She wouldn't be there; no one's there except his friends."

Matt was one of the guys Tats waved at when we came in? Did she even realize she'd passed her whole reason for coming here?

"She's not on the first floor. Maybe she's outside," Jeremy says when we're back in the hallway.

"No, I looked there already."

He's already opening the French doors leading into the backyard. It's strangely still, even though the yard is full of people.

It's the June air, when you can hear every stir in hyper-audio. Maybe that's why everyone around the pool is lying there listless.

"Is that why you didn't want to come to my house that day?" Jeremy is looking at the pool. "Because Farooq was there and he'd see us?"

I can't believe he believes we were together, the monster and me.

Wait, *does* he believe it?

"Jeremy, I wasn't with him; I never was." I take a step back and sit on one of the stone benches flanking the doors. He turns to me.

"But is that the reason you wouldn't come in? You didn't want him to know, right?"

"I didn't want anyone to know, but yeah, I especially didn't want him to know. But not because we were together."

"So if there's nothing between you two, he was just playing me? Why wouldn't you have texted me or something then? To clear it up?"

"I guess I realized that it wasn't going to work for us anyway."

"Okay, so it made sense in your head, and that was enough for you?"

No, no, no. Why is he making this about us? There can be no us, doesn't he see that? "I realized the way I felt wasn't fair to you. Like I said, I didn't want anyone to know about you. Not just Farooq. Because there are these things that are important to me, and I haven't figured out how other people fit into them yet. I'm sorry. I shouldn't have gotten into things. I'm sorry."

"No, it's okay. If that's how it is." It doesn't sound okay, the way he says it. The way he says it opens a space in me, like a skipped heartbeat.

I'm sad.

When it was in my head, it was easier, this thing between us. It was almost better than the real thing because it was neat and could be opened and closed as much as I wanted it to be.

It didn't involve another person's heart. Or two worlds colliding. And Jeremy getting hurt in the collision. "I messed up, Jeremy."

"Don't worry about it now." He shrugs and then goes still. "Shh, look. To your left. Slowly."

I turn slightly. A bird is on the sill of the kitchen window, tilting its head as though listening to something. It's small, and its claws remind me of the one that landed on my palm at the lake.

"Is it a chickadee?" I whisper.

"No, a white-throated sparrow." He lets out a laugh and the bird flies.

"Why'd you laugh? It got scared."

"Because not every bird is a chickadee."

"I know that. Ostriches, chickens, eagles, the list goes on."

"And penguins, right? Come on, let's go find Tats." He laughs again and moves to open the doors to the house.

"Maybe she's down in the basement," he says, heading to a door opposite the French doors we entered through. Music, different from the kind upstairs, blasts into the hall. "This is where Lauren and friends hang."

I follow him down, a stab of worry making me flinch when I hear the door close behind me.

There's no one in the rec room. I turn quickly on the stairs, aware that I'm in a basement with the door closed again, with a guy again, and music so loud.

I'm almost back at the top when I hear Tats. She *is* in the basement. I lean down and look through the banister railings. She's coming out of a room off of the rec room. She sees me and smiles, totally ignoring Jeremy standing at the bottom of the stairs.

"Ready to go, Janna?" She has the weirdest smile on her face.

"You guys want a ride?" Jeremy asks. "I need to pick up something."

"We're going home," I say.

"It's far from here, so don't bother," Tats says, not looking at Jeremy but talking to him.

"It's not a problem," Jeremy says.

Tats turns to him. "We don't need a ride!"

"It's okay, a ride would get us there faster," I say quickly, smiling at Jeremy. "Thanks."

"Fine." Tats goes by and we follow behind.

The ride is silent, with Tats and me in the back like we're being chauffeured.

Finally, I whisper, "I don't think he knew. Jeremy didn't know. He's clueless in this whole thing. He had nothing to do with it."

"I don't believe that," Tats says out loud. "How could he not know his friend was a douche bag?"

I don't say anything. Neither does Jeremy. He probably thinks we're having a private conversation.

"Tats, why'd you go to the basement with them?"

"To make a deal." She's looking out of the window.

"What're you talking about?"

"Janna." She turns to me. "We can't go to the roof anymore. Access denied."

I think about that. "Did they tell on us? Lauren and them? How'd they know?"

"*Now* they know." She pulls the España key chain out of her shorts. There's no key dangling from it. "They've got the key. I gave it to them."

"Tats," I say, uncomprehending. "For what? Matt?"

She laughs and whispers, "Was he there? I didn't even notice."

"Tats?"

"For you, Janna. They're going to leave you alone. They're going to leave my friend alone."

She turns to me, her eyes glistening. They make me lean over and give her a hug so I can hide my own eyes.

Jeremy stops the car at the entrance to our cluster of buildings, and we get out. Tats starts walking, but I move to the driver's window and wait for Jeremy to roll it down. "Thanks again."

He nods. "No problem. See you around then?"

"Sure, as long as you don't scare away the birds." I wave as the window rolls up, and he drives away, a smile on his face.

My phone pings. You never told me your brother's a crybaby.

Lol, why?

He's calling fouls every day. Basketball.

Hey, go easy on him. He hasn't played all year.

"Let me guess, is that from Nuah?" Tats has walked back.

"Yeah, why?"

"Because this." She holds up her phone. A picture of me texting with a smile on my face. I look happy. Like the way happy should look.

"Can I use that for my profile pic?"

"Sure," she says, leaning over to read my texts. "Let's go hang with him. He's playing basketball. Let's go watch."

"At the mosque? Friday night drop-in?"

"So? Is it a guys-only mosque?"

"No. My uncle's not like that and he runs the place. There's girls' floor hockey going on right now too."

"So let's go. We cut the party short." She leaves off saying "for you." *We left the party for you.* "And the night is young! First day of freedom! Let's go!"

I laugh. "To the mosque! YEAH."

Sarah is in the foyer setting up a Ramadan fund-raising drive display.

"I just realized I'm dressed kind of weird for this place," Tats whispers. "Look at that girl. She looks like she's from a fairy tale or something."

Sarah's wearing a high-waisted mint green chiffon dress

paired with a taupe hijab tied short and close to her face, with a chunky white-and-gold necklace, a statement piece, adorning her neckline. She does look royal.

She waves us over. “Assalamu alaikum! Can you girls give me a hand?”

I introduce Tats and we help move a table in between two tall cardboard minaret-shaped cutouts. Each minaret is a thermometer with money amounts replacing the temperature marks.

“It’s a generational contest this year,” Sarah says, pointing at the labels on the minarets. One says ADULTS, the other YOUTH. “We’re going to see who can raise more money.”

“Cool, but is there a scarf I can wear?” Tats asks. I should have remembered that she had on shorts. I should have set her up before we came.

“It’s not a problem, but if you want something to cover with, come with me,” says Sarah. “Janna, can you put out the forms? They’re mixed up in that bag.”

I nod and begin sorting. There are fund-raising forms mixed with other literature. I open a pamphlet that’s titled *Domestic Violence: A Hidden Crime*. At the bottom of a block of writing describing women’s shelters are Sarah’s name and phone number, as a support person.

Sarah and Sausun. I’d thought they were so different from each other but they’re not. They’re super big picture, into causes and things beyond their lives.

In Sausun's case, it makes sense. Her sister is trapped abroad.

It's like she's forced into advocacy. Actually, it makes sense for Sarah, too. She does it for religion.

Something Mr. Ram said comes back to me: the *why* you do something is important. The *Wiyyah*, in Arabic.

Maybe that's why I couldn't do anything about the monster before. The *why* wasn't there.

Because all I felt was this *shame*. Like as if *I* had something to do with it. I don't even know why I felt that.

The shame should have been *all* his but I chose to carry it around this whole time.

What if there are others? Like Sausun had asked?

What if there's someone else, maybe playing floor hockey right now, feeling what I'd felt?

I close the pamphlet. I don't want a single other girl to carry what's only his.

I'm shifting the shame. He needs to feel it.

The doors to the gym off the foyer fling open. The sound of dribbling spills out, punctuated with the bang of the doors shutting.

A bunch of guys, sweaty and laughing, make their way to the water fountain.

The monster's one of them.

He's feeling good enough to come to Friday night drop-in at the mosque? After yesterday?

I drop the pamphlet on the table and look right at him. I want him to see me. I need him to see me, see that I'm here too, that I belong in this space.

I stand because I'm strong enough.

He notices me, from where he's waiting at the water fountain, but looks away.

I walk but my eyes remain on him. I know he sees me moving because he flinches.

The gym doors bang open again and it's Nuah and Muhammad, their T-shirts soaking.

"You okay?" It's almost Muhammad's way of salaams. His standard *You okay?* nods or queries.

"No," I say, heading to Amu's office. "But I will be."

The monster looks up. He's heard me. He moves out of the line for the water fountain, his eyes watchful, glancing from me to the mosque's front doors. Coward.

Through the glass window of the office reception area, I see Nuah near the fountain now. He waves, his face breaking into a big smile on seeing me.

If I need backup, there's Nuah. He found the monster with me on the basement stairwell at Dad's house.

But I don't need backup. I'm enough.

When I come out, Amu is beside me, insisting that he drive me home. He wants to gather as a family.

While he goes into the gym to find Muhammad, I sit on

the couch in the reception room. I need to send a text. I need to give Sausun hope.

I didn't write it out and burn the pages. I said it out loud. It's not mine to carry anymore.

Who'd you say it out loud to?

My uncle.

She sends me a thumbs-up. Then, Too bad you don't make a good Niqabi Ninja. I listened to the recording. An "oozing slime fest"? A "big empty husk of nothingness"?

Too bad back, because that's why I'm texting you. I'm in to help your sister.

Um, why don't you wait to see your audition video? You actually stopped to wiggle your eyebrows at me. Before chasing the perv out of his debut performance.

Fine, I can be the camera/editing gal then.

Fine then.

Muhammad raps on the window and makes a leaving motion. I walk out to the crowded foyer to collect Tats.

She's at the fund-raising table wearing an abaya over her shorts, a scarf around her neck. There's a group of guys from basketball and girls from floor hockey collected around the table.

"So this is the form you fill out," Tats says. "Come on, guys, we can get a head start!"

Sarah points at Tats and mouths, *Where did you find her? She's awesome!* and indicates the YOUTH minaret thermometer. It's at three hundred dollars already.

• • •

"Ya Allah. My little one." When Amu lets go of hugging me, Mom moves in, holding me by my shoulders and looking into my face.

"Oh, Janna, why didn't you come to me?" She gathers me in her arms and I go slack.

There's nothing for my breath to get snagged on inside me anymore.

Muhammad puts a hand out to me.

"Sorry, I'm so sorry," he keeps repeating. "If I'd known about that, that . . ."

He looks at Amu, not wanting to use profanity in front of him.

"Monster?" I say, still in Mom's hug.

"Monster, yeah." Muhammad turns away, his voice quieting.

I reach an arm to him. But I'm still in Mom's hug, breathing.

We walk to Mr. Ram's remembrance gathering the next day. It's hot and Mom wanted me to wear a light dress, but I wore pants. I need a pocket for the mini gummy bears pack that Muhammad gave me the other day.

Tats is wearing a long black skirt. When we near the community center, she stops and pulls a scarf out of her bag.

"For my head, for the Muslim prayers, you know," she says, draping the scarf around her hair. Her bangs and braid peek out of the front and back. "I wanted to be respectful."

I smile. "Mr. Ram's Hindu. But you can keep your scarf on if you want."

Ms. Kolbinsky and Sandra are sitting on a bench right outside the center.

Nuah's by the door.

I walk over to say salaam, gummy bears in hand.

Afterward, on the way out, he tells me the one about the muffin. The one that made Mr. Ram Belly-Laugh smile.

Two muffins were sitting in the oven. One looks over at the other and says, "Man, it's HOT in here!" The second one screams, "AHHH! A talking muffin!"

I laugh, because of the person who's saying it. Nuah.

I'm having a Mr. Ram moment. That day when I left him alone in his apartment, he told me what the poet Rumi had said. That if you love the Divine, you can love everything, be kind to everyone, see someone's joke the way they want you to.

I can't imagine what it means to love everyone. But I'm just going to start right here, by loving a bit more of myself.

And maybe then the rest will follow.

~~Acknowledgments~~ Biblovegraphy

These are the lives consulted, the people who allowed me to write this book. Listed are some of the "books" they've written into my life—things they've taught me through them being them. Thank you.

Ahmad, *I Believe They Can Fly: A Dad's Guide to Rearing Children*
Zuhra, *The Grace Inherent in Grit: A Mom's Memoir*
John, *I Agent-with-Class, What's Your Superpower?*
Zareen, *In the Mind of an Editor Extraordinaire*
Uzma, *BFF Critique Partners For Life: Nurture or Nature?*
Rukhsana, *Paving the Way for Others to Party on the Porch*
Rania, *Kindred Spirits Exist*
Ausma, *Success Has Three Ss: Sincerity, Support, Sisterhood*
Glenna, *How to Read a First Draft and Survive*
Richard, *The Art of Writing for When the Craft Is Boring as Hell*
Leona, *TWELVE: Discovering Student Potential During the Awkward Years*
Shaiza, *Picking Up the Phone at 3 A.M. and Other Friendship Hacks*
Amie, *Check That Off, Sis!!! On Being a Life-Lister Sister*
Zakiya, *The Girl in the Writer's Eye*
MYNA, *Kumbaya Allah: 1980s Memories*
WNDB, *Mission Possible: Mirrors and Windows for Every Child*

Amanda, Sana, Bushra, and Saira, *The Ancient Sister-in-Law Pact: Love and Grace, Always*

Khalil, Khalid, and Zenyah, *That's Not a Phone but a Foot: A Reflection on Patience When Your Aunt Thinks She's Funny*

Sahar, *I Was a Serial Story Tester and Lived to Tell about It*

Johanne, Dawood, and Muhammad, *Chicken Pot Pie for the Soul: 101 Nourishing Conversations*

Anwaar, *Books and the Brother-in-Law: A Podcast*

Shakil, *Baby Brother Starts with a Capital B*

Faisal, *Step-In, Step-Up: A Sibling Support Manual*

Jochua, *Pretty Much, Not Exactly: The Understated Awesome Impact of a Stepson*

Sakeina, *Invaluable Input: A Bibliophile's Meditations on the Shaping of a Book*

Hajara, *Unflagging: A Guide to Cheerleading from the Tiny Beginning*

Bilqis, *A Keen Eye: Wielding Insight and Wisdom-Beyond-Your-Years with Care*

Hamza, *An Introduction to Kindness in the Age of Post-Irony*

Jez, *Love, Simply Love*